# I Belong
## to Y

# The Inside Out Series
# by Lisa Renee Jones

# I Belong to You

## Lisa Renee Jones

**G**

**Gallery Books**

New York   London   Toronto   Sydney   New Delhi

# G

Gallery Books
A Division of Simon & Schuster, Inc.
1230 Avenue of the Americas
New York, NY 10020

First Gallery Books trade paperback edition November 2014

GALLERY BOOKS and colophon are registered trademarks of Simon & Schuster, Inc.

For information about special discounts for bulk purchases, please contact Simon & Schuster Special Sales at 1-866-506-1949 or business@simonandschuster.com.

The Simon & Schuster Speakers Bureau can bring authors to your live event. For more information or to book an event contact the Simon & Schuster Speakers Bureau at 1-866-248-3049 or visit our website at www.simonspeakers.com.

Designed by Ruth Lee-Mui

Manufactured in the United States of America

10 9 8 7 6 5 4 3 2 1

Library of Congress Cataloging-in-Publication Data

Jones, Lisa Renee

I belong to you / Lisa Renee Jones — First Gallery Books trade paperback edition.
pages cm — (inside out series)
1. Man-woman relationships — Fiction. I. Title.
PS3610.O62712      2014
813'.6 — dc23
20140190006

ISBN 978-1-4767-7247-9
ISBN 978-1-4767-7527-2 (ebook)

*To Julie Patra Harrison, my Oriental Shorthair kitkat.*
*When I'm living inside a book, she never leaves my side.*

# Acknowledgments

I am truly blessed to do what I love and to call writing books my "job." I want to thank my readers for making that possible. For the many fans who have joined my street team, The Underground Angels: I am humbled by your support.

Emily and Rae, thank you for all you do daily to support me. Alyssa and Aemelia, thank you for living every deadline crunch like it's your deadline, too.

To the entire staff of Gallery Books, thank you for all you do! I want to give special thanks to Louise Burke and Jennifer Bergstrom for helping develop my career. To my editor, Micki Nuding, who believed in me first and made it all happen: There aren't enough words. You are supportive, insightful, and special in ways I know every author you work with understands.

To Louise Fury, my agent, who is always thinking out of the box, who listens and communicates, and who believes in me even if I forget to believe in me. You rock!

Finally, my husband, who thankfully never expected me to cook anyway, and doesn't cook himself but heats a mean TV dinner at just the right times. He's also exceptional at getting takeout.

*Dear Readers:*

*Finally it's time for Mark's story! I'm so excited to share his secrets with you. And though* I Belong to You *can be read as a standalone story, there are three novellas that really tell the backstory of the relationship between Mark and Crystal. I hope you will consider reading:*

- The Master Undone
- My Hunger—*starts the day after* The Master Undone *ends*
- My Control

*I hope you enjoy!*
*Lisa*

# One

⁓

## Crystal . . .

I'm standing next to Dana Compton at her bathroom mirror, staring at our reflections. My long blond hair touches my shoulders; her short blond hair teases her chin. "I hate that I had to cut it," she whispers. "Damn cancer and that blast of chemo they gave me before my mastectomy."

*Yes,* I think. *Damn cancer.* But I stay positive, hoping she will, too—a feat that's getting harder every day. "That blast of chemo kept you from losing ground when the blood infection made you too weak for your cancer treatments. Besides," I add, "I think you look good with your hair this length. You have such a gorgeous face we can see now."

She gives me a sad smile. "Now you sound like Mark. He said the same thing."

I smile inside at the soft side her son has for his mother; I'm fairly certain I'm one of the few people who have been privy to the real man beneath the hard shell. Except maybe Rebecca. Of course Rebecca. He'd loved her—not that he's confessed such feelings, but the deep, cutting pain in his eyes, the desperateness in him when he touches me but wishes for her, tells me he did.

"Your son loves you," I say. "And he wishes he were here. He tried. He flew me to San Francisco to close the Allure gallery for him."

"I know," she assures me. "And he did the right thing sending you back here when Ava escaped last week. What if she'd targeted you for attack, because you were working at Mark's gallery? We don't know what sick reason she had for killing Rebecca."

She doesn't, but I do. It was for the same reason a brilliant, wealthy artist like Ricco Alvarez had created the counterfeit-art scandal at Allure and the Riptide auction house, not caring about the many lives and employees it would affect: jealousy over Mark and Rebecca.

"Ava needs to be caught and punished," she continues. "Rebecca was a sweet girl."

"It's heartbreaking," I agree. "Like something from a horror movie."

"Yes, it is." She glances back into the mirror. "Speaking of horror movies, I've gotten so thin these past two weeks, it's going to terrify Mark when he sees me. And I need to get these roots done so I'm blond again before he comes home. I'll look more like myself then, and that might lift my spirits."

Since she started daily radiation therapy last Friday, she's been so exhausted that she hasn't been able to do anything. I don't point that out, though. Wrapping my arm around her shoulder, I lean my head against hers and meet her blue eyes in the mirror. "I'll have the stylist come to us. We can have a spa day next Sunday."

"Let's do it at the spa," she suggests, her normally strong voice weak, and her normally rosy cheeks pale.

"The doctor wants you to rest so you'll be strong. And we're only through the first week."

Her lashes lower and lift. "Right. I need to get five more behind me."

Doubt colors the words, and defeat rolls off her in a way I've never felt from her before this week. I really do think having Mark here for her first week of radiation treatments, as planned, would have helped. But he's not, and I am, and it's all a mess.

"Come on," I urge, gently taking Dana's robe-clad arm to lead her back to the bedroom. "Let's go watch *A Walk in the Clouds*. It came in the mail today and I know how you love Keanu Reeves."

"Oh yes," she agrees, wobbling with me past the giant claw-footed bathtub. "He's my younger-man fantasy."

"Keanu's my older-man fantasy," I tease, thrilled that I've elicited a lift in her voice.

"Two birds of the same feather," she says, as she has so many times in the year since we met at a Riptide auction I'd attended.

"Yes, we are," I agree wholeheartedly, helping her onto the bed.

"I'm all for the movie, but aren't the cable and Internet still not working?" she asks as I help her settle comfortably against a stack of pillows.

"Random outages," I say, kicking off my tennis shoes with the intent to join her. "We seem to be in the not-so-random area but they promised it'll be fixed soon."

"Did you call Marianne next door and see if she has the same issue?"

"Yes, and she does."

Thankfully, with Dana lucid again and Marianne being a good friend of hers, she's helping us keep Dana from watching the news until Mark returns. I really don't know how she's going to react to hearing reporters talking about a sex scandal involving Mark, and a connection to the counterfeit-art claims in Rebecca's death.

"The cable company is lucky I'm not myself," she murmurs, sounding groggy. "I'd raise hell."

My lips curve. "I can't wait until you're raising hell again—even if it's at me."

Crossing the room, I stick the DVD in the player in the huge oak entertainment center and grab the remote control. Turning to the bed, I find that Dana's lashes have lowered and she's headed into sleep. With a pinch in my chest, I stare at the woman who's my employer, my friend, and a third mother, so to speak—one with special qualities that really reach inside me and touch all the right places. Normally she looks like she's in her forties rather than her fifties, but today she looks her age or older. She looks breakable.

My fingers curl into my palms. *Damn cancer.* And suddenly, even though Mark turns me inside out, and I end up in bed with him when I say I won't, just to say good-bye over and over again, I want him here. He got her through the blood infection, kept her fighting, and kept his father's fear in check, despite his own. I'm trying to fill his shoes, but fear I'm failing. I don't want to fail.

Grabbing my briefcase to start weeding through the mounds of work, I carefully settle on the bed, wanting to be close if Dana needs me. As my laptop powers up my cell phone vibrates with a call, and speak of the devil—it's Mark. Cautiously slipping off the bed, I punch the Answer button and whisper, "Hello," as I head for the hallway.

"Why are you whispering, Ms. Smith?" he asks, and damn him, even with the snap to his question, and the use of my formal name, which he knows I hate, his voice brings up memories of my visit there last week. Of him crumbling before me, a broken, hurt man; then our naked bodies and his vow that we were done—even though we'd never really started. And the moment he'd grabbed me and kissed me before he put me on a plane, to get me out of harm's way. I'd tasted regret, pain, torment. He'd loved Rebecca. He'd lost her.

"Ms. Smith—"

"I'm staying with your mother and she fell asleep, so I've moved to another room," I reply quickly, stepping into a spare bedroom and pulling the door shut.

"Where's my father?"

"He went to the college campus to meet with his assistant coaches about baseball season."

"Well, that's a relief. I pressured him to attend to his team today, and he told me he couldn't leave her alone with her nurse. If she's the wrong person, we need to replace her."

"No. She's very nice. Your mother is just emotionally wounded right now. She needs extra tender, loving care and I was happy to bring my work here and hang out with her."

"Since I'm still not there as I'd hoped, we need to talk about the staff and the press."

"They're handling the pressure from the reporters remarkably well."

"For now," he says. "But mark my words, money has a way of showing people's true colors. With hundreds of employees, someone will be offered a big payday and they'll take it. Those are usually the people that paint a canvas of lies, too."

I know how easily people hide nastiness behind a shell of niceness. "I'm ready if it happens. But your mother is alert now and I'm struggling to keep the news from her. You have to talk to her soon."

"I'm headed there Wednesday and I plan to stay in New York indefinitely. I'll get in touch with my father and we'll plan to talk to her if she seems strong enough. But don't say anything to her about Wednesday. I don't want to get her hopes up and have some problem keep me here."

Relief washes over me. "Oh, thank God. She's better when you're here. I hope your return means there's news on Ava?"

There is a brief silence, a shift in mood that crackles, before he replies, "From what I understand, you called Jacob yesterday and asked him the same question."

Taken off guard, exhausted, and hurt for reasons I don't try to understand right now, I fight to contain the sharpness of my tone. "Yes," I confirm. "I called your private bodyguard."

He doesn't even try to contain the sharpness in his. "Don't go around me again."

The reprimand hits me all kinds of wrong ways, and I snap. "If you expect me to say, 'Yes, Mr. Compton,' it's not happening. I won't apologize to you for wanting answers. *No.* This isn't even about wanting them. I need them to ensure I can keep holding things together here. I deserve not to be left in the dark."

His silence stretches to the point that I want to scream, though like him, I don't lose control easily. I most certainly don't scream— at least, I haven't for many years.

"Nothing," he finally says.

"Nothing?" Is this one of his many head games? "What does that mean?"

"There's no sign of Ava. She's just vanished."

Shocked he's conceded me this battle, I quickly dive in for more information before he shuts me out. "Did she have the money to leave the country?"

"From what I hear, not enough to truly disappear, not without some help. And the only thing I'm hearing is speculation."

"They still think Ricco helped her, because he believed you were framing her for Rebecca's murder?"

"That's the theory. They're convinced he thought the kid from the coffee shop was her lover, and he helped them run off, perhaps to another country."

I read what he hasn't said. "You don't buy it."

"The kid was going to turn in evidence on her. Why would he run off with her?"

"To buy time with the police?"

"Maybe," he says tightly. "Or maybe she killed him, too."

"Do you think . . . would Ricco actually have killed Ava? Could that be why she's so completely off the radar?"

"If he is responsible for Ava's disappearance, I hope like hell that bastard found out she was guilty, and killed the bitch. It saves me the trouble of hunting her down and doing it myself."

The guttural roughness of his voice reminds me of his vow to kill anyone who hurt Rebecca. "You don't mean that. Mark, you can't—"

"I know what killing her would do to my family. And I already told you, I'm not convinced it was Ricco that helped Ava, anyway."

"But you think someone did."

"Yes."

"Who?"

A pause. "I sent you back there to keep you out of this."

"I'm already swimming neck deep."

"Just control the media and run Riptide. *Stay away* from the rest. If I find out you've done any differently, I don't care how dedicated you are or how loved you are by my mother, I'll fire you."

"Fire me?" I gasp, hurt, insulted, and appalled.

"It's better than having you end up hurt. You've been protecting my family. I'm going to protect you."

"I don't need protection."

"Well, you're getting it. Which brings me to the subject of Walker Security. Their corporate office is in Manhattan, and I've contracted them to take over Riptide's security next week. They'll also be putting men at my parents' building around the clock. Since Blake Walker is still here working with the SFPD to find Ava, Jacob's coming with me to New York."

Tension curls up my spine. "This is extreme. What haven't you told me?"

"I can't stay away when my mother needs me. But where I go, the press follows—in far bigger hordes than you've experienced."

"No. That's not what this is about."

"It's me taking control."

"Of what, Mark?"

"Everything. I'm taking control of everything." His phone beeps. "I have to take that. Call me if anything changes." The line goes dead.

Sinking onto the mattress, I lie on my back and stare at the ceiling. *I'm taking control of everything.* That includes me—or he thinks it does. But it's bigger than that, too. I felt it; I read it between the lines. I replay the conversation, connecting the dots from everything I know to date, and come to the only conclusion I can. This is about the vengeance he vowed—and there are more players than I know. That threat to fire me was to make me back off before I see too much or get hurt. He was so fiercely adamant about protection, there's clearly a risk of danger.

"What crazy, insane thing are you up to, Mark Compton?" I whisper.

## Mark . . .

An hour after we land in New York, Jacob stops the rented Escalade in front of a ten-story gray building nestled within a cluster of buildings inside the center of Manhattan's Rockefeller Center. "I'm not sure how long I'll be," I tell him, reaching for the door.

"I'll stay close," Jacob assures me, his steady, clipped ex-military tone part of his steely reserve.

With a short nod, I exit the rear seat onto the street and into large white snowflakes that quickly cover my hair and my Crombie topcoat. The beginning of a late fall snowstorm is yet another chilling reminder of how far I am from San Francisco and the life I'd worked to create for myself. But the illness my mother fights makes none of that matter anymore. Her living is all that matters.

Stepping under the overhang of the building, I glance at my Rolex to confirm I'm ten minutes early for the nine o'clock private meeting I've scheduled tonight, before I surprise my mother with my extended visit. "Riptide" is etched in gray stone between the large glass doors, and pride fills me. It's the largest auction house in the world, and my mother's creation is now twenty-five years strong—only nine years shy of my time on this earth.

This place is her beast to command and her kingdom of

thousands of employees to relish, but I'm the ruler here now. And I also have to take the helm of my life, and everything around me. I have to be the Master that I lost somewhere along the line—the one who would never allow someone close to him to be hurt, as I did Rebecca.

I key in a code and enter the building, greeting one of the security guards on duty. Mr. Kimmel, well into his sixties, has been here since Riptide opened, and he offers me a quick greeting. "Mr. Compton, sir. I am certain you have made your mother's day."

"I'm surprising her in the morning."

He smiles and his eyes light up. "A good way to start her day, indeed. Will you be staying long?"

"Indefinitely."

"Oh, sir, this is good news that everyone, Ms. Smith included, will welcome." And I have this sense that despite all the negative media about me, he feels I will save the day, or the company—or, hell, the damn world. As if I am unable to fail, as I have too much as of late.

He lifts a hand. "Shall I take your topcoat and briefcase?"

"Just my topcoat," I say, shrugging out of it and handing it to him. "Thank you, Mr. Kimmel."

"No, thank *you*, Mr. Compton." He taps his badge. "I got an offer from Walker Security to stay on when they took over this week. I'm honored to have the opportunity to continue to work with your family."

Having known him since my childhood, and being aware of my mother's fondness for him, I easily reply, "It's we who are honored to have so many years of honest service."

Pride glows in his eyes at my words. He deserves the compliment. I might be hard; I might be demanding. But my mother taught me to commend those who prove greatness with loyalty and fairness.

His reaction to my arrival sets my determination to achieve the goal I'm here to attend to, and my steps quicken as I walk down the long hallway that I know leads to Ms. Smith's office. She needs to know that the Master is back from the bowels of hell. Sex and control make me stronger, which I'd forgotten these past few weeks—with gut-wrenching, heart-shredding results. I eased my rules, and crossed lines for and with Rebecca that ultimately led to her death.

I swore ten years ago that no one by my side would ever get hurt again. Yet in the dangerous gray that lies between black and white, I've already crossed lines with Ms. Smith.

No more. There is no in between.

# Two

‍

## Mark . . .

Stepping confidently into Crystal's open doorway, I find her behind her glass desk, gaze fixed on the file she is studying, her long, shapely legs crossed. Seconds tick by before, in the midst of turning a page, she freezes. Her gaze lifts, landing on me, and she pops to her feet. My eyes sweep the way her formfitting pale pink suit hugs her curves and complements her sleekly styled long blond hair. My cock thickens and heat that I don't deny or dismiss blazes in my veins, allowing myself the right to be unapologetically a man and a Master.

When my gaze returns to hers, I don't hide the predatory gleam in mine. It's part of the message I'm here to deliver. Sex is my release, my way of dealing with life.

"Hi," she says, her stare remarkably unwavering as the sexual tension between us crackles like a live current. "And before you ask what kind of greeting that is," she adds, reminding me of something I'd said to her a week before when we'd burned up the sheets in a California hotel room, "the answer is the same as before. It's my kind."

*Her kind*. The kind that simply doesn't work for me as a Master. But it does, apparently, work for the man beneath the armor I fully intend to restore. I *have* restored.

I shut the door and then motion to the small, round conference table in the corner. "Let's sit." I'm irritated that I'm aware she's wearing the same outfit she'd worn the first night I met her, several weeks ago.

She nods and moves with the same pace, the same confident steps, confirming that she is not my type. As she once said, we're too alike, two bulls fighting for the same red flag. We come together at the edge of the seats, neither of us voluntarily claiming one first, standing toe to toe, our gazes locking.

A band seems to tug our bodies closer; I feel our shared connection in my chest and see it in the dilation of her soft blue eyes. The howl of memories is like a heavy wind that refuses to be ignored. I'd buried my pain over the news of a search for Rebecca's body in Crystal's body. I'd been weak, drunk, hurting. I'd tried to recover with a business-from-this-point-forward talk.

But when I'd walked Crystal, not *Ms. Smith*, to a private jet the next day, I'd needed to touch her, to taste her one last time—the "one last time" I'd never had with Rebecca. My weakened armor had dropped, and I'd pulled her to me and kissed the hell out of her.

And damn it to hell, I want to do that again. But I won't.

Ms. Smith lifts her hand to touch me, the way I've often let her and no one else do, though I still don't understand why. Then she seems to sense the change in me, pulling back before contact.

"How are you?" she asks.

The rasp in her voice edges down my nerve endings and evokes emotions that, on some level, I want to arouse in her, though all I should desire from any woman is passion and lust. Those needs are within the realms I have always controlled, so they are acceptable.

But I sense Ms. Smith wants more. And what I want from her is more—which infuriates me.

"How am I?" My words are as tight as my spine. "Ready to get back to normal. Sit."

Her brow furrows in silence at the command, a prelude to the many battles I suspect are before us, but she claims her seat, as I do mine. Setting my briefcase on a chair, I pull out a document and set it in front of me, intentionally building her expectation as to what it might be.

And I think she knows that, since she refuses to look at it. I narrow my stare on hers, wondering if there's more behind her iron will than growing up in a rich family with dominant men. And in doing so, I see the slightest hint of discomfort in the depths of her eyes, the weakness I'm looking for to push her well beyond her comfort zone.

"I have the answer to my first question," I state. "Clearly, we still want to fuck."

Her lips part in surprise, then a look of incredulity slides over her delicate features as a disgusted sound slips from her lips. "Funny. I thought your first question would be 'How's my mother?' Or 'How's my father?' Or 'How is the staff, after they've taken a beating from the press and customers pounding them with questions?'"

"We've had that conversation three times in four days, including last night. I trust you. That's the point."

"No. The point seems to be us wanting to fuck again."

My lips quirk at her bold statement. "I'll take your lack of denial as confirmation you agree. And us wanting to fuck *has* everything to do with us working together on a day-to-day basis, Ms. Smith."

"Crystal," she amends. "You know 'Ms. Smith' bothers me, since long before we got naked together. Not even the staff calls me that."

"Formality is how I manage and how I operate. It's not a slap. It's not a reflection on us getting naked together. I simply cannot maintain structure with the staff by treating you differently, nor would we be able to avoid questions."

She inhales and lets it out. "Point taken, Mr. Compton."

"Thank you, Ms. Smith." I pause for effect. "My plan is to be by my mother's side as much as possible, and leave you with your present duties if you're agreeable. I'll simply help you navigate the ship in the more treacherous waters."

She nods. "I have a list of powerful clients and prospective clients who represent large dollar figures, and it's taking time to earn the trust that you'd have in one phone call. So I need backup."

"You have it." I lean back and study her a moment. "You treat this company and my family as your own."

"Is that a question?"

"No. I'm just trying to figure out why you're doing it for us, since your own family owns one of the largest tech companies on the planet. That's a lot to walk away from."

"You did the same: Riptide is one of the largest auction houses in the world. And, like I told you, my father and brothers are very controlling, much like you. In fact, I'd say they are equally overbearing."

I arch a brow, amused at her boldness. "You think I'm over-bearing."

"You take pride in being overbearing."

I incline my head. "It works for me. But my mother wrote the book on overbearing—yet here you are."

"It's different. She isn't them."

"But I am?"

"You're arrogant, intolerably bossy, often rude, and infuriating, but—you're my boss, not my family. And I'll point out that you chose to open your gallery across the country, despite being emotionally close to your parents."

"Birds of a feather," I say. "But there's more to your story."

"There's more to yours."

I lean in closer, lowering my voice to a soft rasp. "I never take what isn't given to me freely, Ms. Smith."

She smiles. "Nor do I, Mr. Compton."

The unexpected reply curls my lips. "You are nothing that I expect."

"Because you never expect anyone to be like you. Two birds of a feather. Remember?"

"I'm fairly certain you won't let me forget." We're close, a mere lean-in from a kiss, one I crave more each moment I'm with her.

I lean back before I forget my agenda. "Whatever the rest of your story is, when I look into your eyes I see honesty and sincerity, qualities I value more than ever. Qualities I owe you in return. That means giving you a clear understanding of who and what I am—because the past few weeks have not been an example of those things."

Her gaze lowers and she says softly, "I know I'm a gateway to a place you're using to cope with . . . things." Then she looks at me.

17

"Maybe I even *am* that place. You've just lost someone important to you. You fear losing your mother to cancer. So anything you feel with me is about *them*, not me. Sex is an escape for you.

"And it is for me, too. It's how I've handled the emotion all of this creates in me. So I don't need or want your guilt. We're clear on everything."

But we're not; the muddied water we're traveling is dangerous. Worse, she makes me want to believe we *can* continue. But she brings out a part of me I don't want to exist; if I let it, I *will* deserve the guilt.

"If we're clear up to this point," I reply, sliding the contract across the table, "then you understand why it's so important that we're equally clear on what our relationship is or isn't going forward."

Her eyes hold mine and she swallows hard, before her gaze drops to the contract. She stares at the first line, "Master and Submissive Contract," for two beats and then calmly hands it back to me. "I told you. I will never be your submissive."

"This is how I operate." A contract is about my responsibility for her well-being, being in charge of everything that she is and does. Yet that's not really what I want right now. I want lust, desire. Short, intense BDSM sessions that let me exert the control I need in the rest of my life, strengthening me—but right now I'm too far to the other side to make that happen.

"This is how you operate," she repeats slowly.

"Yes. The only way."

"It's not how I operate." She stands up, in full rejection mode.

I push to my feet as well. "Have you ever *been* a submissive?" I ask, intentionally pushing her buttons. "Did you have a bad experience, and that's why you're resisting?"

She makes a frustrated sound. "All you need to know is that I will never be one with you."

She walks away and I have to clamp down on a sudden urge to grab her, pull her to me, and demand to know what the fuck she meant. *She is not for you,* I remind myself. *She is not for you.*

She puts the desk between us. "I'd like to get back to my work now."

Her voice quivers with hurt—not my intention, and proving how bad this could get if it continued. And what's bad for us would also be bad for my mother. Slipping the contract back into my briefcase, I go for the close, standing directly across from her and pinning her in an unwavering stare. "Submitting to me would teach you things about yourself that I know, and you don't."

The hurt disappears, replaced by red-hot anger blazing from her eyes. "You know about me? Seriously? You don't even know about *you* right now."

Goal achieved. Believing that I'm an asshole lets her hold her head high; lets this end on her terms.

I press my hands on the desk, leaning toward her. "Oh, Ms. Smith," I purr, "you'd be shocked to know just how well I know myself. You'd be even more shocked to know how well I know you. After fucking under my rules just once, I'd own you."

She presses her hands to the desk and leans forward, too, yet I see her bottom lip quiver. "Fucking me," she bites out, "*pleasing* me, doesn't make you own me."

My blood heats with desire. "Sounds like a challenge to me."

"One you'd fail," she assures me.

"Should I remind you yet again, how easily I made you beg me to lick your—"

"Don't," she warns calmly. "Don't keep pushing me." She

straightens her spine and crosses her arms. "I'm done. We're done." She sits down and pulls her folder in front of her. "I'm getting back to work."

*Control.* She wants it desperately, but we both know it's mine. I've won, despite my body's scream that the only win would be bending her over the desk and burying myself inside her. I curve my lips as if I'm amused at her efforts, though I'm not. "Carry on, Ms. Smith," I say, arrogantly enough to singe every control-freak nerve ending she owns as I turn and head to the door.

As my hand touches the knob, she says, "Objective achieved."

The simple words are as good a power play as any I've ever delivered. Intrigued despite myself, I turn and arch a brow. "Objective achieved?"

"You had a message to give me tonight, and I got it. You love your family too much to risk letting us become a problem. It won't. As I've said before, we didn't happen."

*We didn't happen.* She'd challenged me with those words right before I'd followed her to a restaurant bathroom and proved I could make her say, "Mr. Compton, please lick my pussy." I didn't like her words then, and I don't like them now.

"Denial is weakness," I tell her. "It means that I'll have you tied up and tormented before you know it. I'll own you before you can blink. You need to come up with a better plan, or you'll belong to me in no time. Unless that's what you really want."

I leave, giving her no chance to reply.

## Crystal . . .

He disappears into the hallway, his musky, spicy, deliciously provocative scent lingering. After his footsteps fade, my shoulders finally slump and my breath gushes from my lips. I knew this was coming, and thought I was prepared. I'd spent the last few days telling myself that I'd *welcome* the day that he pushed me away, because he'd gotten under my skin. But I hadn't been prepared for his trying to turn me into a mere contract that expires—and it scares me that he still affected me after he gave it to me. He's still everything I don't want, and somehow everything I crave.

No. *No.* I shove off the desk. The man I just dealt with is not the man I crave. He is not the man I've known these past weeks, the man I've started to fall for in a huge way. The one who has a tender side, who's vulnerable yet strong.

This man is cold and hard, an arrogant asshole, and I should welcome these realizations. Falling in love with a man who's grieving for a woman he'd loved and lost is nothing but a heartache. And Mark Compton is *not* a man you let tie you up, or he's right: He'll own you. I've worked too hard to find myself and my freedom to let that happen.

He doesn't know me—not even close. And he's just done me a favor. Now we're both where we need to be: in control of ourselves, not each other. We're done.

# Three

Mark . . .

I'm cold inside and out as I exit Riptide, for reasons that have nothing to do with the snow that's now blowing in fierce gusts. As I slide into the Escalade, Jacob eyes me in the rearview mirror. "Everything okay?"

"Fucking beautiful."

"Does that mean go to the hotel, or a bar?"

"Sex is my drug, not booze." Especially not scotch, considering the last time I'd drunk-dialed Ms. Smith and flown her to San Francisco. "Go to the Omni on Madison Avenue."

"Got it," he assures me, tapping his GPS.

He pulls away from the curb, and during the three-minute drive I replay my encounter with Ms. Smith. By the time the hotel doormen open our car doors, I tell myself there was no other way than making her hate me. This woman sees beneath my skin, and the sense of freedom in being unable to hide from her is dangerous. Instead of containing what I feel in some moment, when she's

23

nearby, I get lost in it and in her. She makes me weak enough to forget my control. And I think it's pretty clear I'm not one of her better choices, either.

Jacob and I enter the white-tiled lobby, a sparkling chandelier above our heads. Due to the late hour and the weather, only a few patrons are sprinkled across the room. "The front desk," I say when I don't see any manager I recognize. At the counter, the clerk quickly looks up the alias I've registered under, as I did during my mother's blood infection, and sees the flag on my file. As I follow the woman leading us to a private office, Ms. Smith's *"I'm a gateway"* plays in my head, causing a twist of guilt in my gut. She'd have ended up hating me anyway, no doubt rightfully so.

The manager who helps us is no one I know, a pretty blonde whom I barely register outside of her remote resemblance to Ms. Smith, who seems to want to play around in my head. She does whatever check-in computer work that is needed while Jacob engages her in conversation to ensure our privacy.

The woman is efficient and quick, as is Jacob's glance at our room numbers and the knowing look of disapproval when he sees we're on different floors. Leveling a stare at him, I dare him to challenge me and he gets the message. We cross the quiet lobby to the elevators, the silence between us lurking, not comfortable.

I hired his team for a specific list of reasons. That list does not include ensuring that I don't carry out my vow of vengeance, spoken in a moment of torment in front of his boss. But the news that Rebecca was most likely dead and in the Bay, knowing that she'd struggled for years with nightmares of drowning in the Bay, had been torture.

We enter the elevator, riding to his floor in silence. "My room at eight in the morning," I say when the elevator halts. "That should give us plenty of time to get to my parents' apartment and then the hospital for my mother's treatment at ten."

Jacob punches the button to hold open the door. "I've been thinking about tomorrow. You mentioned the press had tracked you to your parents' apartment during your last stay, even though the apartment had a private garage that should have prevented you from being detected. I can't help but think someone on the building staff is being paid to tip them off."

"What are you saying?"

"Your mother wasn't aware of her surroundings the last time you were here, but she is now. Since you haven't warned her yet about what's being said in the news, and you were pleased with the hospital's protocols for high-profile visitors, I think you need to surprise your mother there."

My lips thin. "I don't like it, but I'll do it. Change the meet-up time to nine."

"Check. My gut feeling, and they're never wrong, is to talk to your mother sooner rather than later."

"I don't like how that sounds."

"My gut feelings saved my life many times in the service."

I inhale and let it out, wishing like hell I had time to let my mother recover from her treatments before she has to deal with any of this. "I'll expedite the talk, but I need to pick the right moment. In the meantime, I need you to get me past the leak in my parents' building."

"Already on it. I have backup coming to the hospital tomorrow, to cover you while I meet with the apartment security head." The elevator buzzes in protest of Jacob holding the button. "My time is up." His lips curve on one side.

As the steel doors close a cluster of thoughts rushes at me

almost instantly, and I force it away, leaving my mind blank. It's all about control.

The ding signaling the twenty-first floor sounds and I go to my regular suite, turning on the living room/office fireplace before three rapid knocks sound on the door—my regular bellman. Before placing my bags in the closets, he offers me a large yellow special-delivery envelope with my name typed on the front.

Adrenaline rushes through me. It's the information that I've been waiting for for a full week. Feeling like I finally have ammunition for the vengeance I fully intend to enact, I double his tip and send him on his way.

Once I'm alone again I slip out of my jacket, loosen my tie, and settle onto the living room couch. Opening the envelope, I find a stack of papers and, conforming to my request of complete invisibility, a disposable phone with a number taped to the back. From this point forward, there are no names. He is "Doc," a nickname he uses for his precision at delivering whatever his clients need. As far as he's concerned I'm nobody, which suits me well.

Setting the phone aside, I begin going through the comprehensive documents. Everything I could ever want to know about Ryan Kilmer, from birth until present, including a complete list of all business transactions his thriving real estate business has ever made. Squeezing my eyes shut, memories jab at my mind of the many times that I'd invited him and Ava into Rebecca's and my most intimate moments. She'd hated them both, which was why I'd chosen them. To make her hate me. To make sure she didn't want them. And I did it all under the guise of Master. I was such a bloody fucking asshole.

Cursing, I push to my feet, walking to the glass door and stepping into the blast of snow and wind, intentionally tormenting myself. My hand closes on the freezing railing, a punishment for my actions, though I can never punish myself enough. Before me there is only white and gray, a flicker of lights muted in the core of the murkiness.

Ms. Smith asked who I thought had helped Ava, and the answer is Ryan. Fucking Ryan. I don't give a damn about his alibi for the night Rebecca died.

And considering our many profitable business transactions, I can think of only one motivation for Ryan's actions. The same as Ava's for killing Rebecca, and trying to kill Sara. Pure envy. Maybe of me and Rebecca, or perhaps of the power the club had become for me. I, of all people, know how easily jealousy forms and the poison it inevitably becomes. I curse again and turn my face to the blurred sky.

I shouldn't have done a lot of things I did where Rebecca was concerned. And I should have done a lot that I didn't. Ultimately, everything that has happened is my fault—but I'm not the only one who is going to pay.

I silently vow that by morning, I'll have a plan to unravel Ryan's life and his money train. And then I'll dial that phone, and let the real games begin.

It's three in the morning when I finally lie down, having left a message for Doc to call me. In my hand is Rebecca's journal. And as many times as I've promised myself that I won't read more, I can't help myself. It makes me feel like she's still alive. It makes me feel guilty and hate myself. It makes me focus on doing right by her in death, if not in life.

I flip open a page, to an entry I've read before and I know will shred me, and start reading:

*Lunchtime, Friday*

*Another nightmare. They were gone for months and now they are back, tormenting me as much as ever. I bought a book that said I should write them down to start understanding them, but they still mean nothing I can decipher in any way. But I keep writing them. So, here goes . . .*

*It started again with me hanging from a railing on the edge of a cable car that's somehow operating without a driver, and my dead mother is with me. We're both on the step hanging off the side of the car, but several feet separate us. As the car slowly climbs a hill the air is calm, but my emotions are in a frenzied dance. I remember how I felt as I write this. I don't seem to be able to see what I'm wearing, and for some reason I need to know. It's a silly detail that seems irrelevant, but maybe it's symbolic of some event in my life. . . . I really don't know.*

*My mother isn't smiling in this version of the nightmare, and she did when she first started visiting me. She looks angry, but ten years younger than when she died. The long, sleek brown hair she'd lost during her lung cancer battle is back; her pale skin absolutely luminous. Then I had the sudden realization that we weren't alone. A man in a suit is sitting near the back. There's never been anyone but my mother and I in these nightmares, and a sense of foreboding overwhelms me. I strain to see this new visitor, but his face is oddly in the shadows.*

*The car begins to top the hill and my mother hisses, "Don't look at him."*

*I cut my attention back to her and now her hair is short and thin; her body is thin, her skin now ashy. Memories of her lying in a hospital bed fighting for her life come back to me. "Who is he?" I ask curiously.*

*"Just don't look at him. He's dangerous. He's poison."*

*"Who is he?" I demand.*

*"No one I ever want you to know."*

*And then it hits me. "My father. Is this my father you refused to tell me about, even on your deathbed?"*

*"There are things it's best you never know," she says, repeating what she'd told me then. We start rolling down the hill and she lets go of the rail, balling her fists at her chest. "Do you know how much your anger hurt me when I was dying?"*

*"Grab the pole," I order, panic rising inside me. Our speed increases and I repeat more urgently, "Grab the pole!" We hit a bump, and I scream as she tumbles to the street and then vanishes.*

*Deep, evil male laughter radiates through the wicked wind that lifts my brown hair. My gaze goes to the faceless man and I climb up the step, past the seats, to the center aisle. The car is racing down the hill, too fast for the rails, and I have to grab the edge of the seats on either side to steady myself. "Stop laughing!" I demand, but the laughter just gets louder and louder. "Stop laughing!"*

*Anger and confusion collide in me, and I don't even think about the danger to myself. I rush at him, charging forward, but when I get to him he vanishes as my mother had. He's gone, as if he were never here.*

*Suddenly the car jumps the rails and takes flight. I gasp, trying to catch my balance, but I fall, sliding down the middle aisle. Scrambling for a grip somewhere, anywhere, I manage to grab the steel bottom of a pole and hold on. Hanging on never saves me in these nightmares, and I remember being conscious of that fact, but unable to fully conceive it. I want to live. I want to survive. (I think that maybe I will survive when I fully grasp the meaning of these nightmares.)*

*Squeezing my eyes shut, I prepare for what I know comes next. The cold splash hits me like a shock of pain. It's so real, and it never gets easier, no matter how many times I've done this before. I never accept death. As the freezing bay water seeps through to my skin and bones, I swim, trying to find an exit before we go underwater and the trolley drags me down with it. But I can't get there quick enough, and I'm shivering, my teeth chattering, as the roof is upon me, my hand pressing against it. Inhaling, I draw in a deep breath a moment before the force shoves my head under the water. I'm near a door. I'm going to get out this time. With one hard pull on a pole, I jerk forward to the exit. And all of a sudden my mother's there, her eyes shut, hair floating upward. She's dead. Like I'm about to be. And then everything is black. . . .*

*That's the last thing I remember before I sit up in bed, gasping for air, the real world coming back to me. I'm in "his" bedroom, in his bed; the spicy male scent of him is everywhere, a sweet jolt of reality.*

*My Master's hand comes down on my back. "Easy," he says. "You're okay." He pulls me into his arms and holds me tightly, stroking my naked back, which still tingles from the flogger he'd used on me before bed. And I want to be tied up again, have him take me to a place that leaves no room for the fear I'd felt in those moments underwater.*

*I whisper his name, the name I never dare write for fear someone will find this one day here at the gallery and read my words—but I said it then. I had to, and he didn't correct me, as if he knew how much I needed him to be just him, and real—for us to be real. For*

*there to be more to us than a contract. And sometimes, like in that*
*moment this morning, when he's holding me, when he's gentle in a*
*way I know he's not with anyone else, I let myself believe that we*
*are more.*

*He leaned back then, stroking the hair from my eyes as he*
*promised, "I'm here. You're here. We're okay." But that gnawing feel-*
*ing I've been battling, that we wouldn't be okay for long, had already*
*returned and I can't help but worry that's what my nightmares are*
*telling me. I'm about to lose someone else I love. Him. Us. Lately I*
*feel like I've already lost me, like I don't know who I am anymore.*
*Like Rebecca Mason is just a girl who used to exist and left nothing*
*behind worth remembering.*

*He laid me down and made love to me, then. Not fucked me,*
*not flogged me. Made love. And it turns out I needed that far more*
*than the flogging. For just a little while, all those other feelings faded.*
*A year ago, that tenderness would carry me for weeks—but now, only*
*hours later, I need more.*

I wake at 8 a.m. to the alarm and Rebecca's journal lying on my
chest. For several minutes I stare at the ceiling, replaying some of
the hundred drowning entries, most of which involve me in some
way. Scrubbing a hand through my hair, I set it aside, although letting go of it cuts me deep in my soul.

I want her back. I want to fix what I didn't do right, though
I'm not even sure where the right and wrong began and ended.
Maybe at hello. But I'll never get the chance to find out.

Pushing to my feet, I walk to the bathroom. I need to look
myself in the mirror, to face my sins and my emotions, to rebuild
my armor and the Master I've lost. Maybe that happened at hello,
too, and I just didn't realize it.

By 8:45, I'm dressed in a custom-made black suit with a red tie, chosen because it's my mother's lucky color. While I haven't believed in luck in a very long time, she does, and that's what matters.

Going to the desk I used to plot Ryan's demise, I seal the documents back into the envelope, then walk to the closet and squat down in front of the hotel safe. After placing them inside, I lock it securely. Returning to the desk, I dial from the untraceable cell phone, frustrated when I get the beep of voice mail. Leaving a message that could bite me in the ass later isn't an option, so I end the call.

At nine o'clock, Jacob is at my door in a black suit and a trench coat. He announces, "It's snowing like a forest fire outside."

I arch a brow at the contradictory statement that somehow makes sense. Taking my Crombie from the entryway closet, I step into the hallway, letting the door slam shut as I start walking. Ready to get to the hospital and see my parents. Even more ready to take action than I was last night. I'm done with sitting back, waiting, wanting, burning to death from my own lack of control.

The elevator opens and Jacob and I step inside. "Anything I need to know about this morning, Bossman?" he asks, using the nickname the Allure staff back in San Francisco often call me.

"I want one of your men shadowing Crystal around the clock."

"Suspicion or protection?"

"Protection. She's too close to my family and business to assume she won't become a target."

"Starting when?"

"Today. And it's not enough for you to just be on alert for Ava. Find her and whoever's helping her, before she finds us."

His jaw is set hard. "We're working on it."

My eyebrow goes up. "No denial that she's working with someone? I thought you were programmed to repeat that police rubbish?"

"More like, told not to encourage you to rip anyone's throat out in the name of vengeance."

"But you're telling me that you think there's more to Ava's disappearance? Despite that order from your boss?"

"Yes, I do. And they do."

"About damn time you grew some balls."

"I assure you, Mr. Compton, I have balls the size of Texas when I need them. I can also promise you that, despite downplaying it to you, Walker Security is working every angle that could represent danger to you or your family, or even your reputation. They aren't ignoring any possibility where Ava is concerned, or taking anything for granted where safety is concerned. They're damned good—which is why I joined them."

The elevator doors ding open and we step out, then head toward the lobby doors. "Do you have any new information you should share?"

"Nothing on Ava, Ryan, or Ricco that helps us at all."

"Would you tell me if you did?"

"Not if I could rip their throats out for you and call it justice, to spare you the aftermath."

"I'm not sure what to make of that answer."

His stoic expression doesn't change. "I do that to people." He continues: "I don't like the setup here. There's only one door in and out of the hotel. If the press gets too heavy, it'll be a trap. We need to move."

Just then the hotel manager spots us from the bellman's desk and rapidly moves in our direction.

"That's Ralph Reed," I explain of the forty-something dark-haired man in a brown suit approaching. "The hotel manager. He's been around for years, and the hard set of his jaw and his brisk stride means there's a problem."

"Whatever it is, it just happened—because I met with him about my security concerns earlier this morning."

Fighting the urge to curse at what's certain to be a delay, I glance at my watch. "We have less than an hour to get to the hospital."

"We'll get there," Jacob assures me.

"Spoken like a tourist," I reply. "You don't know the city at this time of the day and in bad weather."

"Mr. Compton and Mr. Parker," Mr. Reed says as we meet mid-lobby. "Excuse me for getting right to the point, but we have a . . . situation."

Jacob motions to a corner. "Let's step to the side, where we aren't as exposed."

"Of course," the manager agrees.

I hold up a staying hand. "I have to get to the hospital. What's the situation?"

"Someone claiming to be with the press was asking for you this morning. I've questioned my staff about the leak, but no one is claiming responsibility."

"Did you get the name of this person, or their press credentials?" Jacob immediately asks.

Mr. Reed's lips press together. "Unfortunately, no. The doorman did try, as did the bellman's desk."

"Did they confirm that Mr. Compton's staying here?" Jacob asks.

"Absolutely not," Mr. Reed assures us. "We took great precautions to keep Mr. Compton's stay as invisible as possible. However, he is quite well known among the staff."

"Is there security footage of this visitor?" Jacob asks, pounding away at the issue, which is commendable, but the seconds are also pounding away at my watch.

"We have cameras everywhere," Mr. Reed replies. "I can arrange the footage."

"Call me when it's ready," Jacob instructs. "You have my card. And if it can be emailed, please do so."

I insert, "Right now, I need to be somewhere."

"Of course," Mr. Reed says, sounding apologetic. "I'll be in contact in the next hour."

I'm already stepping around him and heading toward the door by the time he's finished the sentence. Jacob again falls into step with me and I say, "Clearly, you aren't convinced it's a member of the press asking around about me."

"My motto is proof before acceptance."

I don't ask where that comes from. I've looked in the man's eyes. I've seen the hardness that only going to hell and pulling yourself back gives a person, and I approve. People who've been through a bloodbath and survived are the strongest, and I expect nothing less than Hercules by my side when it comes to protecting my family and employees.

We step outside to find the Escalade has been pulled around and is waiting for us, the storm gusting wickedly. I wave away the back door a doorman opens for me, choosing the front instead.

Jacob joins me and glances at me, his face expressionless as he starts the engine.

"You aren't my driver," I tell him, answering the question he hasn't asked. "And I prefer being behind the wheel, especially in the city." I eye my watch. "Step on it."

We pull away from the curb into blizzard-like conditions, the traffic as heavy as the snow on the bumpers. I'm not going to make my mother's treatment by car. When finally we begin to move, I direct Jacob to a subway stop and tell him, "Meet me at the hospital. Tell them your name and I'll have them bring you to me." I open my door.

"Wait. Where the hell are you going?"

"I'm taking the subway."

"That's risky with someone looking for you," he points out. "Let me park—"

The light turns and I get out, slamming the door shut as horns start blowing.

# Four

Mark . . .

I hold on to a pole in the crowded subway car. I've had to take three trains to reach the hospital, all done in only fifteen minutes. It would have taken an hour on the city streets.

The train halts and as the crowd moves toward the doors, a flash goes off too close to me for comfort. I look for a camera or cell phone being directed my way but find nothing. Giving up, I exit and head for the stairs to the street, bothered by the flash that my gut tells me was directed at me.

I reach the hospital five minutes later and quickly arrange entry for Jacob through the secure entrance reserved for visitors of high-profile patients. It's now just ten minutes until my mother's treatment time. Rushing out of the elevator on her floor, I head toward the private room we've arranged for her to use before her treatments. Headed toward me, rolling an empty wheelchair, is my mother's radiology nurse. Just seeing that chair, and thinking about seeing my mother in it again, rips a piece of my heart out, but Reba is still a sight for sore eyes. She's close to my mother's age and has a knack for challenging every stubborn word my mother speaks—of which there are many—while still making my mother love her.

"I'm so glad—" she begins as we meet outside the cracked door of my mother's room.

I hold up a finger, stepping to her side. "She doesn't know I'm here."

She smiles warmly and pulls the door shut. "She's going to be elated. I'll give you a couple of minutes to see her, but we have a tight schedule, so make it quick. Your timing is perfect. Apparently she tried to refuse to come this morning."

"Refused? That's new. She's been all about getting this behind her and getting back to work."

"Even the strong feel weak at times, and believe me, cancer is the beast that can make that a truth. The blast of chemo your mother was given just before the mastectomy was a lot for most to handle, but yet she weathered both procedures well. But we just couldn't give her as much time after that blood infection to get stronger as we would have liked to ensure she didn't go backwards now. Considering everything, I'd say she has a right to feel beat up."

I nod. "Hopefully I can help her get past this."

"From what I understand, you were her rock during the blood infection. Having you here will be good for her. But be warned; she's lost more weight since you left."

"How much?" I ask, concerned. "She was too thin two weeks ago."

"About five more pounds, but it looks like ten on her already frail frame."

"Is that from the radiation?"

"Mostly the aftermath of the blood infection, but she says she's too tired to eat. I think it's depression. We can talk more while she's in treatment, but I want to get a counselor to talk to her. We need to convince her it's a good idea."

"I'll convince her," I say forcefully, not about to let my mother stop fighting. She's always been my unbreakable rock. I'll be hers now. "Whatever she needs, we'll make happen."

"I know you will. I'll be back in five minutes." She motions to the wheelchair. "Maybe you can coax her into this?"

"Consider it done." My fingers curl around the chair's handles. She opens the door a crack again, then walks away. Steeling myself for what might wait for me inside, I nudge the door open a bit more and pause.

"If I skip this week then I'll be stronger next week," I hear my mother say, and even her voice is frail.

"Dana," my father starts, his voice a reprimand usually reserved for the game of baseball.

"I need to be stronger this week, Steven," she argues. "Mark just learned about Rebecca. He's going to need the support you'll have to give him. You can't do that if I'm this weak."

"Eat and you'll be stronger," he says.

My mother is actually worrying about me when she's fighting for her life, and it triggers two words in my mind: "Control" and "Master." That's what my family needs me to be now. I have to be their pillar.

I find the mental armor I've put on at will for ten years now and roll the chair forward, calling, "I hear you need a driver." And as I take in the sight before me, I've never been as thankful for that armor as I am now.

In this mode I'm able to slow down my mind, processing what I see in a controlled fashion despite only seconds passing. My father hovers beside my mother's greenish blue hospital chair, his gaze fixed on her, his normally muscular body looking gaunt, the streaks of gray in his light brown hair more predominant than just two weeks before.

My mother in the chair, her blond hair now thin and cut to her chin, her face gaunt, her body no more than a hundred pounds under her hospital robe. A wave of pure fear overcomes me and the control I'd shackled is faltering, as it has often these past two weeks. I'm going to lose her, too. I'm going to lose my mother as I did Rebecca, and I swear I feel the darkness of hell begin to swallow me right there in that room.

I tear my gaze from my mother to give myself a moment to breathe, and my gaze lands on Ms. Smith, kneeling on the floor beside my mother, her hand covering my mother's thinner one.

Her long blond hair is a striking contrast to her red silk blouse, which I know she wore for the same "good luck" reason I wore my tie. Our eyes collide and our combative conversation from last night fades away. Effortlessly, she is in every crack I haven't sealed in the armor, her strength supporting mine.

"Mark!" my mother exclaims. Her expression is pure happiness; the light in her eyes washes away the darkness of hell. She tries to stand, and my father grabs her arm at the same time that Ms. Smith grabs her knees, holding her in place.

"Dana, no," Ms. Smith warns at the same time my father says, "Wait." He gives me a look, appealing for help, the steel once in his gray eyes terrifyingly absent. The man I've known as a quiet strength is nowhere to be found. He's terrified.

And I get it.

"Stay put, Mother," I order, abandoning the wheelchair to squat down beside her. My knee touches Ms. Smith's, and the tension that rockets through my body is as unwelcome as the way she sees too much. I take my mother's hand and tease, "Still trying to run races, I see."

She doesn't laugh. She presses her free hand to my cheek and studies me. "I haven't seen that look in your eyes in over a decade. You were closer to her than I realized." Her lips tighten, the way they do when she's fighting an emotional response to something. "I never wanted to see it again."

Swallowing the knot in my throat, I am amazed that she still sees me this clearly. I draw her hand into my lap. "I'm one hundred times better being here, I promise you," I say, not offering a denial she rightfully wouldn't believe. "But I won't be if you're *not* here. I need you here. I need you well, and skipping treatments won't do that."

"I need a break. And—"

"The façade of feeling better is dangerous," I warn, firming my voice. "Take the hits and be done with it."

"That's what I keep telling her," my father inserts.

She glowers over her shoulder at him. "I was worried about both of you," she tells him, then turns to me again. "How long will you be here? What's happening with the police?"

"I'll be here indefinitely—so we have plenty of time to catch up."

Surprise registers on her face. "Indefinitely? But what about Allure?"

"I'm not worried about Allure. I made arrangements to be away as long as needed."

She doesn't look convinced. "You're sure?"

"Positive enough to have a realtor finding me an apartment."

"You can stay with us," she says. "Our place is huge. We won't even know you're there."

"I might just buy a place here," I tell her, instead of admitting that I'm a magnet for trouble. "No matter what, I'll be close." I lean back on my haunches. "Reba will be here to pick you up any second. Let's get you in the chair."

Ms. Smith takes that as her cue to stand, but loses her balance. Instinctively, I reach out and catch her arm before she ends up sprawled on the floor. She grabs my arm in return, and what I feel between us is too present and powerful to dismiss. I have failed to end what I started.

## Crystal . . .

As I stare into Mark's eyes, I try to remember the anger I'd felt last night—and this morning. He's like Dr. Jekyll and Mr. Hyde, and right now he's the man I'd been falling for, the man who cares for his family with such deep love that he tore down the walls I'd erected early in life.

He stands and pulls me up with him before his hands, those big, wonderful hands, slip away, leaving me aching for their return. Fifteen minutes ago, I would have sworn that I never wanted him to touch me again.

"Thank you," I say, and while he only nods, there's appreciation in his eyes for my being here for him and his family.

We break eye contact to find his parents staring at us. If Mark notices, he doesn't act like it, merely reaching for his mother's arm. "Let's get you up before Reba has my hide for delaying her schedule."

As if she were waiting to be announced, Reba enters the room with an "Are we ready?"

"We are," Mark assures her as Dana settles into the chair. "Right, Mother?"

"No," his mother retorts. "But I'll go."

It hurts my heart to hear this vibrant, powerful woman sound like a punished child.

"Grumble, grumble," Reba teases. "Boy, am I ready for you to order me around again so I can tell you I'm not your employee." She gestures toward me. "That's what she said this past weekend, too."

I smile. "Only I *am* her employee, so I do have to take orders."

"Actually," Mark amends too softly, "you're mine now."

My gaze jerks to his intense gray one, and heat flushes my skin at the possessiveness there. Unbidden, the memory of him saying "I'll own you" is in my mind. My chin lifts rebelliously, delivering the message "*No one* owns me, and that will never change, most especially not for you."

His father moves between us, giving me a blessed chance to breathe. "I'll push my wife," he tells Reba. "We'll talk baseball on the way to the treatment room, and she'll tell me everything I'm doing wrong with the team."

"It's the pitching," Dana immediately says, catching on to the bone he's thrown her. "You have no one with the level head that Mark had on the mound."

"Yeah, yeah," Steven replies, pushing her toward the door. "So you've told me for ten years—and I might remind you that I've won four championships?"

*No one with the level head that Mark had on the mound.* I stare at the doorway as they disappear into the hallway, remembering a similar comment on another occasion. It's hard to imagine Mark playing a game of any sort, though competitive and focused fits him to a T.

"What are you doing here?" Mark snaps, shocking me back into the moment and the sudden realization that we're very much alone.

The tormented look in his eyes is gone; the steely gray from the night before is back. I'm baffled, unsure what is real and what's a façade. But I've dealt with powerful, controlling men all my life, and I know when they're fishing for a certain reaction, whatever it might be—and he's not going to get it.

Clamping down on the hurt and simmering anger, I reply, "I stopped by McDonald's to bring McMuffins for the nurses. While I was here, I figured I'd stop in and say hi."

"No one likes a smartass, Ms. Smith."

"Better a smartass than an asshole—Mr. Compton. I've been here before all of her treatments."

"You should have called me. I need to know the business is in order while I'm here by her side. Who's running Riptide now?"

My simmering anger begins to burn in my belly. "You barely returned my calls for months on end, when I was often desperate for guidance—and *now* you're questioning how things are being run? For your information, Mr. Compton, I taught myself, and taught myself well. When I come here to support Dana and Steven, I arrive at Riptide at six in the morning to ensure the day is organized and nothing slips through the cracks." I draw a hard-earned breath. "If this is about my refusal to sign—"

"It's not." His words are more of a reprimand than a reply. "However, a contract would have established boundaries we now need to otherwise address, for a productive working relationship."

It's all I can do not to recoil as if slapped. The reaction is too intense; a flash of a long-lost memory I don't want to remember. Somehow he's hit an emotional spot I never want touched. Ever.

"Boundaries?" I ask, my voice radiating emotion despite myself. "How's this for boundaries? Your father called me this morning because he hadn't heard from you, and your mother was refusing treatment. I went to their apartment, and we double-teamed her to get her here."

I shake my head. "You truly excel at being an asshole, Mark Compton. But you're the asshole your mother needs. You give her strength. You make her fight. And if that means you have to revel in your assholeness, so be it. I'll tolerate you for her sake."

He arches a brow. "You'll tolerate me?"

"That's right." I feel steadier now, already recovering from my flash down memory lane. "Though I'll need a big pink bottle of Pepto in my desk drawer, and some wine by my bedside." I snatch up my purse, tote bag, and coat from a chair on my way to the door. "She'll be out in half an hour. I'm going to work."

I head down the hall to the private elevators the staff has us use to avoid the press. After slipping on my coat and replacing my heels with snow boots from my oversized tote bag, I punch the call button for the car. He's such a complete jerk—the kind only a foolish woman would pine for. Maybe I have more of my biological mother in me than I thought.

The doors open and to my unwelcome surprise, Jacob is standing before me, looking all G.I. Joe with his buzz cut and hard-set jaw. Edginess radiates off him, the way I'm certain that anger must be bristling off of me.

"Crystal," he says, punching the button to hold the door as I enter. "Is Mr. Compton here?"

My brows dip. "Aren't you his bodyguard?"

"Exactly." His jaw clenches as he seems to clamp down on something he's about to say. "Is he here?"

"Yes. Don't worry. His mother's in treatment, and your client is safely tucked away in her private room."

A hint of relief flashes in his eyes before they go hard and focused again. "And you're going where?" he asks, a demand in his voice that I really don't need right now.

"To work," I say, stepping into the elevator.

"I'll ride back down with you." He lets go of the button and I turn to face him as he does the same with me. "We're arranging to have security around the clock for you," he informs me. "I'll wait downstairs with you until my backup arrives, then he'll accompany you to work."

"What? No, that's not necessary. No one has bothered me; I don't want or need a shadow."

"Now that Mark's here, that will change. The press will chase him down and do what they can to twist him in the headlines."

"No," I repeat as the elevator opens, and go down the hall to sign out at the guard desk. Jacob does the same as I head for the back door.

But Jacob is on my heels. "Mr. Compton wants this to happen."

I turn to face him. "He doesn't control my private time. And he said nothing to me upstairs about it."

"I'm sure he has his mother on his mind. He told me to handle it. Think about this, Crystal. You're close to the family, and that means you're a target. He just wants you to be safe."

I tamp down my anger at his calm words, and think about why this is all happening. Someone is dead. People have committed crimes, and it's not the first time the harshness of jealousy has hit this close to home. I know what it makes people capable of.

I briefly close my eyes. Damn it. I'm making rash decisions about my safety, which could affect other people's safety. The fact that Mark Compton rattles me into this state of illogical thought reignites my anger, but I'm not a fool. And I have a bad feeling that there's a lot more going on with Mark, and this investigation, than I know about.

With a deep breath, I say, "I'll provide my own security. My family has its own service. I'll get it in place right away."

As usual, he doesn't react. "I'd feel better if we did the job, so we know you're safe."

"My father is a perfectionist. He hires people that you'll approve of."

His jaw clenches just enough to give away his displeasure. "I'll talk to Mr. Compton. In the meantime, we'll cover you. My backup should be here any minute, then you can leave."

"I have a critically important eleven o'clock meeting that I can't miss."

"Crystal—"

"As in many millions of dollars at stake for Riptide. Go take care of the Compton family. I'll take the subway—busy trains with lots of cameras."

"I can't let you go without coverage."

I recite my route, and what stop I'm exiting. "Have one of your people meet me on the street if you really think it's necessary. I'll be there in twenty minutes."

"No subway. I'll put you in a cab, then have one of my men at Riptide meet you at the curb."

"You saw the weather and the traffic. I can't be late—and time is ticking as we argue."

"I need you to take a cab," he insists. "Even if you're late."

"It's *millions.*"

"I heard you."

I frown, uneasiness sliding down my spine. "What the heck is going on, Jacob?"

He pauses for a few moments. "Mark didn't push the security issue before you left because he didn't think it was a real issue until his presence in the city was known. I got a call as I was walking inside. The press is all over Riptide. Somehow they heard Mark is in town."

I press my fingers to my temple. "This is a billionaire client I'm meeting, and he's threatening to pull his auction items because of the scandal now waiting to greet him at our door."

"Our team is clearing them out, and it's close to being under control, from what I hear. But I don't want to risk you being ambushed. Try to push your meeting back an hour."

I'm already pulling my phone from my purse. "I'll call on the way there. I can't risk not reaching them, or him arriving before me to a mess. I can't lose this client for Riptide, Jacob. I'm not sure Mark would save me over him."

His jaw clenches and unclenches. "Let's go, then." He takes my tote bag. "I'll ride with you. The Comptons are safe here, and the man on his way will cover them." He moves ahead of me and pauses at the exit, waiting for me to join him. Then he shoves open the door, cursing under his breath at the cold blast of air. "Sorry. Thin California blood is going to be the death of me."

I laugh and laugh harder as he looks completely miserable for the short walk to the subway, though he still hovers protectively. When we're finally on a train, people all around us, the two of us clutching the same pole, Jacob tells me, "He rode the subway this morning. That's why I wasn't with him."

"Who? Mark?"

"That's right. We were stuck in traffic and he said we weren't going to make the hospital in time. I stopped at a light and he took off." He grimaces. "I'll have a driver and ride in the backseat with that man from now on, I can promise you that."

"Why are you telling me this?"

"Because you're caught right in the eye of the storm swallowing that man whole, and probably more capable of influencing him than anyone."

"Me? I can't even get him to consistently call me by my first name. I have no control where's he's concerned."

"You know that's not true, and he needs a voice of reason right now. And I believe you are that voice."

He's giving me far more than I expected. "Why would I need to influence him?"

"You know why."

My stomach rolls. "Please tell me he's still not talking about vengeance, like he was right after Ava escaped."

"I had an exchange with him this morning that all but confirmed he is."

My fingers tighten around the pole. "What did he say?"

"It was inferred, but the look in his eyes said everything. He's after blood."

"He'll destroy his family if he ends up in jail."

"He could end up dead. We aren't completely certain Ava is acting alone."

"Who else is involved?"

"I'm not prepared to say anyone is. We're exploring options."

"So you think Mark is after vengeance, and you think someone else is involved. You know nothing."

"Saving lives means taking preventative actions."

"But you have no proof Mark is personally after Ava or anyone else," I state, making sure I understand properly.

"Not yet. But my boss, Blake, lost his fiancée while they were both undercover on an ATF mission. He actively sought vengeance on the man responsible. And despite his brothers being an ex-Navy SEAL and ex-FBI, and both having suspicions, they never knew until he was in the middle of trouble."

"Again, why are you telling me this?"

"You seem to be able to get through to him."

I laugh without humor. "He's an asshole, Jacob, and I told him so this morning. No one gets through to him except maybe his mother, and you can't tell her. She can't handle this now."

"You've seen behind that wall, just like I have."

"I don't know what's real with him anymore."

"Believe me—what's beneath the surface, good or bad, is always what's real." He continues: "I see what you're doing to help this family. I just want your eyes open."

We fall into silence. I've known a variety of controlling people—some who balance it with compassion like Dana, others with their own variety of poison. Which type is Mark? "I never wanted to see you hurt like this again," Dana said to him this morning. What happened before?

I'm still pondering that question when Jacob and I exit to the street. While the snow has slowed down, the wind is fierce. We hunch into our coats and travel two blocks with brisk strides. Then we turn right, bringing the gallery into view. I'm relieved to see a walkway roped off with movie-theater-type poles by the front door, with guards on either side. The crush of reporters Jacob mentioned is now gone.

"Your team works fast," I say approvingly, just as Jacob grabs my arm and a mic is shoved in my face.

"Ms. Smith, we understand Mark Compton is back in town. Do you know what his relationship with Rebecca Mason was?"

Jacob shoves me behind him. "No comment at this time." He begins a terse exchange with the reporter and his crew.

Worried about what's behind me, I turn, pressing my back to Jacob's—and gasp as I find a hooded man standing so close that his hot breath reaches my cold cheeks. His face is partially draped, but I still manage to home in on two things: his hard black eyes, which radiate meanness, and the deep scar down his right cheek.

# Five

Crystal . . .

As I stare into the stranger's eyes I reach behind me and grab Jacob's coat, as if holding on to him will somehow make this man go away. "Who are you?" I ask, trying to memorize his face. Full lips. Lines by his eyes and sun-darkened skin make him look to be in his late forties though he might be younger.

"Who do you think I am?"

"A reporter?" I ask.

"No. I am not a reporter."

"Then . . . who?"

"Who indeed."

"Do you know who I am?"

"Doesn't everyone who watches the news?"

It's not a real answer. It's a cat-and-mouse game. "What do you want?"

"The list is long. But then, isn't everyone's?" The stranger's lips twist in an evil smile and then he just . . . leaves.

I blink, confused.

Jacob suddenly grabs my wrist and pulls me around, starting to walk rapidly toward the door. I dig in my heels. "Wait! There was a man."

"What man?" He turns to face me. "Where?"

I scan the area, but he's nowhere to be found despite the sparsely populated sidewalk. "He's gone."

Jacob tightens his grip on my wrist, as if he's afraid to let go of me—and at the moment, maybe I am, too. I double-step, relieved when we enter Riptide. Just inside, Jacob corners me, putting his back to the reception area and several security guards. "Tell me about the man."

"He came right up to me, right in my face, and stared at me. He was right up on me and we had this odd exchange." I shove up my sleeve and glance at my watch. "I need to tell you after my meeting."

He shoves down the hood of his jacket. "Tell me now."

I sigh, knowing determination when I see it. I repeat the exchange and he shows no reaction.

"He was probably a reporter we pissed off when we cleared the front door," he says after a short pause.

"No. I don't think so."

"Why?"

"Just a gut feeling. I have to get ready for my meeting."

"Just don't leave without one of us with you."

"I don't plan to."

He steps back, giving me space to depart. I check in with the receptionist before heading down the hallway to my office, being waylaid by at least four staff members who want to talk about the press disaster and putting off their questions until later.

In my office I quickly hang up my coat, freshen my makeup and hair, and then sit down at my desk. Then, and only then, do I let myself process that last exchange with Jacob. He doesn't think the man with the scar was a reporter, either.

At eleven o'clock, my file for the meeting is in front of me when my phone buzzes from the front desk. The receptionist announces, "Your father is on line one, and your brother Scottie is on line two."

I sigh. "Tell my brother I'm talking to my father and then going into a meeting. And buzz me, please, when Mr. Prescot arrives, no matter what." I grab line one. "Hi, Dad."

"What the *hell* is going on at that place you're working at? I want you out of there."

I press my fingers to my temple. "I warned you about all of this."

"The news is creating a much worse picture than you did."

"I don't even want to know what that means right now. I have a meeting I have to be at my best for. I can't think about anything else right now."

"I mean it, Crystal. I want you out of there."

"Be proud of me for managing all of this, instead. I'm managing it with the skills you taught me."

"To work for me, which ultimately is for you—not for someone else."

"Dad, please. You know Dana Compton matters to me and that she has cancer. Would you really want me to desert her now?"

He huffs out a breath. "I selfishly want to say 'yes,' and if this gets worse, I might just go run that place myself to get you out of there, or send one of your brothers."

He's not joking. What was I thinking, when I considered having him provide my security? He'd go nuts if he knew about the hooded man or Mark's desire for vengeance. "I'm fine," I say firmly. "This is not some mom-and-pop shop. This is the largest auction house in the world, with world-class security, and I'm gaining invaluable experience here."

He sighs. "At least while you're there, your liking for artistic men can be fed with ones who pay their own bills."

I groan. "Not that again."

"I can't take another wannabe starving artist or, Lord forbid, another wannabe rock star, like that Jake fellow you wouldn't let go of in college."

"If you continue, I might have a seizure from the repeating conversation my brain can't take." My phone sounds again, and the receptionist says, "Mr. Prescot is pulling up to the building now, per the security staff."

"Thank you," I say. "I'll come and get him."

"Prescot," my father says. "As in Larry Prescot?"

"The one and only. And he's no happier about this situation than you are—so let me go prove that I learned from the best, as in you, and save his business. I meant it when I said I was getting invaluable experience here."

"A far cry from tattooed rock stars, my dear. I owe Dana Compton more than a few favors, starting with this one. Tell Prescot you're my daughter."

"You know I don't like to name-drop."

"Trust me, baby. Tell him. And call me when you get home tonight."

"It'll be late."

"Text me if I don't answer, so I know you're safe."

"I will," I promise. "And can you tell the rest of the clan I'm okay? Scottie already tried to call. I'm sure Daniel will be next."

"I'll tell them I talked to you. Whether you're truly okay is up for debate."

"I am."

We've just said our good-byes when my cell phone buzzes with a message from Mark. Dinner tonight. Eight o'clock at my parents' house.

I stare at the message. He acted like I didn't belong at the hospital this morning, and he's given me no update on his mother. Now he's demanded, not asked, that I be at dinner. There are so many things I want to reply with—but I want to see Dana. That's all that matters. I type Okay.

Okay? he replies.

Grimacing, I don't even try to hold my fingers in check. Sorry, sir. Yes, sir, Mr. Compton, sir.

He doesn't reply. Perhaps what I see as being a smartass again, he perceives as a real concession. My mind goes back to the restaurant bathroom he's so focused on and I squeeze my eyes shut, replaying his hands on my waist as he sets me on the counter and spreads my legs before ripping off my panties, teasing me with his fingers but not his tongue. And oh, how I wanted his tongue. He'd made me choose between his fingers, his tongue, or his cock. When I'd chosen his tongue, he'd ordered me to tell him to "lick me." Then it had been, "Lick me, please." Then, "Please lick my pussy, Mr. Compton." I'd tried to resist and failed. I'd said the words, and he rewarded me with an orgasm, leaving me with a satisfied smile on his face and my panties in his pocket.

Something my father often says comes back to me: People who are being manipulated rarely know it until it's too late. What if Mark's Dr. Jekyll and Mr. Hyde routine is all a plan to get me where he wants me, tied to a bedpost? I glance down at my reply.

Sorry, sir. Yes, sir, Mr. Compton, sir.

What if that kind of submissive answer is exactly what he wants from me? And not just in the office.

He was right. We need boundaries—and they won't all be ones that he likes.

# Six

Crystal . . .

The day zooms by with one challenge after another, and before I can blink, I'm in an Escalade with Jacob, to drive me to dinner. "Is all well in your neck of the woods?" he asks.

"As well as can be expected," I say, shrugging out of my coat and setting my tote bag on the floor.

"Did you arrange security through your father?" he asks, moving the gearstick into drive.

"No. I realized that someday, one of you is going to have to protect Mark from me. Since he intentionally provokes me, it seems fair that he should pay for what's essentially his own protection, not mine."

Jacob chuckles. "Yes, I suppose he should." He pulls out onto the street.

"Any news on Ava?" I ask as we reach the stoplight.

"Nothing," he says. "But since Blake's working with the police in California, we'll know if anything turns up on that end."

"Do you think she's dead?"

"I really don't know."

The frustration in his tone tells me he's giving me the truth. We fall into silence for the rest of the drive, and I think of the way Mark immediately whisked me to an airport after finding out about Ava's escape. I also remember the taste of fear, regret, and guilt in his kiss. And I think of how those things must be magnified now that he's here, with people around him who could be hurt if Ava shows up. It has to be destroying him—yet he couldn't stay away. Will he ever be able to stop looking over his shoulder if Ava isn't found?

As Jacob parks in the private garage of the seventeen-story Fifth Avenue building where the Comptons reside, I've begun to think about Jacob's certainty that Mark is after Ava himself. And with my new perspective, I can't help but wonder if, given the same risks and lack of answers Mark is faced with, my sanity wouldn't require I look for Ava myself, as well.

Jacob motions to my door. "One of my men is approaching on your right, Crystal. You're in such deep thought I didn't want him to scare you."

"Oh," I say, not realizing how checked out I've been. "Yes. Thanks."

Jacob exits his side of the vehicle and my door is opened by a tall man with long blond hair tied at his nape. Despite his dark suit, he looks more like a rock star than a lethal weapon. He offers me his hand, his sleeve rising up enough to offer me a glimpse of the tattoo on his wrist. "Asher is my name, Ms. Smith. I'm with Walker Security."

Jacob rounds the hood to stand beside us, and Asher turns his attention to him. "I've let the Comptons know you've arrived, and the service hallway and elevator have been cleared. No one should know she's here."

"Good," Jacob says, on edge and ready for any problem.

"Why are we taking the service elevator?" I ask. "The building's security is excellent; no one gets in without invitation."

"We have reason to believe that someone from the staff gave the press tips the last time Mark was here," Jacob explains.

"Did the press come here today, too?" I ask.

"Yes," Asher confirms. "Early this morning."

My brow furrows. "Then how could the leak come from here? Mark hadn't shown up yet."

"But we had talked to the apartment and arranged security," Asher replies. "And the word from some of the staff is that there have been issues for other tenants in the building."

"Asher here has a way of making people drop their guard," Jacob says. "He's going to find out who it is."

Asher smiles. "It's the tats and ex-rocker background. They think I'm still that guy."

Jacob points to the door. "Follow Asher. I have your back."

Does he expect bullets to start flying? All of a sudden, I'm not sure Jacob's claim of knowing nothing about Ava is true.

The elevator opens and Jacob follows me inside, keying in a security code for the fifteenth floor, which Dana and Steven own. "When you're done," he says, "call me and I'll come up and get you."

"I will. Any idea who's going to be my security person?"

"Since you'll have protection at Riptide, and Mark will have protection both here at his parents' and while he's at work, I'll be able to stay point man for both of you, using backup as needed. At night we'll have someone see you to your apartment, and we'll be on call if you need to go out."

Tension rolls through me. "I really hate every move I make being monitored, but I know it's necessary. And you've already seen the dynamic between me and Mark, which makes you the best one equipped to protect Mark when I snap."

He doesn't laugh as I expect him to. The elevator stops and he holds the doors open. "Yes, I know about the two of you, as does Blake, but to every possible extent, we'll keep the relationship private."

"It's not a relationship."

His eyes narrow slightly and he looks like he wants to say something, but he only pauses before saying, "Call me when you're ready to leave."

"I will. Thank you, Jacob."

"My pleasure," he says, allowing the door to shut.

The instant that he's out of sight, I cut to my right and go down a glossy, pale African wood hallway, nerves fluttering in my stomach. At the door I skip the buzzer, in case Dana has fallen asleep, knocking lightly instead. When it opens Mark is standing there, the knot to his red tie several inches down his shirt, his jacket off, his collar loose. I feel a jolt of pure heat as every nerve ending in me comes alive, and I quickly lower my lashes before he notices. Despite my certainty that a man like Mark Compton could never reach me emotionally, despite how he's behaved in the past twenty-four hours, I am still devastatingly drawn to him. It must be a biological defect that I crave a man who's destined to shred my heart.

"Ms. Smith," he says, and the snap in his tone jolts me to the core. I look at him, giving him the control he wants over me.

In that moment he owns me as he's promised, and Lord help me, as I look into the steely hardness of those gray eyes and find a predatory gleam, part of me wants to be owned by this man. I'm wet with the idea, my nipples aching, and my knees weak. He knows it, too. I see it in the glint of satisfaction in his eyes, and the freedom he feels to lower his gaze for an inspection that goes from my toes to my head, lingering in the more erotic regions. I swallow hard, feeling every second like a stroke of his hand, the lick of his tongue. I'm in big trouble, which he confirms when he grabs my hand and pulls me hard against his hard body.

"We need to talk," he announces.

My hand flattens on the wall of his truly impressive chest. "Yes, we do," I say, sounding remarkably firm, despite all the places he's making warm and tingly.

He stares down at me, his expression unreadable. But the thundering of his heart beneath my palm tells me he's powerfully affected by me, too.

"No time like the present," he finally murmurs, taking my hand in his bigger one and pulling me inside.

"Not now," I say. "Not here."

"Now," he insists, and the intimate way he laces his fingers with mine stirs odd feelings in my chest.

"Your mother—"

He pulls me forward and in a few steps we're inside the elegant library, where walls of books are illuminated by droplights from a high ceiling. I turn to face him, not sure what to expect next with his changing moods.

He shuts the door, and before I can blink, he's advanced on me and I'm against the wall. His hands are pressed to the wall above my head, but he doesn't touch me. And I want him to. Too much. So damn much.

"Topic number one," he says tightly. "You aren't using your own security people. You're my responsibility."

My irritation is instant. "I am *not* your responsibility."

"Don't push me on this, Ms. Smith."

"You know what? It *is* Ms. Smith to you. And don't order me around like I'm your submissive. I didn't sign your damn contract."

"I think we're both clear on that fact."

"And you were right: We definitely need boundaries."

"I won't have my security process compromised by outsiders who aren't fully accountable to me. You're using my security team. Subject closed."

"Spare me the dictator routine. I already told Jacob I'd use your people."

"When?"

"On the way over here."

"Why?"

"Because you and my father would be like the *Clash of the Titans*. You and I clash enough on our own. We don't need to add more to the mix."

His eyes sharpen. "Is that what you call what we do?" he asks, his voice a rough, low tone that creates a tingling in my nipples. "Clashing?"

I swallow hard, trying to control the heaviness of my breathing that I fear he's already noticed. "You have a better name for it?"

"Many words come to mind. Should I start listing them?"

"No," I say, certain I won't approve of his choices. He glances at my mouth, and I suddenly remember the spicy, delicious way he tastes. Instinctively, my hands flatten on the hard wall of his chest. "Don't kiss me," I warn. The heat darting up my arms tells me how bad an idea touching him was.

"But you want me to," he says, his hands sliding to my wrists, and somehow he makes it darkly erotic. This isn't one of our spontaneous moments that we dismiss the next day. This is different, uncharted territory.

He leans closer and I splay my fingers on his chest, applying pressure. "I said don't."

"Because you don't want me to, or because you're afraid of where it will lead?"

"Because I said it. That's the only reason you need."

"Yet you didn't deny that you want me to."

"Eve really wanted the apple, and look where it got her."

"If anyone's being tempted by a poison apple"—his head lowers, lips close to mine, breath warm and tempting on my cheek—"it's me."

My fingers flex against hard muscle. "Mark—"

"I think it's because you're afraid of where it might lead, of the power you think it might give me over you."

I try to tug my wrists away but he holds me easily, a gleam in his eyes. "I never fell into bed with you," I say. "I was captive to the emotions you were feeling, feeding off those. You don't have the power over me."

"No. You have the power. That's what you don't understand. *You* have the power—or I wouldn't be lying in bed at night remembering how you taste." He pauses for effect. "And I do remember how you taste. All of you. Every last inch. Your mouth. Your neck. Your nipples. Your—"

"Stop it," I hiss, knowing exactly what he was going to say next. "I know what you're trying to do."

He inches backward, releasing my wrists, and taking the promise of a kiss with him, those gray eyes resting keenly on my face. "What am I trying to do?"

"This is a game. It's manipulation."

"I want to fuck you. Many times. Many ways. How is that manipulation?"

"One minute you want to fuck me. The next—"

"I *always* want to fuck you. I just want to do it my way. With your pleasure at my mercy. Your hands tied up. Your legs tied up. Your clit on my tongue."

"Stop."

"Why? Am I making you wet?"

I glare, my only defense against an answer I'm not going to give him.

"I'll find out myself," he says, dragging my hemline upward before I know his intent.

I grab his hand and my skirt. "Don't even *think* about it."

"We're both thinking about it."

His cell phone rings and he stiffens, drawing a deep breath before his hands fall away from me and he steps back a good foot. He pulls out a phone I haven't seen before and quickly answers, "Give me a minute." He covers the receiver. "I need to take this," he informs me.

I manage a nod despite my reeling senses, but his energy has changed, and his eyes harden along with his voice as he adds, *"Alone."*

The slap of the dismissal shakes me to the core, jolting me into a flicker of a memory of the past I never wanted to visit again. I shake my head, trying to rid myself of the flashback. Mark Compton really *is* the apple. He's stealing my control, to create his own.

I leave the room, pulling the door shut behind me. "The end," I whisper. I will not let him play these games with me.

## Mark . . .

I watch Crystal leave, and am cursing at the look on her face before she's gone. Then I curse the damn disposable phone that chose the worst time to ring—when I should be glad that it stopped me from doing something we would both regret. I hadn't meant to do what just happened, and that's a problem. My plan to make her hate me won't work if I can't keep my damn hands off her.

Punching the Answer button, I say, "Give me good news."

"Kilmer started the morning out with some devastating financial news that he spent all day trying to correct, but failed."

"What happened to no names?"

"It leaves room for confusion, and I know you don't like confusion. Trade out the phone. Text me the number and I'll call you from another line."

"Fine. What other news do you have for me?"

"There's chatter about Ava in some of my circles."

"What kind of chatter?"

"She was seen at a dive motel known to be popular with unsavory types, since they keep no records."

"When? Where?"

"The day before yesterday. That's all I know. I'm meeting the source tomorrow."

"You don't know if she's still in Cali?"

"No."

"Was she alone?" I ask.

"According to the information I was given, she was with a known mercenary."

"A mercenary. By choice or as a prisoner?"

"My source wasn't willing to disclose the information."

"Let me guess," I say through gritted teeth. "He wants money. Translation: You want money."

"Another ten K."

I'm irritated, but if Ava's befriended a crazy killer, I need to know. "Ten K up front. Another five-K bonus when I get answers."

"I can live with that arrangement."

"I'm sure you can. I'll transfer the money later tonight."

"Then you'll have answers tomorrow. This might be a good time to think about what you want me to do with Ava when I have her."

"Find her. That's what matters right now." I end the call and tuck the disposable phone in my pocket to retrieve my regular cell, punching in Blake Walker's number.

"I have a reliable lead that Ava is alive and well," I say when he answers. "What have you heard?"

"From whom?" he asks, ignoring my question.

"I'm not willing to disclose that information."

There's a short pause. "You're going after her on your own," he says. It's not a question. "You still want vengeance."

"I'm keeping my ear to the ground to protect my family."

"Then give me your contact's info, and let me protect them for you."

"I pay you to protect my family—and so does San Francisco law enforcement, since they've now contracted you as well. And I trust your people, Blake. But if your family could be in danger, would you wait for someone else to protect them?"

Considering he'd confessed to me his own vigilante quest to kill a man who'd murdered someone he loved, we both know the answer. A beat passes. Then two. "Just promise me you'll give me a chance to act on anything you find out before you do."

"I promise to be as transparent as you," I say, making it clear that I'm aware he's dodged my question about what he knows about Ava. "And you make sure your staff is vigilant about watching for unusual threats."

"We were in airport security right after 9/11. We know how to look for the unusual. But I need an assurance that you won't act——"

"Just do your job, Blake, and make sure Jacob pays special attention to Crystal Smith."

"I'll call him when we hang up."

"Good. Do that." There's a knock on the door. "I need to go."

I end the call as my father pokes his head in the door enough for me to see his blue and red team jersey. "Everything okay?" he asks.

"Fine," I say, stashing the phone in my pocket and walking in his direction, wondering if Ms. Smith said something to make him think otherwise. "Just a quick business call."

"Your mother's asking for you," he says, and I sense nothing beneath the comment. "The Chinese food was dropped off downstairs. Jacob is bringing it up." The doorbell rings. "That'll be it. We're eating in our bedroom. Your mother doesn't want to try to go to the table. She's afraid it will wear her out."

He disappears, and I face what is inevitable. A cozy dinner with me, my parents, and Ms. Smith, whom I just told I want to fuck. I'm treating her like a damn yo-yo, which is wrong and I have to fix it. Based on how upset she was when she left, perhaps I already have. Calculated anger was one thing, but that was pain—the very thing she's tried to help me get past.

"Mark!" my father calls, and I scrub the roughness of new stubble, joining him and Jacob in the hallway. "Get the rest, will you, son?" my father asks, his arms loaded down with bags.

"Got it," I say as he heads toward the bedroom. "You heard that Ms. Smith changed her mind about using us for security?" I ask Jacob softly.

"I did. Royce Walker was going to talk to her tomorrow if she didn't change her mind. We dodged a bullet on that one. He never asks. He tells you as he rolls over you. And Ms. Smith doesn't do well with force."

"No, she doesn't," I say, "which is why her sudden change of heart seems a bit too easy. What reason did she give you for agreeing?"

"She said it was to protect you."

"How so?"

"She says if you keep intentionally baiting her into arguments, you'll need protection from her, so it's only fair you should pay for it."

I laugh. "She knew you'd repeat that. So tell me: Who's baiting who?"

Jacob lifts his hands. "I plead the Fifth, considering I have to protect you both. I'll leave it to you two to wrestle out your differences."

"Hmm. That's a visual I can't quite get my mind around."

"Creative visuals, a lethal weapon when I want to be one, and I grill a great steak. My specialties, at your service. Can I get you anything right now?"

"I'll settle for Chinese right now."

"Have it your way," he says, turning to leave.

I back up and kick the door shut, and the security system

automatically locks it. I walk the short distance to one of the two master bedrooms and find my parents on the massive oak bed while Crystal stands at the small conference table my mother uses in place of a desk. As she removes food from a bag, Crystal's gaze lifts and finds mine and the detachment in her stare speaks volumes. I'm right. I hurt her, and I did it in some deep, cutting way I don't fully understand.

Quick to look away, she finishes emptying the bag as I cross the room to join her. "I hope you're going to eat tonight, Mother."

"It sure smells good," she says. "The first thing that has in a long time."

"Excellent," I say. "I believe I have the drinks." I halt directly across from Ms. Smith and set my bag on one of the two chairs.

She places a container in front of me. "Cashew chicken."

"How do you know it's mine?" I ask, trying to get her to look at me again.

Her lashes lift. "You just seem like a cashew chicken kind of guy."

"I told her," my mother informs me. "She gets the same thing."

"So you're a cashew chicken kind of girl?" I ask.

"And her birthday is next week, too," my mother adds. "November twenty-third. One day after yours."

"But you're about a decade older than me," Crystal says, giving my father his food.

"Older and wiser."

She snatches a drink from in front of me and passes it to my father, a combative energy between us. "Younger and more versatile."

My father roars out laughter. "I do believe our son has met his match, Dana."

71

"That's why I hired her," Dana says as Crystal kicks off her shoes and walks to my mother's side. "She doesn't stand down to anyone except me."

Crystal sets a tray over my mother's lap and then places her food and a soda on it. "Now eat, and I want nothing left. You need to gain weight."

I laugh and settle into my chair. "I guess you're right. She backs down to no one."

Crystal returns to the table and it's all I can do not to watch every move she makes. Once she's across from me again, opening her plasticware, I say, "Versatile, but unwilling to try new things."

"Old and incapable of thinking outside of the same box."

I want to drag her back into the library and fuck her right now. She glares a warning at me over the way I'm looking at her, but my father and mother are absorbed in jabbering away, and I ignore her. "We need to finish our talk."

"We did. Or I did. I'm done, Mark Compton. The End."

She means it this time.

# Seven

Mark . . .

"What do you think, son?"

"About?" I ask, jerking my gaze to my father.

"How about coming and watching some of the pitchers throw this weekend with me? Dana says she and Crystal are having a girls' pampering day on Sunday."

I arch a brow at Crystal. "Oh?" The more I see her closeness to my mother, the more curious I am about *her* mother.

"We have a stylist coming in for hair and nails," she says, her lips curving as she looks at my mother. "It's going to be fun."

"I can't wait," my mother says, dragging her hand down her hair. "I think it'll make me feel a little more human."

"So what do you say, Marky boy?" my father presses. "We on for some baseball?"

"You have practice on Sunday?"

"A pitching camp. I really could use your input."

Fighting the feeling that I can't face this part of my past right now, my lips manage a curve and I say, "Sunday it is, then."

The light in my father's eyes is my reward. "We can go by that burger joint by the practice field we used to hang out at. Good memories."

He's right. They were, and I don't want to let one bad piece of my history destroy some of the special moments I've shared with my father.

"I was thinking," my mother says, and her solemn tone draws all of our gazes as she sighs and starts again. "I was thinking about Rebecca, and how young she was and how young you were when life got all twisted. Things change so quickly. Life is here and gone, and—"

The jab to my gut plunges deep, and I lower my eyes, fighting the emotions by beginning to count, leaving room for nothing else. *One. Two. Three. Four. Five.* When my gaze lifts it collides with Crystal's, and I see the question in her eyes. She wants to know what my mother is talking about . . . and part of me wants that one person whom I can actually tell.

"Everything happens for a reason," my father tells my mother. "We just don't know what it is until later. But I'm betting that you'll inspire a lot of people to fight when this is over."

*Everything happens for a reason.* He'd said that to me way back then, too. I was certain that my future had been ripped away from me as a lesson. It made me become stronger for everyone else around me, to ensure no one else got hurt. But what reason is there in Rebecca dying? How can there ever be a reason for that?

I push to my feet. "I'm going to get ice. Anyone else?" All eyes have shifted to me, and they all call bullshit, "you don't

74

want ice, you want space." "No?" I ask. "Okay then." I leave the room wondering how "Okay then" even got into my damn vocabulary.

Walking down the hall and past a large living area, I pause in the center of the massive kitchen, leaning on the black rectangular island counter. My head drops toward my chest and I start counting to keep myself out of my own head, so I can walk back into that bedroom. *One. Two. Three. Four. Five.*

"Mark."

I squeeze my eyes shut as Crystal's voice stirs an odd sensation in my chest that somehow eases the ache in my gut. Desire rockets through me, and I tell myself it's about fucking and control. I need it, and she's my safe zone outside of the club.

"Are you okay?" she asks when I do not speak.

When our gazes meet the jolt is as unwelcome as it is intense. She feels it, too. I see it in the slight widening of her eyes, the way she curls her fingers into her palms on the counter across from me.

"You were furious with me a few minutes ago," I say. "Why are you standing here now?"

"I'm not one-dimensional. I can be furious and worried at the same time."

Unable to squash my intrigue over the unknowns of her past, I agree. "No, you aren't one-dimensional. Nor are you simply a rich girl who wants to prove something to daddy."

"Thank you." She crinkles her brow. "I think."

We fall into silence, a hum of electricity charging between us. "I still go back to you saying 'The End' to me a few minutes ago. You meant it this time, too. That doesn't translate to you standing here."

"Neither does much of what you do, where I'm concerned."

"You're absolutely right. It doesn't. What does, though, is sticking to 'The End.' What doesn't is how badly I want to drag you into another room and fuck you right now."

She shakes her head. "It's not me you want. It's someone who'll sign a contract and be your outlet and bridge to control. You left that bedroom thinking about the impossibility of a reason for Rebecca's death, beyond your self-blame and guilt. You need that bridge."

There is banked pain lacing her words, and a hint of the earlier anger I'd seen in her eyes. I could make those things go away by telling her what she's said isn't true. I could tell her she's gotten under my skin. But I don't even know who the man beneath the surface is right now. I've destroyed two women. Crystal doesn't deserve to be number three.

"Is everything okay?" my father asks from the doorway, repeating Crystal's earlier words.

"Yes," I say, my gaze lingering on Crystal before I push off the counter, hands going to my hips. "We're ready to talk to Mom about what's been going on."

"We are?" Crystal asks, sounding surprised. "Tonight?"

"We can't risk her finding out from somewhere else," I explain.

"She'd feel betrayed," my father adds.

Crystal gives a choppy nod. "Yes. I can see that. But I am not looking forward to telling her."

"None of us are," my father says. "Right now, though, she wants us all to eat together. And since it's the best chance we have of getting some food down her, I say we wait until after we've finished. I don't want to jeopardize her appetite."

"I'm all for getting food down her," I say. "She's skin and bones."

76

"I've been force-feeding her what she does eat," Crystal adds. "The nurse suggested some high-calorie protein shakes. I tried that, but she hates them."

My father starts to turn, then pauses. "By the way, Crystal, Larry Prescot called me just before you got here. You won him over. Thanks for calming him down before he got to Dana."

"My pleasure."

He disappears into the hallway and I grab Crystal's arm. "How okay is Prescot?"

"Very."

"How can you be sure?"

"I threw out my father's name—something that I normally would never do."

"But?"

"I was on the phone with my father when the receptionist buzzed to tell me that Prescot had arrived for our meeting. My father overheard and insisted that I drop his name. I reminded him that I'm adamant about succeeding on my own merits. But I'm also not one to foolishly ignore resources when backed into a corner, and I was. Prescot was being a total jerk. I knew we were about to lose the business."

"So you broke your rule."

"I did. And it was an amazing turnaround. Prescot suddenly remembered the many ways people have tried to paint him as a monster in the media, and became sympathetic rather than judgmental. I called my father afterward, and it turns out that Prescot enjoys the benefits of his secretary beyond her exceptional organizational skills, and his wife of twenty years doesn't know."

"But your father does."

"Yes. And now, so do we."

My lips curve. "Sounds like I owe you and your father a thank-you."

"All you'd get in return from my father is a demand that I quit my job. He hates me working for anyone but him, especially now with all this bad press."

"Is he afraid it will overflow to him?"

"No. He's afraid I'll get hurt."

*Me too,* I think. *Me too.* "And what did you tell him?"

"I told him I'm his daughter, not his possession. He doesn't own me any more than you do, and neither of you gets to claim responsibility for my happiness. That's all mine."

As she leaves the room, I stare after her in silent agreement. I'm not responsible for her happiness. But I'm not going to be responsible for her misery, either.

Twenty minutes later, my mother has told us all about her treatment and recited several dirty jokes one of the techs told her to calm her down, one of which doesn't please me. "I'm going to have to defend your honor and punch this guy tomorrow."

"Oh please," my mother says, waving me off. "It's funny."

My father snorts. "I gave up defending your mother's honor after the car mechanic incident when I was out of town."

"What's the car mechanic incident?" Crystal asks.

"You'll never look at my mother the same way if we tell you," I say.

"The guy was trying to rip me off," Dana says. "So I told him I was going to stop by the sex shop and pick up a dildo so he could screw me extra hard."

Crystal bubbles over with laughter until tears flow down her cheeks. "That's priceless," she says, her voice now a sexy rasp, which has me looking at her lips and thinking about all the places I'd like them to be tonight. "There's never a dull moment with you, Dana," she says. "And I'll still respect you in the morning."

We all laugh, my mother included, and the sound is music to my ears. "I can't believe I've been up so long," my mother says afterward.

My father and I exchange a look, followed by me and Crystal. It's time. We have to talk to her. While my father clears her tray, I stand up and go sit on the edge of the bed beside her. Crystal moves to the opposite side, beside my father.

My mother scans our faces. "If this is an intervention, I can't give up the drugs. It's a doctor–approved addiction."

I take her frail hand in mine, wishing like hell this conversation weren't necessary. "I need to talk to you about something."

"All right, son. I'm listening."

"I'm here, which means the press is, too. I need to warn you about what they're saying."

"Go on," she says, lacing her fingers in front of her.

"Ava's defense team are after their version of O. J. Simpson, Hollywood lights and all, uncaring of who they hurt in the process."

"That's not good," she murmurs.

"But it's nothing we haven't dealt with before," Crystal points out, "with all the money and power that runs through the gallery."

"And even one of my ballplayers, who took a payoff from a pro team long before he went pro," my father says.

"Just tell me what you need to tell me," my mother says, her attention on me.

"Before Ava's escape," I continue, "her defense team was desperate to counter her confession, which they claimed was made under duress, and driven by me."

"You? Why you?"

"They changed their story a number of times. First, Ava said she confessed to protect me."

She gasps. "Do you mean—"

"Yes. She accused me of killing Rebecca, but the police have cleared me and they now have proof of Ava's guilt."

"And?"

"Her legal team threw out a lot of random nonsense when trying to get the murder charge dropped. Everything from a sex scandal, to a sex club, Rebecca blackmailing me, and Ricco saying I set him and Mary up to shut him up when he had almost figured it all out."

My mother sits up. "What? Do they actually believe you'd ruin our business to set him up?"

"Easy, Dana," my father says. "Easy."

"Nothing is getting ruined," I assure her.

"In fact," my father adds, "Larry Prescot called me today to express concern and relay how pleased he is with Crystal."

"I'm finding in general, as we talk to people and explain things," Crystal adds, "they become more supportive, not less."

"Ricco's trial is in January, so we'll have to endure his accusations then. In the meantime, the press keeps trying to make headlines with all the nastiness Ava's defense threw out before her escape."

"Like a sex club and sex scandal."

"Nothing anyone can prove. It's just talk."

"Nothing they can't prove," she repeats. "*Is* there a sex club?"

I draw a breath and let it out. "It's a cigar club to the public."

"So there is a club."

"Elite. Expensive. Members only."

"And your role is?"

"I own it."

She turns to my father. "You knew?"

"Not before this Ava fiasco."

At his reply, she glances at Crystal. "And you?"

"Mark warned me," she says. "He never let me get sideswiped, so I never missed a beat when questioned."

My mother's gaze comes back to me. "What kind of sex club?"

"Elite—"

"You said that."

"BDSM and fetish."

Her hand goes to her throat. "Do you have a club here?"

"No. That was never an option and it still isn't."

"And Rebecca and Ava were members?"

"Yes," I reply.

"What else do I need to know?"

"Ricco had a stalkerlike obsession with Rebecca. The police suspect he helped Ava escape because he thought she was innocent, and that I killed Rebecca. There's now speculation that Ava is missing because he found out the truth and killed her."

"So, we have press now. We'll have press again when something turns up on Ava, and again during the trial."

"That about sums it up."

She stares forward, and it's as if she's shutting a door, withdrawing from me and everyone in the room. "I need to rest now." Defeat laces her words and radiates off her.

I did this to her. I made her hell deeper and darker. "I'm not going to let this hurt Riptide," I promise. "I *won't* let that happen."

She looks at me, her bottom lip trembling in a way I have never seen before. "I said I need to rest, Mark." She looks forward again.

I suck in a breath, fighting the icy knot in my chest. She thinks I'm going to destroy everything she's worked for. But deep down, I knew she'd think that. I knew she never truly trusted me. It's a big part of why I left New York.

Pushing to my feet, I leave and go to the library, and walk straight to the double doors at the back of the room. Opening the door, I step onto the balcony, the bitter cold gusting around me. I do exactly what I did last night and walk to the rail, pressing my hands to the cold steel. She believes I'll let her down. This city, this world I'm in now, is all about a past where failure nearly destroyed me before. Instead, it destroyed someone else. It's happening again, and this time, the someone else is my mother.

"Mark. It's freezing. Come inside."

At the sound of Crystal's voice, I squeeze my eyes shut. She's too close to all of this—to me. I'd send her away if it wouldn't destroy my mother. "Go home," I say, needing to think.

"No. You can't stay out here and—"

I turn to her sharply, noting the way she hugs herself, shivering against the cold, and I harshly snap, "*I said,* go home, Ms. Smith."

She stiffens, sucking in a breath. She blinks once, then twice, before the same expression I'd seen in the library crosses her face, followed by a moment of panic. As if she knows I've seen it and she doesn't want me to. Then she wordlessly departs. I squeeze my eyes shut again and tell myself it doesn't matter. Better she be angry or hurt now, than dead or burned alive in the hell I'm living.

I hear the front door open and shut, and the sound cuts through me like a blade. She's trying to ease my pain, and I'm creating it in her. "Damn it," I whisper, and follow her.

In the hallway outside I find Crystal's back to me, her phone to her ear as she says, "Yes. Right now please, Jacob." She turns to face me as I pull the front door shut, anger and more hurt burning in her gaze. I'm burning as well—with lust, desire, a need for this woman that's like no need I've ever known. My plan to drive a wedge between us hasn't worked. Control isn't staying the path. It's adjusting and moving forward.

"Go away," she hisses.

"I can't do that," I say, advancing on her as she drops her phone inside her purse. She tries to move away but I grab her wrist. "Call him back. You aren't leaving like this."

"Sending me away upset or angry is your specialty. You should be reveling in your success," she says bitterly.

I back her against the wall, framing her hips with mine, my hands flattening on either side of her. "I don't want you to leave."

She grabs my arms. "I'm getting tired of you trapping me like this. It's a bad habit that has to end. And I can't do this yo-yo thing with you anymore, either." Her hands flatten on my chest, intensifying the hunger that she takes to places I never allowed myself to go before.

"Neither of us can," I say. "We want each other. That was my point in your office last night. You said sex was your release, too. We're letting desire get twisted with emotions driven by my mother's and Rebecca's situations."

"Translation: I sign the contract and I become your submissive. You control me."

"A contract isn't an insult." Needing to get past what had been intended to drive her away, I continue: "It's a level of commitment most people don't even give to their marriages. And you're confused about what submissive means in the BDSM world. *You* have the power." I turn us so that my back is against the wall, fitting her soft curves against my body, molding her pelvis to my thick erection. "*You* decide what we do or don't do. And even then, you can change your mind with one word: stop. Like now. I'm going to let you go though I don't want you to leave. I'm asking you to stay and talk this out, but it's your choice." I lift my hands, no longer holding her to me.

A conflicted look flashes over her face but she doesn't move, her fingers flexing on my upper arms where her hands have settled. "I'm not signing a contract."

"I never wanted you to sign the contract. The point was—"

She shoves out of my arms. "To push me away? How could I forget? Of course you don't want a commitment. And I don't want one, either." She runs her fingers through her hair and looks at her trembling hands. "So why am I shaking from adrenaline and emotion, and so confused that I barely know my name? Why, Mark— or Mr. Compton, or just 'Mr. Asshole, Sir'? Why am I feeling like this? Because I feed off your emotions and pain, and you play with mine." The elevator dings and it's only a matter of seconds before Jacob appears. "My life was in order before you. Now it's a mess. Thank you, Mark Compton."

Footsteps sound, and I hold up a hand. "Give us ten minutes, Jacob," I order without looking at him.

"No," she calls. "I'm coming now." Her jaw clenches and she

levels me in a stare. "Goodnight, Mr. Compton. And remember: There are cameras everywhere, and a snitch on the staff. Don't follow me." She turns and leaves.

I start after her and then stop, running a hand through my hair. "Fuck!" She's right. I can't risk a scene that ends up in the news and on my mother's doorstep. Once again, I have no control.

# Eight

‹────⁘────›

Crystal . . .

I'm still shaking when Jacob and I reach the garage, and I keep telling myself to hold it together until I'm home. Jacob opens the door to the Escalade and I slide inside. I've never had a man affect me like this before. Never.

Fortunately, Jacob senses how ready to blow I am and we remain silent for the drive to One Beacon Circle, the high-rise where I live. Once there, he insists on escorting me to my fiftieth-floor apartment, which my father had purchased with the insistence that he wanted me safe, and that it fit his portfolio. I'd agreed on the condition that we bought a small unit and I made the payments—payments that, thanks to Dana and Riptide, I've been doubling for six months straight.

I'm ready to go inside when he stops me by handing me a business card. "Obviously you know you have top-notch security here in the building. But if you need to leave, even for a soda from the corner store, call this number."

Glancing down at the card, I read the name Kara Walker and give him a curious look. "I thought you were remaining my point person?"

"I'm still available, but after some internal discussions with my team, we've decided a woman might make it more comfortable for you to be shadowed."

My jaw sets. "She's Blake's wife, isn't she?"

He grimaces. "You sure picked up on that quickly. Yes. She's Blake's wife."

"I can't help you with Mark," I tell him. "We're done. I'm done. So if Kara has bigger fish to fry, let her at them. Don't pull her off a job for me, or keep her from being in San Francisco with Blake."

"Blake wanted her with you. And no matter what, you're in close contact with the Compton family, able to stop a potential problem before anyone else."

He's right, and I nod. "Fine. I've got her card."

"And you have my number, too."

"And Royce's and Blake's. Why don't you give me Luke Walker's? Then my phone can have a Walker family reunion." I hold up my hand. "I'm sorry. I'm feeling suffocated and not myself."

"No apology needed. I think anyone would be overwhelmed under the circumstances, and far more so than you've been. I'd suggest you call Kara tomorrow and go over your schedule for the next few days, or weeks. It might help you to feel you're not constantly reporting to someone. Then she can discreetly be available when you need her."

"I will. Thanks, Jacob. I really appreciate all you've done, and I know Mark does, too."

He gives me a mock salute and starts down the hall. I shut the door and lock it, then lean against it and shut my eyes. I remind myself yet again that I'm caught up in the emotions of everyone around me, Mark especially. What I feel for him is not what I think I feel. He's simply a smoking-hot man who grabbed my attention. The man oozes sex when he walks into a room. Our sexual chemistry is off the charts and I want him. Or I did, when it was simply sex, not some kind of control game. I do not love Mark Compton. The ache in my belly is about pain and loss, some mine, some that of those around me who need me to carry some of the burden for them. I *do not* feel anything else.

At nearly midnight, I'm sitting in my bedroom by a huge window overlooking the lights of a never-sleeping Manhattan; I'm still in my black skirt and red shirt, with piles of paperwork in my lap. I'm exhausted from working through the details of next weekend's auction. I've pushed myself to keep working, trying and failing to prove that Mark cannot invade my thoughts. Nor can I get rid of the fear that I'll never overcome what is between us, and how it will affect me and Dana.

Smelling like Mark, all musky and deliciously male, isn't helping me forget having his hard body pressed against mine, or his declaring in quite graphic terms his desire to "fuck me." My nipples tighten and ache in frustration. The man is an asshole who used me and then, instead of owning up to it, offered me a contract he knew I wouldn't take.

Running a hand through my hair, I head to the bathroom and turn on the water in my giant oval tub, pouring in my favorite jasmine-scented bubbles to wash away all evidence of him. Stripping off my clothes, I let them pool on the gray tiled floor and walk to the granite counter to put my hair into a ponytail. But for a moment I stare at myself, my chest clenching as I see my biological mother in the mirror. She died at twenty-eight, the same age I am now—and I was only nine when I leaned over her and begged her to get up.

Nausea churns in my belly, but I tell myself not to shove aside the brutality of the memories that have been fighting their way to the surface due to my fear of losing Dana, too. I need to remember the poison of blind love. My hand goes to my throat. *Love.* Where did that word come from? I'm not in love.

I turn away from the mirror, afraid of what I might discover. No smart woman falls in love with a man who's grieving for another woman. A woman who has every right to be grieved, and missed.

I turn off the water, and I'm preparing to step into the tub when my doorbell rings. My heart lurches with fear and dread. No one can get to my apartment but the security staff or someone I've approved to come up. No one would be at my door at this hour if something wasn't wrong, and the possibilities race through my mind. Dana is worse. Ava's been found. The press is doing who knows what.

I grab my hot pink silk robe from a wall hook and tie it around me, worried about what awaits me at the door. Rushing from the bedroom, I flip on a light and speed toward the door. "Who is it?" I call.

"It's Mark."

My entire body quakes with the sound of Mark's voice. Why is he using his first name, not "Mr. Compton"? And why do I care, when his being here in the middle of the night can't be good? I yank open the door. And Lord help me, the blast of alpha, tormented man steals my breath and weakens my knees.

His arm is high above his head, pressed to the door frame. His red tie doesn't even have a knot anymore. His white shirt is wrinkled, his jaw shadowed, and his blond hair a rumpled mess.

"What's wrong?" I whisper. He looks worse than the night I arrived in San Francisco to find him halfway through a bottle of scotch. "Is Dana—"

"My mother's fine. She went to sleep right after you left." His lashes lower, then lift as he does a sweep of my body, lingering at my chest, where my nipples are no doubt puckering beneath the thin silk.

I hug myself to cover my near nakedness. "What's happening, Mark?" My lips purse. "Correction. Mr. Compton."

His bloodshot eyes meet mine. "Mr. Asshole will do."

"I was angry when I said that."

"You were right. I'm an asshole. I'm sorry."

I shake my head as if it's filled with cobwebs. "What? You're . . . sorry?"

"Yes. I'm sorry, Crystal."

I don't miss the use of my first name rather than Ms. Smith. "I don't understand. What are you sorry for?"

"Absolutely everything. I had no right to drag you into my hell—and once I did, I couldn't seem to stay away from you. I even blamed you for my lack of control, because no one sees me the way you have. *No one,* Crystal. I had to get control over myself. And that meant control over my addiction to you."

"Addiction?" I'm shocked that he would ever use such a word, let alone in reference to me.

"That's right—and I don't have addictions. But I don't know what's real right now, and that's not fair to you. So I presented you with a contract last night, knowing how you'd react."

I swallow the knot in my throat. "I see," I manage softly.

He scrubs his jaw. "No. No, you don't see. I want you, Crystal. *No.* It's more than that. I *need* you—and I've never felt that way about a woman; not even Rebecca. You have no idea what guilt that creates in me. Maybe I'm displacing the emotions I had for her to you, which would make me an asshole. I don't know. I just know that I'm not in a place that's fair to you. And since I couldn't seem to do the right thing, I went to your office to make you hate me so *you* would. So I couldn't get the chance to hurt you."

Everything hard inside me melts. Here is the man I've fallen for, the one capable of honest emotion, no matter how damning it might be. I step forward, closing my hand around his shirt. "Come inside before my neighbors hear us."

His feet are set hard, his body unmoving. "No. I want you too much to be able to come in and not touch you."

"Good," I whisper.

He grabs my wrists, warmth climbing up my arms at his touch. "You're not hearing me. I'm going to hurt you if we keep going like this."

"Don't give yourself so much credit, and me none," I chide.

"Crystal," he says softly, as if he knows that I'm deflecting so I don't have to admit the truth. Because he's right. He is going to hurt me—but it's too late to turn back now.

I lace the fingers of my other hand with his, relieved when he allows me to lead him inside. He shuts the door and locks it, leaning against it as I had, and still fighting his emotions.

The torment in him is familiar. It is how he comes to me, perhaps even *why* he comes to me. And like him, it is my weakness. Perhaps he senses how familiar the emotion is to me. Perhaps that emotion is the true bond between us, one destined to carve me into pieces. I've begun to think Mark is my drug, a high that has consequences, but I can't seem to care.

I step to him and he reaches for me, lacing his fingers into my hair. My skin tingles at his touch and then his mouth is on mine, his tongue stroking into my mouth. In one hot lick, he has me moaning; in two, I'm melting into his hard body, my fingers reaching for the buttons of his shirt.

He reaches down, his fingers wrapping my wrists, tearing his mouth from mine as he holds them between us. "This isn't about one night anymore, Crystal. If I stay, I won't walk away again. I'll try to own you," he warns. "I want you that badly."

*Own me.* I don't know why there's a burn in my belly at the words I'll never allow to be fulfilled. He's using me to survive the loss of Rebecca, and when I'm with him, there's no room for the juggling in my head. "You won't ever own me, Mark. But I can handle you trying."

"You didn't think I could make you tell me to lick your pussy in that bathroom, either. I'm demanding, and I'll push and push, and push some more. I'll put you on your knees because I can. I'll make you beg because I can." His hands go to my shoulders. "I'm going to ask for more than you ever thought you would give."

*Yes. Please.*

Oh God. What is he doing to me? "And if I won't give it to you? Then what?"

"I'll find a way to convince you."

"I have limits," I say, unsure why I can't just say "no."

"I'll erase them."

"You'll fail."

"I won't fail."

"That's arrogant."

"It's confidence."

We stare at each other, and it's like looking into a mirror. I see how he controls what he can to compensate for what he can't. And how that means he needs to control me, so I won't control him. We're two people who seem to everyone else to have blessed lives, but both of us live in glass houses, captive to the same stone. And that stone is a trauma in our pasts.

I don't want to be captive to that stone anymore. I don't want to win the battle over my limits. Life can be gone in a moment, lost to fear and regrets.

I push away from him. "In the hallway outside your parents' apartment, you said that I decide what we do or don't do."

"Yes. Convincing you doesn't mean forcing you. You can always say no."

"You'll just change my mind," I say, and it's not a question.

"Yes," he agrees.

Those words, coupled with his honesty tonight, allow me to give him a pebble of my trust. I'm not ready to let go of my stone. And I'm not sure I will, if he doesn't let go of his. But he's let me see a side of him that I don't believe anyone else has. I haven't abused that trust, and it's time to find out if I'll get the same in return.

I inhale and let it out, reaching to my sash and untying it, and the cool air sweeps beneath the silk to caress my hot skin. Mark's eyes are burning embers, sparking in the room. He steps forward and my heart begins to race.

As he holds my stare, his index finger parts the silk farther, finding my skin before dragging a line up and down between my breasts. Goose bumps rise, tightening my nipples into aching balls of need. And just that easily I am weak in the knees, wet with desire. I want his hands on my breasts, his lips on my nipples, but I get neither.

His palms slip beneath the robe, caressing it away from my body. It slinks downward, teasing my skin as it drops into a sultry puddle at my bare feet, leaving me naked while he's fully dressed. Leaving me exposed for his viewing and for his taking, vulnerable in ways I wouldn't allow myself to be with another man. And I am both terrified and aroused, waiting for him when I swore I'd never wait for any man.

But I wait, and this pleases him. I see it in the possessive burn in the depths of his eyes, but there's more there, too—there is relief, as if he'd been hanging off a ledge and I just lowered him a rope. And maybe I have, or I am, but somehow he's reached inside me and found that piece of me that I deny but can never escape, a part waiting to implode. He, too, is saving me.

Finally he reaches for me, dragging me against him, his hands cupping my backside as he lifts me. Instinctively, my arms wrap around his neck, my legs around his waist, and his palms flatten on my back, holding me as if he's afraid I'll escape. We stay like that for long moments, and the sea of turbulence between us fades into calm, then sizzles into a fire. In this space, in time, no matter how delicate the seams, I am woven into his life and he into mine.

He starts walking toward my bedroom and I bury my face in his neck, inhaling that spicy, sexy scent of him. Then he sets me on the edge of the mattress, my fluffy white down comforter hugging my naked body as he kneels in front of me. He slides my legs apart, his hands gliding up and down my naked thighs, my sex tightening, the wet heat slicking my flesh.

"I don't want this to be wild and out of control tonight. I want you to wake up knowing that *we* made this choice together—not circumstances. Tonight is about trust, something I tore down when I used the contract to push you away." He pulls the red tie from his neck and holds it between us.

I straighten, my spine stiff with a jolt that tells me my past is here, in vivid living color. This is too fast, too much. "I don't want to be tied up."

His fingers caress my cheek. "Relax," he says gently. "I'm not going to tie you up. I want to blindfold you. That's all."

I wet my suddenly parched lips. "Blindfold," I repeat.

"Yes. That way, you can stop anything I do with more than words. You have the control. I have the pleasure of ensuring your pleasure.

"This is where you say yes or no," he says, and then firms his voice, a command in the depths as he adds, "Say yes."

"What are you going to do to me?"

His sexy, sometimes brutally wicked lips, curve. "If I told you, I'd ruin the surprise. Say yes, Crystal." The command is firmer this time.

That intense arousal and fear have returned, drenched in adrenaline. This is how it feels facing fears that I haven't allowed myself to acknowledge. And I want to face them. I shut my eyes. "Yes."

"Look at me when you say it, so I know you mean it."

I'm comforted that a simple "yes" isn't enough to satisfy his need for my agreement. My eyes meet his and I repeat, "Yes."

He searches my face for a moment, and then wraps the tie around my eyes, covering them. Then his lips find my ear. "Stay and don't move. Just listen. It's a remarkable way to awaken your senses. And don't speak unless I tell you to speak. Understand?"

"Yes."

"Yes, what?"

"Yes, I understand."

I wait for him to speak again, but he doesn't. It's almost as if he waits to see if I truly *do* understand. My fingers curl into the blanket and I can feel his hot stare on my body as intimately as I would his mouth. There is something intriguing about knowing and not seeing. Something arousing about craving and not being satisfied. There is movement; sounds of what I think is the rustle of clothing. Of this wickedly hot man undressing, and I squeeze my thighs shut against the growing ache I feel. Silence falls then, and time ticks by eternally and I open my mouth and shut it. It's a test, I think, but the question it raises is confusing. By passing it, am I proving I'm in control of me or that he's in control of me?

"Stand up," he says.

Suddenly, the answer to my question doesn't matter as much as relief to my body. I do as he says.

"Take three steps forward."

I do it and stop, and I can feel his body heat. Then there's a shift in the air, and I think . . . I think he's circling me. No. He's behind me. Suddenly his hands are on my waist, as if he feels like I might dart away.

"Say my name."

"Mark."

"Again."

"Mark," I repeat.

"Mr. Compton," he commands.

"No."

"Say it."

The command is sharp, and so is my reply. "No," I hiss.

"Do you want me to fuck you?"

"Yes, Mark, I do."

He pulls me against him, my back to his chest, his hands covering my breasts, fingers teasing my nipples. "Say my name."

"Mark."

"Stubborn woman," he growls, and tugs on my nipples.

"Ahhh." I moan at the force of the tugs. "Ahhh. It . . . hurts." He rolls them, tugging again, and the pain begins to turn to pleasure. My lashes lower and I feel my body melting into his. At the same moment, his fingers slip between my thighs, into the slick heat there, and I almost come from the touch.

"You're wet, Ms. Smith," he murmurs. "So very wet. I think you really do want to fuck. Or maybe you just want to come."

"Yes. Please."

"Say my name." His fingers slip away from my sex, while the other hand glides from my breast to settle on my waist.

Frustration rolls inside me and I whirl on him, ripping away the tie from my eyes as I all but yell, "Mr. Compton."

He laughs and pulls me to him, the thick ridge of his erection against my hip. "Very good, Ms. Smith. That's how you answer every command I give you while we're fucking tonight. That way, every time you say 'Mr. Compton' to me tomorrow at work, you're going to think about my fingers between your legs and on your nipples—and so am I."

# Nine

Mark . . .

I watch the understanding fill Crystal's light blue eyes, feel the softening of her body against mine a moment before she whispers, "Oh. Yes . . . we will."

"And I plan to give you even more to remember, before this night is over."

Her gaze drops to the thickness of my erection. She wets her lips and my shaft jerks with the impact of the seductive lick, and the many places she is taking my imagination. I guide her fingers and wrap them around the base. While I normally prefer not being touched, since that allows me control, I already crossed that boundary with Crystal in the past—and I crave her hands and mouth all over me, everywhere. Anywhere.

My grip tightens and her gaze lifts, her eyes laden with desire, those lush, beautiful lips that I've just fantasized about angled toward me. In a blink, hunger consumes me. *She* consumes me, and

I can't remember why I thought that was a problem before. I don't want to remember. I just want her.

Twining the fingers of my free hand into the long, silky strands of her hair, I drag her mouth a breath from mine. "What are you doing to me, woman?" And then I claim her mouth.

My tongue strokes against hers, caressing, taking, drinking in the warm, sweet taste of her. She is one part willing woman, two parts challenge. I know I'll never fully control her, and the very thing that would have made her wrong for me in the past is the very thing that makes her what I want and need now. She is freedom. She is passion. She is the safe place where I can be the man I've tried to deny beneath the Master persona, and failed. It's why I failed Rebecca; it's how I turned emotion into dangerous games. I had no idea how much I needed the freedom to simply be me.

Crystal's fingers tighten on my cock, and it's nearly my undoing. Tearing my mouth from hers, I promise, "I have a never-ending list of the wicked things I'm going to do to you, but right now, I just need to be inside you. Stand with your back to the footboard and your hands on top of it."

Her swollen, deliciously kissed lips curve as she replies, "Yes, Mr. Compton." It's not the way a submissive would say the words. It's a challenge, and even more, it's a promise that she plans to use those words to taunt me in the future.

My blood thickens with the sultry words she's turned on me, and I watch her walk to the bed, her beautiful ass a portrait finer than any of my many masterpieces. She turns to face me, her eyes colliding with mine as she presses her hands behind her onto the footboard. Her breasts are thrust high in the air, the nipples puckered in tight little balls. She's all about challenge and seduction—and though she doesn't know it yet, she's going to pay for taunting me, and I'm going to enjoy every second of it.

I reach for my pants and remove my wallet, retrieving the one condom there. Sex hadn't been on my agenda tonight; my apology had. I roll the condom over the thick pulse of my shaft, then in two long strides, I'm in front of Crystal. My hand settles on her tiny waist with intentional possession. I meant what I said when I told her I wanted to own her, and not just her body.

My other hand goes beside hers on the footboard, and I lean into her, binding her without a device, my chest hair cradling the stiff peaks of her nipples. An easy shift of my body, and I settle my cock between her thighs, denying us both by avoiding that sweet, warm spot in the V of her body. A Master worth his salt knows how to build tension and work the passion to explosive, absolute pleasure.

"Do you really think you can taunt me and get away with it?" I demand, my voice soft but lethal.

Her chin lifts, defiance in the depths of her eyes. "Who said I wanted to get away with it?"

"So you *wanted* me to make you pay?"

"I just wanted you to hurry up and fuck me. It didn't work. You still aren't fucking me."

I press my other hand to the footboard, trapping her with my body, my cheek pressed to hers. "Consider this a warning," I say, inhaling her sweet, floral scent. "There's a price for taunting me. A punishment."

"What do you mean, punishment?"

"I have a very creative imagination. Nipple clamping, flogging, or just a good spanking."

"No," she whispers, panic in her voice as she jerks her upper body, unable to move away. "No, I won't—"

"But I will," I promise. "And you'll want me to, I promise—or I won't do it."

"Can't we just—"

"No. We can't *just.*" I dip my fingers into the dripping wet heat of her sex. "Your body says you like the idea of me punishing you."

"Your hard cock is between my legs. Of course I'm aroused."

"Me punishing you *is* me arousing you." I dip two fingers inside her.

She moans, her lashes fluttering. "No."

I pull out of her, moving my hand to her hip. "No?"

"I mean yes. Or—" I arch a brow and she lets out a rush of air. "I don't want you to spank me, flog me, or whatever else you dream up. So please just fuck me already, *Mr. Compton.*"

I slide my hand up her back and arch her into me. "There's no such thing as 'just' fucking." My lips caress hers. "Not with me. Not with you."

"I think you might want too much," she says, sounding breathless.

"Not too much. Just what I said before: more than you thought you had to give. But you can. You will." I press my cock to the lips of her sex, then drive deep into her, my hands cupping her backside. "But one day, you'll know my hand on your gorgeous ass and you'll wish you'd known it sooner." I thrust into her hard and fast, one time, two—

"My arms," she pleads. "Mark, I'm can't hold myself—"

I wrap an arm around her, anchoring her. "Let go," I order.

"No. I'll fall."

Her words blast me with a dark emotion that aches and burns in my chest and belly. I don't just want this woman's trust. I want to *deserve* it. "You won't fall," I promise, my words rough, vehement. "I won't let you."

She blinks up at me, her expression softening as she whispers, "I believe you." She lifts her arms, wrapping them around my neck before repeating, "I believe you."

Her promise eases that ache inside me, delivering a sense of purpose and rightness that I haven't felt in too long to remember. I slant my mouth over hers, kissing her, claiming her, taking every drop of the passion I feel in her and demanding more. And she gives it to me, meeting every lick, every touch with one of her own.

Lifting her, I carry her to the side of the bed, laying her on her back and coming down on top of her, drowning in the collision of our eyes. The connection I feel, which I didn't know I *could* feel after all of these years, shakes me to the core. And in this moment, I admit what I've only suspected before. I have been lost, and in some way, this woman has found me.

I kiss her, tasting her in a way I have never let myself taste, rocking into her body, her soft moans and the way she arches into me thickening my cock. I feel every thrust up and down my spine, every touch of her hands in every part of me, in ways I'm not sure I've ever allowed myself to experience. She touches me eagerly, without restraint, and it drives me over the edge. I drive into her, wild with need. Burying my face in her neck, I pump against her as she arches upward, meeting every thrust of my hips with her own. There is only this frenzied need between us . . . until her fingers dig into my shoulders, and she stiffens. Her body spasms around my cock and I am one part relief, one part regret as she drags me with her, and my release is on me, shaking me with the impact, as she shudders beneath me.

Finally, we collapse into sated exhaustion, me on top of her, not wanting to let her go. It's as if there's a floor beneath me with a gaping hole, and a cyclone pulling me through to the other side, and she is the calmness that keeps me from falling through.

Finally I lift up on my arms, and my eyes meet Crystal's.

"Mmmm . : . hi," she says.

I laugh. God, when's the last time I laughed while I was inside a woman? Never. "Hi?" I ask in disbelief. "What kind of—"

"My kind," she says, smiling. "If you're getting up to throw out the condom, go and come back. I'm not letting a Master off with one orgasm."

"I'm not letting a submissive—"

"But I'm not your submissive. Now go, before you get punished," she teases.

I pull out of her, feeling the moment like a shock wave, and the way she bites her bottom lip tells me she's feeling it, too. I am in so much trouble, yet I can't seem to care. Tearing my gaze from hers, I walk into the bathroom and toss the condom in the toilet, intending to return to the bedroom. But when I turn, I see the tub filled with bubbles and inhale the sweet scent of the flowers that's always on Crystal's skin.

My mind flashes with an image of Rebecca sitting on the edge of my bathtub back home in San Francisco, spreading her favorite rose-scented lotion on her body. No. It had been *our bathtub*. She'd lived with me, though I know she never really felt she belonged there. Everything had still been about the contract. The fact that it had an end date and that I'd insisted she keep her apartment was always there between us. I wanted to take care of her, and I wanted her in my life. What I hadn't wanted was to fall in love, and so I didn't.

I scrub a hand over the tension in the back of my neck. I was too shut off emotionally. I thought if I didn't love her, neither of us could get hurt.

"Damn it," I murmur, glancing up to find Crystal standing in the doorway, a deliciously naked distraction that I need right now.

"Either you have a vibrator in your pants, or your phone is on silent and ringing," she announces. "If it's a vibrator, I can do that myself." She turns and leaves me with a view of the perfect backside that I'm definitely going to spank sooner rather than later.

"A vibrator or my phone," I repeat, and I actually smile again.

Going into the empty bedroom, I catch a glimpse of her exiting into the living room area. I assume she's going after her robe, which, considering I don't have another condom, is probably a damn good idea. I grab my pants off the floor, dig out my phone, and find a text from Jacob. Headed to room for some shuteye. Kara Walker is on duty. 212-555-7789.

She must be Blake's wife, hell-bent on stopping me from acting on my claim of vengeance. I clamp down on my anger. Though I can never right my past wrongs, I can do the right thing now. That means avenging Rebecca and making sure no one else gets hurt. As long as Ava is out there somewhere, I can't be sure either of those two things will happen. And I won't allow anyone to get in my way.

# Ten

Mark . . .

Seeking out Crystal, I pass through her modern art deco–style living area, with white furniture and red and white abstract paintings by a famous artist whose work I'd never have on my walls. While brilliantly talented, he's an absolute prick. Following the sound of music and singing, I head to an open archway. Stepping inside I find a compact, square kitchen of rich navy blues and grays. Behind the cooktop on one end of the stainless steel island is Crystal, wearing her pink silk robe as expected. She's holding a spatula, completely focused on whatever's in the skillet while singing "You Shook Me All Night Long" by AC/DC.

I lean on the door frame, entertained by the adorable expressions she's making while absolutely rocking out. Seconds tick by and still she doesn't look up. "You're cooking at this hour?"

She jumps and looks at me, holding her fist to her chest for a moment. "You scared me." She laughs, and the smile that follows is genuine and infectious, much like my mother's. Picking up her phone, she punches a button to turn off the music. "I guess it was a little louder than I realized. I didn't even hear you come in. And yes, I'm cooking. Apparently threats of spankings make me hungry."

"Especially if you do it all night long," I tease, mimicking the lyrics, intrigued by her willingness to be so direct about a topic that makes her uncomfortable.

Her cheeks flush a rosy color. "If the lyrics were 'you took me in four minutes,' I'd have been humming even if I was alone."

"I think I should be the one to hum to that." I walk to the seat across the counter from her and sit down. "Pancakes?"

"Really good pancakes with chocolate chips. You do like chocolate, right?"

"I do. Some might even say I have a sweet tooth."

"I'm not asking what that means."

"Really," I say. "I have a sweet tooth. Candy, cake, you name it. I force myself to savor it only on the holidays."

"I have one, too, but I'm not that controlled about it," she says. "I treat myself once a week, and lately that's been a box of my favorite cereal on Saturday night about midnight. I don't have time to cook."

"Because you're obviously a workaholic," I say, wondering if being adopted makes her feel she always has to prove her worth. I'm not adopted and I feel that pressure.

"But I always cook on the holidays for my family. It's a tradition now. I grew up in a house full of men with busy schedules. If I didn't cook, no one did, so everyone is used to me making certain things."

"You were adopted into a family of all men?"

"That's right." She fills two plates with two pancakes each and sets one of them in front of me, one in front of the empty seat next to me. "Angela Smith was killed in a car accident the week before my adoption was final." She turns to the fridge behind her.

"You've got to be fucking kidding me."

"It seems impossible, doesn't it?" She sets two cans of Diet Sprite on the counter. "Sorry, that's all I have in the house. I haven't been home much."

"This is fine," I say, popping the top and getting back on topic. "So Smith was grieving and in shock, and still went ahead with your adoption?"

She rounds the island and sits down next to me. "Yes. Looking back as an adult I know how amazing that is, but Angela had been a foster child like I was—only she was never adopted. They'd been poor when they had my brothers, and now wanted to help someone in need. And to them, that meant rescuing an older child who had limited chances to get adopted." Her voice tightens. "I think . . . I think going ahead with the adoption was my father's way of keeping Angela alive. I think he sees her in me."

"Now I *really* want to meet your father."

She smiles. "He's a good man. An arrogant pain in the ass sometimes, who's overprotective, but still a good man. I think you'd either get along very well with him, or the two of you would want to throttle each other."

"I'm not sure if that was a compliment or an insult."

"Simply stating the facts," she says, handing me a bottle of syrup.

I set the syrup down. "How old were you when he adopted you?"

"I was fourteen. I'd been in foster homes for five years," she responds, taking the liberty to pour the syrup for me, which for reasons I can't explain makes me want to pull her close and rip the robe off her. I refrain only because I want to hear the rest of her story, and we have no condom.

"How did you end up in a foster home at nine?"

"My mother died, and my father wasn't a fit parent," she says quickly and without looking at me, attending to the syrup lid with a little too much focus. "But it ended well." She glances up at me. "I was raised by a powerful, controlling father, who bred my older brothers into clones, who now worry about me as much as he does."

"So your father never remarried?"

"He did, but not until we were all out of the house." She motions to the pancakes. "Try them. It's a recipe I love; they taste like chocolate chip cookies."

I'm still focused on her. "How do you like your stepmother?"

"She's very loving to my father, and good to all of us."

"But?"

"There really isn't a but. She's a good person and passionate about charity work."

"But you don't see her as a mother," I say, starting to see how she's bonded with my mother, who always wanted a daughter but couldn't have more kids.

She jabs a piece of pancake with her fork. "She and I are night and day."

"Translate that to a real answer."

"She's very submissive to my father."

One side of my mouth quirks up. "I'm suddenly seeing the irony of this conversation."

"You started it, not me."

"Yes. Maybe I should shut up and eat." I take a bite of the pancake. "You're right. Chocolate chip cookies, and good ones, at that. You can run a company *and* cook. What else is up your sleeve?"

"I can sing."

"I'm not sure I'd agree with that one," I tease.

She smirks. "I think you should shut up and eat again." She pops the lid to her drink and turns somber. "Anything else happen with Dana after I left?"

I inhale at the memory of my mother's withdrawal during our conversation, then let it out. "No. Like I said, she fell asleep. I went outside into the hallway and paced. My father found me and gave me a pep talk, then proceeded to ask if I was fucking you, and that was it."

She sets her fork down and gapes. "Your father asked if we were—"

"Fucking. Yes. He's worried you'll break my heart."

She shakes her head. "He did *not* say that."

"No. I made that part up."

"What did you tell him about us?"

"That, as of earlier tonight, I wouldn't dare to stand close to sharp objects when you were around."

She presses her hand to her forehead. "Oh God. What did he say?"

"He told me to apologize to you."

"For what?"

"He didn't care what I did. He just said to apologize. He claims that's how he's stayed married all these years. Then he went back inside the apartment."

"Does your mother know?"

"No. But after I told her I own a BDSM club tonight, she'd probably say I'm not good enough for you."

"That's not true. She loves you, Mark. Her reaction to what you shared tonight was about how helpless she feels—not about you. She's always better when you're here."

"Her reaction didn't say 'trust.'"

"She's fighting cancer, and she just heard you own a BDSM club. It was overwhelming."

I grab her knees and turn her to face me. "I handed over management of the club to someone else."

"You don't have to tell me this."

"No, but I want to. I started it seven years ago, but it was never about sex to me, and my sexual partners were few."

She tilts her head and studies me. "If the club wasn't about sex to you, then what did it mean?"

"Being the ultimate Master in control. And I know that sounds arrogant, but it wasn't about ego."

"Then what was it about?"

I pull back, letting my hands fall away from her. "I don't know anymore."

She gives a slow nod. "I understand. I didn't mean to push for too much." She starts to turn and I grab her legs.

"You didn't ask too much. But things that made sense for a lot of years suddenly don't anymore. That's why I came here tonight. I don't know what this thing is between us, but I've done so much denying in the past—and this feels like it's the only thing honest in my life right now."

She leans forward, her hands settling on my arms, and I can almost feel her touch calming the storm that's been raging inside me for weeks without end. "Whatever this is or isn't, you made sure it's honest when you came here tonight."

I give in to desire and pull her off her chair and between my legs. "I assume since you're fucking me, you aren't seeing anyone else."

She glowers. "*Now* who doesn't know how to filter?" she asks, reminding me of what I'd said to her the first day we'd met.

My fingers flex on her back. "I need to know."

"There's no one else." She hesitates, opening her mouth, then closing her lips.

"You want to ask me, too," I say.

"I don't want to pressure you."

"Why not? I'm pressuring you. So you deserve to know: When I needed an escape last week, I didn't go to the club or call someone I knew from the club. I flew you to San Francisco. I don't want anyone else."

"If that changes, just please tell me."

"I don't and it won't," I say, pushing to my feet. "And if you don't know that, then I haven't done a good enough job of showing you." I scoop her up and start walking toward the bedroom. I might not have a condom, but I have a tongue, and I plan to use it well. I need her to know that I'm a changed man before she's faced with the full impact of my many sins against Rebecca—sins I fear she'll never forgive me for. I know I won't.

I wake to the soft glow of morning light through the bedroom curtains and the vibration of my phone on the nightstand, but with Crystal curled against my side I'm not quick to respond. For several moments I'm unable to move, *unwilling* to move, certain that the few hours of peace we've created together are about to end. I grab the phone and glance at the time, 7:00 a.m., then the caller ID, noting Jacob's number.

Crystal shifts beside me, leaning up on one arm, her long blond hair a tousled, sexy mess. "What is it?"

I hit the Decline button and set the phone down. "Jacob. Probably wanting to know our travel plans this morning. I'll have to go by my hotel and change on the way to the hospital. And I know my mother will insist I go to Riptide today to help secure the business—so we can plan on riding in together."

"I should have gone in early today," Crystal says. "There's a huge auction next Saturday I'm in the middle of planning."

"Now there are two of us to bring it all together, so you can ease up on the hours a bit."

She nods. "I think it would go a long way for you to talk to the staff and assure them everything is okay, too."

"You're barely awake and already talking business."

"It's inbred. In my house, we talked stock market reports before we brushed our teeth."

"Mine was sports in one ear and fine art in the other—but at least I learned to multitask." My cell starts ringing again and I sigh. "He's not giving up." I answer the call without looking and say, "I didn't know you had a wake-up service."

"At your fucking service." I sit up at the sound of Blake Walker's voice as he adds, "Time to get up, because I have news. Corey, the kid who ran off with Ava, was dropped off at a hospital a few hours ago—beaten badly enough to be in the ICU."

"And? What did he say?"

"They aren't telling us anything yet."

"They? Why aren't *you* talking to him?"

"Because I'm in San Francisco—and he was left at a Long Island hospital."

My blood runs cold. "That's just a forty-minute train ride from here."

"Which means whoever beat him is there, too," he adds.

My grip tightens on the phone and I stand up, certain that whoever did this wants me to know.

"I'm on my way to Long Island," Blake adds, "but I'm not

coming alone. Detective Grant is coming with me, because it's a conflict of interest for me to question you about Corey, since I'm on your payroll."

"Then you shouldn't have gotten greedy and taken both jobs."

"Ease up, man. I'm on your side. I didn't know Rebecca, but I read her journals and feel like I did. And I trust myself to do her justice more than I trust the police, who have a district attorney motivated by the election year pulling their strings."

I inhale and exhale. "If you think that hearing you and half of San Francisco read her journals is going to console me, you're not as smart as I thought you were."

"I'm a lot *smarter* than you think I am. I know you, man. I *was* you. I held my fiancée in my arms while she bled to death with a sliced throat, because I was minutes too late to save her. And it happened because I let her stay in harm's way for reasons I can never forgive myself for. I know where your head is—and you need to step back, before you don't have that option anymore. Let me handle this."

His words chill me to the bone, and I press my fingers to my temples, fighting the fucking burning in my chest and eyes. What the hell is happening to me? Where is the man who could shut everything out? "What does Grant want?"

"You aren't going to comment on anything I just said?"

"Not now."

He's silent a moment. "Fine. We'll talk when I get there. On Grant, let me be clear before I go on: I've said nothing to him about your motivations toward anyone or anything. But the kid was dropped in New York, and you were close to Rebecca— which gives you motivation to act on her behalf, since she can't."

I run a rough hand through my hair. "In other words, call my attorney."

"I would."

Frustration rolls through me. "Being close to Rebecca made me a murder suspect. Though I was cleared, now I'm a suspect all over again, for the same reason."

"It's fucked-up, but that pretty much sums it up."

"I've been with Jacob around the clock for weeks."

"That doesn't mean you couldn't have hired someone. And you and I both know that you did."

"The kid was going to turn in evidence on Ava. He's a hero, as far as I'm concerned. And the police have to know that I'm not foolish enough to drop him this close to home." I walk into the dark bathroom, snatch up a towel, and wrap it around my waist.

"Or they think you're smart enough to know that would be the obvious assumption."

I grind my teeth. "In other words, Grant and I are about to go around the block a couple or ten times again. Well, just tell him to be careful. There's a fine line between questioning and slandering, with this much press involved and the livelihood of a business at stake."

"I've had that conversation with him, believe me. But the guy's pretty 'who gives a shit?' He's a problem."

"I'll deal with him. You just find Ava before she hurts someone else. And in case that's not clear enough, let me be more direct: Keep my family and employees safe. Or I swear to you, Blake Walker, your brothers will be looking for vengeance on your behalf—and I'll come stand on their doorstep and tell them to bring it on."

"You're living in hell, so I'll pretend you didn't say that. We're adding extra men to the operation and tightening surveillance where we can."

"But you still have no clue where Ava's at."

"No." He hesitates. "Look, man, I might be on the right side of the law, but I was undercover in one of the biggest drug cartels in the world. I know how to play dirty. Connect me to whatever underground contact you have. I'll make it count."

"Not a chance. I'm going out to Long Island. I'll meet you there."

"Forget it. They won't let you near the kid, and my brother Luke is headed down there now. If Corey talks before I get there, Luke will be there to make it count."

"I don't like how this is going down. Someone is sending me a message."

"None of these people I'm dealing with are fools."

"But?" I sense there's more.

"But it's an election year, and the DA in San Francisco needs this to go away. That's why you need to consider sharing anything you know with my team—and letting us help."

"I'm sick and fucking tired of hearing about the election year."

"You and me both—but it's a fact we can't escape. So let me help. Be straight with me, and let me make sure they don't use you as a fall guy."

"What happened to conflict of interest?"

"Fuck conflict of interest, if they try to make you the fall guy again. I'm pulling up to the airport now. Luke will call you if he finds out anything. And just a heads-up: The detective is flying in with me, but he's going to go straight to you. My brother Royce, who's former FBI and still well connected, will be there if he crosses any lines. Just make sure the ones you and I know that you're crossing stay hidden. And keep Crystal the hell away from it, so she won't go down if you do."

"There's nothing to keep her away from," I say, being careful not to have anyone admit anything.

"Denial," Blake says. "I did it, too. It can be dangerous. Remember that."

He's hit a raw nerve, and I grind my teeth. "Just have Grant call my cell when he arrives. I don't want this near Riptide or my parents."

"My team will do our best to keep him and all of this away from both. I'll call you when I land."

He ends the call and I lean on the sink, my hands on the counter, head dropped forward. It seems the tables are turned. I'm going after Ava and Ryan, and someone is coming after me. Most likely Ava and Ryan, who've proven killing isn't beyond their scope.

I dial Jacob. "I assume you know what's happening?"

"Yes. That's why I was calling you."

"Have my things at the hotel brought to Crystal's."

"All of them?"

"Yes, and the sooner the better. But I'll need to go by and clear the safe, so we need to leave here at about eight thirty. And I'll be going to Riptide with Crystal after the hospital."

"I'll have them there in thirty minutes."

"I'll be waiting," I say, ending the call, and I prepare to get dressed and seek out privacy to reach out to my underground contact. Turning, I find Crystal standing in the doorway, hugging her silk robe to her body.

"What's happening?"

"The kid that left with Ava was dropped off at a hospital, badly beaten. No one knows by whom, and he's in ICU and can't talk yet."

"But he's alive, so that's good, right?"

"Yes—but he's also here in New York."

Her eyes go wide. "Here? How did he get here?"

"Everything is a mystery at this point, but Blake's on his way here to question him when he can speak. Apparently a detective from San Francisco is also headed here to talk to me."

"You? Why?"

"I cared about Rebecca and this kid was dropped here in New York, so they see it coming together as a motive. And since I've been under supervision with a security person at all times, they think I hired someone to do it."

She draws back slightly. "Please tell me you didn't."

"I didn't." I'll kick Blake's ass for telling her about my vow of vengeance.

"That's it?" she challenges. "Just 'I didn't'?"

"It's a straightforward, honest answer."

Her eyes narrow. "Then why do I feel like it's complicated?"

Because nothing these past few weeks has been simple.

I close the distance between us. "I'm moving in with you. My things will be here soon. And I need to go downstairs and attend to some business."

"What? Did you really just tell me you're moving in with me without asking?"

"There's no question to ask. Somebody wanted that kid to be dropped off here because I'm here. I was cautious about my plans, which means someone is watching me—and doing a job no amateur could."

"Who? Ava? Is she that sophisticated?"

"No. That's the point. And I'm not leaving you alone to end up like Rebecca. End of story." I try to step around her.

She grabs my arm. "So, what? Now I'm your responsibility? Is that why you came here last night? To get close and make sure you can keep your guilt at bay?"

"As I showed you last night, I'm not someone who fakes emotions. I don't even fucking *want* to have emotions. But yes, you're my responsibility, and don't even bother to argue that point with me. I will protect you, even if you end up hating me in the end."

She inhales and her lips tighten. "What business do you have to attend to?"

"Business."

"Got it. Your business is none of my business, but you're now living with me. Glad to know we're being honest."

She lets go of my arm and I fight the urge to pull her close and explain, but I resist. Blake's right. There's more to this than just protecting her. If the police are about to be on top of me again, the less she knows, the better.

Letting her go, I walk into the bedroom and begin to get dressed. I grab my pants and pull them on, reaching into my pocket to remove the disposable phone to see a missed call. I glance up to find Crystal staring at it and me.

She says, "Vengeance isn't business. And it isn't protecting your family or me." She disappears into the bathroom and turns on the shower.

I don't go after her. If I'm right and that kid was dropped off here to turn up the heat on me, this *isn't* vengeance anymore.

It's war.

# Eleven

Mark . . .

Once I'm dressed, I take the elevator down to the lobby. Certain there will be security feeds anywhere in the building, I head toward the exit, only to be intercepted by Jacob just before my escape.

"I thought we weren't leaving till eight-thirty?" he asks.

"We aren't. And how did you find me?"

"It's my job, one that you expect me to do well."

"While I won't argue that point, I don't require assistance at the moment. Just make sure my things make it to Crystal's." I shove open the glass door and exit into a gust of arctic air, wishing like hell I had the coat I'd left in Jacob's SUV last night.

Hunkering down against the wind, I grab the disposable phone and punch in my contact's number. He answers on the second ring and says, "Ava was last seen in a Mexican border town near El Paso, Texas, three days ago. The clear assumption is she's escaping to Mexico."

"If she was going to Mexico, she could have done that in California. Was she with the mercenary you told me about?"

"Yes. And from what I understand, she had her tongue down his throat."

This is not good news. "So she's not a prisoner." To avoid the elements, I step under the awning of a retail store sharing space with the apartment building.

"It's hard to say with this guy," my informant says. "He could be using her for a little pussy before he slices her throat. He's that vicious."

"Or she could have him pussy whipped."

"Doubtful," he says. "I'd bet my right ball he's the one pulling her chain. You don't get under this guy's skin. He'll scalp you for trying."

"I need a name."

"A.J. Wright."

"Any known connections to Ricco Alvarez?"

"You've had me focused on destroying Ryan Kilmer, so not that I know of. But Ricco Alvarez has the kind of money this guy would demand, and he's suspected of helping her escape."

"If Ricco found out she killed Rebecca, he wouldn't still be helping her."

"Who says he is? Maybe he told A.J. to kill her, and A.J. is just playing with her for a while before he does."

"Until I have proof, I'm not ruling out any options. That means Ryan, Ricco, and even Ava meeting A.J. on her own are still on the table. And you can stop looking for the kid who ran off with Ava. He ended up in a hospital here in New York, so beaten up he's in the ICU."

He whistles. "Someone was telling you they're on your doorstep."

"Exactly. Find A.J. and Ava and see if there's a connection to Ricco. And yes, I know it will cost me."

"I expect a wire today for what you owe me."

"Words aren't proof. You'll get the money when I get proof that A.J. is with Ava, and Ava is alive. And I want everything you have on A.J.."

"Not a problem. The hotel manager where they were staying likes extra money under the table. He took a photo. I have a man in New York. I'll have a file delivered to your hotel to avoid electronic signatures."

"No. I'm moving locations. Deliver it to Riptide. Make sure you put 'Confidential' on the front."

"It'll be to you this afternoon."

"Then you'll get your wire this afternoon."

"And you'll be happy to know Ryan Kilmer has another blow awaiting him today. That money-laundering scandal you wanted linked to one of his primary properties is sure to put him back on the police radar."

"Good. Include details in the paperwork you send me. But most importantly, find Ava and A.J." I end the call and head back toward the entry to the building, glancing at my watch. It's already eight o'clock. We need to leave for the hotel to clear the safe in thirty minutes to be sure we make the hospital in time to see my mother before her treatment.

I quickly enter the welcome warmth of the lobby, my long strides eating up the path to the elevator. If I end up with proof that Ava's alive, I have to tread carefully. I won't go to the police and let them screw up a chance to catch her. I have to get to her before she gets to me and the people I care about.

Once I'm back on the fiftieth floor, I'm keyless and forced to knock, vowing to remedy that situation quickly. "Who is it?" Crystal answers after a good minute.

"Me," I say.

The door cracks open but she doesn't appear. I step inside to find her walking away, her hair wet, her skin damp, with nothing but a towel covering her. I'm in the hallway, locking the door in an instant, in hot pursuit. I catch her just as she rounds the corner to the living room, snagging her wrist and pulling her around to face me.

She whirls on me. "Damn it, Mark, let go."

"Not a chance," I say, pulling her to me, inhaling her sweet, floral scent, which is becoming as addictive as she is.

Her hand flattens on my chest. "When I'm pissed, don't touch me."

I flatten one hand on her back, molding her to me. "I have to touch you. That's just it—I have to. And that's not familiar to me. I'm trying to be honest here, Crystal. And I'm asking you not to push me on some things right now, and don't shut me out. I'm doing what I feel I have to do—but you're the one thing keeping me grounded."

Her fingers curl on my chest. "You're riding grief and guilt, Mark. And you're scaring me."

"I'm not going to do something foolish, but I'm also not sitting back and letting you or my parents get hurt. If anything happened to you or them right now . . . I would lose it. And I wouldn't be responsible for my actions anymore."

She wraps her arms around me. "I'm scared for you, Mark. Let the police handle it."

A knock sounds on the door and I kiss her, a deep, possessive claiming, before I start to set her away from me.

She grabs my arm and wraps her arms around me again. "I want to be here with you and for you, and I'm not shutting you out. But I'm also asking you not to shut me out."

"Whatever I do is for your protection." There's another knock and I kiss her again, hard and fast, and this time I set her firmly away from me, turning away to end the conversation. "Who is it?"

"Jacob."

I glance over my shoulder to make sure Crystal's no longer standing there in a towel, to find nothing but the towel remaining. My groin tightens. She's sending me a message and it's loud and clear. She won't be dismissed, and it worked. I unlock the door, pulling it open to reveal Jacob and my bags. I have only one thing on my mind. *Her.*

I wave Jacob forward, and he rolls a cart inside. "Where do you want them?"

"Just leave the cart. Come back in about twenty minutes and I'll be ready."

"Will do. Luke Walker wanted me to give you a message."

Unease rolls through me. "And that would be what?"

"The kid started talking before he got there. He has no idea what was said, only that they asked a lot of questions about you."

"Are you saying the kid accused me of beating him up?"

"All Luke knew was that you were the focus of the questioning."

I inhale and hold in the breath a moment before I say, "I need to make a phone call. We'll go by my hotel after the hospital, on the way to Riptide." I glance at my watch. "It's eight twenty. Be back here at nine."

I snatch up the towel and turn away, already grabbing my phone from my pocket and dialing my attorney, Tiger. The door opens and closes, telling me Jacob has left. I wait through a series of rings and get voice mail, which doesn't please me.

I say, "Call me when you get this. I might need you in New York. And yes, I know it's going to cost me. When have you ever been cheap?" I end the call and stuff my phone back into my pocket. Clutching the towel, I stare down at it. Everything inside me wants to go find her and fuck her. Everything inside me just wants her, period. Selfishly. Completely. In the face of danger she shouldn't be a part of.

But it's too late. If I send her away, fire her, alienate her, and tell my mother why, her safety would still be at risk. There is no way to be sure she's safe except to keep her right here, right now.

A dark edginess I know all too intimately begins to overtake me, a part of the Master that has been long buried hard and fast in the act of sex.

Aware that time is ticking, I stalk toward the bedroom and open the door. It's empty, the bed still a mess from where we slept. *Together.* I don't know how it's happened, but since the day I met her, she's become such a part of my life that no matter how I fight it, or her, she's in my blood—a part of why I exist. Yet so is Rebecca. I don't understand it, and I do not like things that I don't understand.

I walk into the bathroom to find Crystal in her pink robe, finishing her makeup. Memories of Rebecca doing the same freeze me in place, as I realize the intimacy this means I have now with Crystal. And I like it. I like it in a way that I never allowed myself to with Rebecca—which rips at me like a chain saw.

Crystal's eyes meet mine, and I know she's seen what I feel. My ability to hide my emotions has gone to shit, along with my ability to deny they exist—at least where she's concerned. I have that sense of connection with her. It's a vulnerable moment, and I find myself fighting the rawness of the emotions it stirs. My cock thickens, the need for sex and release—my way of coping with what I don't want to exist—hitting me hard and fast.

"We're leaving at nine, instead of eight thirty," I say, walking past her to the shower. After stripping down, I open the door to turn on the water and don't wait for it to warm. Stepping forward, I let the cold water wash over me and turn my back to Crystal, pressing my hands on the wall.

"Mark."

Her voice whispers over my nerve endings and my body doesn't seem to care how cold the water is. I want her. "Not now, Ms. Smith." I grab her shampoo and soap my hair, the damn flowery scent surrounding me. I rinse it off but it's too late; the scent is all over me. I wipe water from my face, smooth my hair back, and turn to the damn wall again, smelling roses and jasmine mixed together. Rebecca. Crystal. Confusion.

The door opens, telling me Crystal has ignored my dismissal, but what's new? I cut her a hard look over my shoulder. "What part of 'not now' do you not understand?" I ask, my eyes traveling her naked body, her tight little pink nipples, and I growl low in my throat with the thickening of my cock, turning away to let my head fall forward.

"Oh dear God," she gasps, "the water is freezing." In a moment the cold becomes warm, like my blood.

"Go away, Ms.—"

"Crystal," she corrects as she ducks under my arms to rest on the wall in front of me, her hands settling on my chest and turning my warm blood to hot.

Grinding my teeth, I compel myself not to touch her. "Damn

it, woman. Don't you get it? I *fuck* when I'm in a bad place. That's what I do. I fuck, and I need to fuck *you* right now."

She wraps her arms around me, my erection pressing against her hip, and it's torture, absolute torture, not to touch her. "Then fuck me," she whispers.

"What part of 'we don't have a condom' have you forgotten?"

"I'm on the pill."

"And you didn't tell me last night," I say, part a demand for explanation and part accusation.

"You told me you always use condoms. I knew that made you safe for me, but I wasn't sure you'd think it made me safe for you."

"How many partners?"

She blinks. "Partners? Oh. Partners. One without a condom, and I lived with him for over a year. He was clean. I made sure of it, and just to be clear, I'd never go without a condom for a one-night stand. Or even several, like we were. But now you're—"

"Moving in with you," I say, wrapping my fingers around her neck, pulling her mouth a breath from mine. "That means you belong to me now."

"No," she says. "It means—"

My mouth slants over hers, cutting off her words, my tongue pressing past her lips, delving deeply, possessiveness rising in me so intense that it's a living, breathing thing. I hate the man she lived with. I deepen the kiss, wild hunger rising inside me, driven by darkness and the self-blame that I've lived with for ten years. What am I doing with Crystal? What the *fuck* am I doing?

I turn her into a corner, my hands on her shoulders, and step back enough to loosen her grip around my waist. "You should get me the hell out of your life, before I destroy you like I did Rebecca. Tell me to leave."

She laughs without humor. "Like you'd listen?"

"Damn it, tell me to leave, Crystal," I demand.

"Your staying or leaving doesn't impact the premise of your demand, which seems to be that I have no control over myself. That's wrong. I decide who destroys me, not you, Mark Compton."

"You think Rebecca didn't say that?"

"Apparently being a Master has confused you, or made you a little too arrogant for your own good. I have a mind of my own."

"That's what she said."

Her hands go to my arms. "And she left you, Mark. That's not a woman who lost her backbone or her own mind. She wasn't too weak to survive you and whatever you think you did to her."

I tangle my fingers in her now damp hair. "You don't know everything. You were right when you said I'm an asshole. I am." I turn her to the wall and lean in close. "You want me to stay?"

"Yes."

"Are you sure?

"Yes. I want you to stay."

"Then you need to know who and what I am. I'm going to spank you and it's not going to be gentle. And in the future I will flog you, clamp you, and torment you in ways that you have never dreamed of. Still want me to stay?"

"Mark—"

"*Do you* want me to stay?" I ask, rubbing her backside to get the blood flow where I want it.

"Yes. I do."

I keep rubbing, warning her with my touch, preparing her. "Do you understand that means I'm going to spank you now?"

"I—"

"Do you—"

"Yes. Yes, I understand."

I don't hesitate. I squeeze her backside, caressing for several seconds, and she stiffens. "Relax or it will hurt more." She doesn't, and I command, "I said, relax your muscles."

She makes several heavy, gasping sounds, but her body eases. Not giving either of us time to think, I spank her. One firm smack is followed by another, and another. Seven total, enough to leave a burn but no pain in its aftermath. The instant I'm done, I turn her and force her to face me.

She won't look at me, and I don't make her. I don't want to see what's in her eyes. I just want to take away the sting and give her the full experience, the full erotic pleasure this can be—not just the shock and pain. My fingers tangle into her hair, lifting her mouth to mine, and I kiss her, and damn it, she doesn't taste like anger as I expect. She tastes like forgiveness and understanding that I don't deserve. It's me who becomes angry now, me who knows who I am, when she still doesn't seem to understand. Guilt, so much fucking guilt, claws at my insides, at my mind.

I wrap my arms around Crystal's waist and lift her. Her legs close around my hips and I bury my cock inside her, the only place that gives me any peace. She leans into me, her arms clinging to my neck, her sweetly scented hair teasing my nostrils, the now-hot water blistering my back.

And I want it to. I want the punishment, understanding Chris Merit and his craving for the whip now in a way I never have before.

Tightening my grip around her waist, I pull her down on my cock, thrusting upward. She moans, and I don't even recognize the sound that comes out of my throat in response. I force us into a rapid pump, counting with each of the motions. One, two, three, four. I grind and thrust until finally, finally, I find that place where everything fades into erotic sensations, and I expect Crystal to be this nameless body . . . but she isn't. Somehow, some way, in the dark place of pleasure I don't deserve, I am aware that it's her. I pull her closer, cupping her backside, holding her tighter.

She leans back to look at me, as if she senses the desperation that I don't want her to see, but can't hide. I see no contempt or blame in her eyes. I see the same understanding I tasted in her kiss, and the rush of pleasure borders on pain. My balls tighten, the edge of orgasm coming with unexpected force. Another thrust, another pump, another sound I don't recognize from myself follows.

My lashes lower and my head sinks to her shoulder, hers to mine. Spots sprinkle the darkness behind my closed eyes, the intensity of being inside this woman almost too much to bear. *She* is my escape, not the sex, and it's a terrifying reality. I need her. I want her. I can't seem to let go of her.

"Oh God," she pants, her lips brushing my earlobe in a rocketing sensation I feel in my cock. "Mark, I—"

She spasms around me and I pull her down hard on my erection, thrusting hard and deep. My release comes in an intense rush, and suddenly we're both leaning against the wall, and I barely remember when I pulled out of her, or when her legs left my waist to settle on the floor. Or why we've huddled into the corner.

When reality comes back to me we stand there, staring at each other, the awareness of what has passed between us far more forceful than the water pounding on my back.

Her hand comes gently to my cheek. "You didn't make Ava kill Rebecca. Stop blaming yourself."

"I just spanked you, and you're comforting me?"

"Did you spank me because it's erotic, or because you wanted to scare me away?"

"I don't know," I say, and it's as honest as I've ever been. She's as honest as I've ever been in every possible way, and I find myself needing to know this is real. That something in my life is real. "What I do know is that I invited Ava and Ryan into my and Rebecca's bed, even though I knew that she hated my sharing her. And hated them in particular."

Shock rolls over her face. "Why would you do that?"

"Our contract said I could make that choice."

"That's not an answer. Why would you *do* that?"

"Because she was breaking down my walls. I needed to raise them back into place—yet I hated sharing her. So I selfishly made sure the only people who fucked her besides me, never had a chance to take her from me. It was my asshole way of being possessive while I held her at a distance. But Ava wanted me, and I'm sure Ryan wanted Rebecca. I created the jealousy in both of them that led to Rebecca's murder."

"You really think Ryan was a part of it."

"I know he was somehow involved."

"*He's* really what's motivating your anger and need for vengeance, isn't he?"

"I considered him a friend. He tried to bury me with the police. He did bury Rebecca, and I'm going to force him to confess."

"How?"

"Don't worry. Killing him doesn't interest me. Even torturing him wouldn't last. I have other plans. Like I said—tell me to leave and I will." I push off the wall and exit the shower.

"Mark," Crystal says, but I don't want to hear her logic and reason.

Grabbing a towel, I dry my hair and wrap it around my waist.

"Mark," she calls again.

I walk into the living area and roll the cart with my bags into the bedroom. There I grab a garment bag and set it on the mattress, and remove a suit, shirt, and tie.

I half expect Crystal to appear and tell me to leave, but she doesn't. Maybe she doesn't know what to say to me. But I need to know what she has to say, what she thinks. I need her forgiveness.

Like I need what I can never have. Rebecca's forgiveness.

# Twelve

### Crystal . . .

I turn off the shower, replaying the first bite of his palm on my
backside. *He spanked me.* I can't get my mind around the reality of
it—or Mark's confessions. Far more emotionally frazzled than I let
on, I wait, expecting flashbacks from the past . . . but they don't
come. They just . . . don't. This experience hasn't triggered memories, yet his harshness in his parents' library did. It says something
to me about what I felt from him then and now, and that explains
how I was aroused, not afraid.

But what he did to Rebecca . . . I'd never tolerate such things,
but his reasons, though flawed and even unforgivable in many ways,
were honest. And I'm not sure he's been honest with himself in a
long time. I'm pretty sure I haven't been with myself, either—and
maybe that's part of our bond. He admitted things to me that he
hates about himself, and he's claimed he needs us to be the one honest thing in his life. And I think that translates to his need to have
someone in his life who trusts him, when he doesn't trust himself.

And there it is. The reason I said "yes" to the spanking.

On some level, I'd known it was about trust.

Shaking myself, I step out of the shower. In a rush of activity, I dry off, attend to my hair and makeup again, and finally pull on tights and a red dress with a belted waist and a fitted skirt. With a deep breath, I prepare for whatever I might feel when my eyes meet Mark's, and I enter the bedroom. He is nowhere in sight.

Exiting into the living area, I find him standing at the floor-to-ceiling window just outside of my dining area, which connects to my living room. He's on the phone. "From what I understand," he says, "the first thing the police did when Corey woke up from his beating was ask about me." He pauses. "My thoughts exactly. I need my attorney here, not in San Francisco. I'll pay whatever it takes to get the plane here tonight."

Easing out of the room, I allow him privacy and return to the bedroom. Noting the open garment bag, I walk to it and stare down at the contents, contemplating all I've experienced this past hour. No matter what, I have feelings for this man, and I know in my heart that he needs to have a safe place to heal and to let go of his anger. I remove several suits from the bag and carry them to the closet, shove my clothes to one side, and hang up Mark's things.

After finishing the task I come face-to-face with Mark, and I'm jolted by the dominant force of his presence. His blond hair is still damp, lying in ringlets around his classically handsome face, and his amazing body is perfection in a dark blue suit paired with a red tie.

He glances at the empty garment bag and the closet, then back to me. "What are you doing?"

"Making sure you know I'm not ordering you to leave."

"Then you're not as smart as I thought you were."

"On the contrary," I say, unfazed. "I'm not as shallow-minded as you apparently think I am. I can see beyond my own hand."

He arches a brow. "And my hand?"

Unbidden heat simmers in my stomach, and I don't understand this reaction—or many of my reactions to Mark Compton. Shoving it aside, I softly add, "I can see beneath your skin."

His eyes darken as he steps closer, our knees brushing. "Who was he?"

"Who?"

"The man you went on the pill for."

"Does it matter?"

"Yes."

I believe his need to know is just about being a control freak, and I don't hold back. It's not some golden secret, especially around Riptide. "Nathan Monroe."

He arches a brow. "As in the new 'it' artist?"

"Yes, though I dated him while he was still a starving artist. When he found success, it went to his head. He became a conceited jerk. The only plus in his corner afterward, at least per my father, was that he could finally pay his own bills."

"He hit big six months ago. So you broke up when?"

"Five months ago, and your mother cheered me on as I dumped him. She'd helped me get him some notice."

He stares at me, his expression unreadable. "I've always said my mother is the biggest bitch on the hill, and the kindest flower in the garden."

"I get the feeling her son has the same characteristics."

"I'm no flower, sweetheart."

My stomach flutters with the unexpected endearment.

"In fact," he continues, "you've all but called me the same conceited jerk as your ex."

A knock sounds on the door and, unwilling to let this end yet, I step so close that I can feel his body heat. "You can be," I agree, "but the difference between him and you is that he really *was* a jerk. You use arrogance and control to hide the real you. But I've seen you. I know you."

He stares down at me for several beats before his hand closes around the back of my neck and he crushes my mouth to his in a long, deep kiss. Then he says, "In a way, no one else has. No one. You know that, right?"

"Yes," I whisper. "And you know I'd never betray that trust."

The air shifts between us, and I can almost feel the bonds between us weaving tighter. "If I didn't, I wouldn't have told you what I did in the shower, nor would I be standing here." He leans in to kiss me again, his mouth almost to mine when his phone rings, and another knock sounds on the door.

We both groan. "I'll get the door so you can get your call," I say.

He sighs and releases me, reaching into his pocket to remove his phone. "Are you in Long Island yet?" I hear him ask before I turn down the hallway.

As I reach the door another knock sounds, and I ask, "Who is it?"

"Jacob."

I unlock the door to discover that beside him is a pretty brunette with warm brown eyes who is dressed in black slacks and a black silk blouse. She extends her hand to me. "Hi, Crystal. I'm Kara Walker."

I take her hand and, being someone who has instant vibes with people, I already like her. "Hi, Kara," I say, stepping to the side to allow them to enter. The door shut, I ask, "Is Kara taking over for you today, Jacob?"

I don't miss the slight flex of his jaw as he answers. "No," he says. "We're both escorting you to the hospital."

Suddenly, Mark's need to stay here to "protect me" hits home. "We need two escorts?"

"Better to be safe," Jacob says noncommittally.

I cross my arms. "What don't I know that I should?"

"The question is more like, what don't *we* know that we should," Kara replies, keeping her voice low, clearly to keep Mark from overhearing.

"That's exactly right."

We all turn at the sound of his voice to find him standing at the end of the hallway, the look on his handsome face as irritated as his tone is as he adds, "Stop worrying about an angry claim I made about vengeance after hearing Rebecca was dead. Start worrying about where the *fuck* Ava is. Answer that question, and this all ends. Then we'd have justice, and no need for two bodyguards."

Mark and I ride to the hospital in the back of the Escalade, with Kara and Jacob in the front. Without the prior day's snow to contend with, it's a short twenty-minute drive. The silence in the vehicle is uncomfortable, Mark's reprimand of Jacob and Kara sitting with us like an extra companion. Yet one thing stands out for me. The way Mark's knee rests against mine, and the words he told me: *You're the one thing keeping me grounded.* He's on edge, and I'm guessing it's about that phone call he took.

Jacob parks the truck and he and Kara open their doors. When Mark reaches for his, I grab his arm. "I need to talk to you alone for a second."

His eyes narrow on mine for a moment before he calls out to Jacob, "We need a minute."

Jacob and Kara shut their doors and seal us inside. Immediately, I turn to Mark and settle my hand on his leg. "What's wrong?"

His attention goes to my hand on his leg, lingering there before I'm fixed in an unreadable gray stare. "Were you aware that I don't allow people to touch me?"

Confused, I stutter, "W-what?"

"I don't allow people to touch me. Except you." He covers my hand with his own. "That first evening you picked me up at the airport, you kept touching me, and I let you. I didn't know why then, and I don't know why now."

I'm still confused. "You mean no one after Rebecca went missing, right? She obviously touched you—as did previous partners."

"I never let her touch me freely. It was part of the Master/submissive roles we played."

Emotion wells in my throat at the certainty that to Mark, BDSM is far more than the pleasure and games. It's a disconnect, a withdrawal from everyone but his parents. But then again, he lives in another state. Isn't that a withdrawal, too?

"You know you're inviting me to ask you why," I say cautiously.

"Playing the Master role helps me control what I feel, and when I feel it. Except, as I said, with you."

"I just happened to be in the right place when you needed someone."

"I've tried to tell myself that, but there were other people just as present, and other ways I could have dealt with all of this. I kept returning to you. I *keep* returning to you."

"Is that what's bothering you right now? The way that I've seen more than you want me to see?"

"No. It's about me having the control I need to ensure my mother doesn't see too much of what I'm worried about." His lashes lower and he inhales. "I don't know what the fuck is the matter with me."

I cover his hand where it covers mine, and the fact that he lets me means so much more than it had before. "It's called being human," I say. "It's the curse and blessing we all face."

He looks at me. "I used to believe I managed it better than others."

"You do. And you're demonstrating that by actually being in the moment." I remind him of his own words. "What we deny owns us. You can't control what you don't first own and face. You simply delay the moment it owns you." I tilt my head to study him. "You weren't like this when I went to answer the door to let Jacob and Kara in. Did they overlook something that set you off?"

"It's a general frustration that I'm paying so damn many people to get no answers. That, and the kid woke up before Luke got to the hospital. The police are questioning him, and I have no idea what's being said."

I think of the extra phone he keeps so guarded, and that, along with the sense of helplessness I read from him right now, feeds my worry that whoever he talks to on those calls is trouble waiting to happen. "Mark, about that—"

"It's late," he says, glancing down at his watch, and I have this sense of a door shutting. "Thirty minutes until treatment. We need to go inside."

I don't push, because he's right. But I think Jacob is right, too.

Mark's navigating dark and stormy waters, and I'm either going to pull him out, or drown with him. I don't know which.

Jacob and Kara frame us as we stop at the security desk by the private elevators and sign in. A few moments later we crowd into the rather small elevator. "Stay in the waiting room," Mark orders them when we exit onto the treatment floor. "I don't want my mother any more upset than she already is."

"I'll stand guard downstairs by the security desk," Jacob says, "and let Kara hang out up here."

Kara glances from me to Mark. "If you have to tell your parents I'm here, you can always say that Crystal and I bonded when Walker took over Riptide, and I'm working a job here at the hospital. It's not a lie; I am. It just happens to be you. And if Crystal and I have coffee together, that will reinforce it."

Mark grimaces but I nod. "Your mother is always after me to have a social life, so this is perfect. It works."

He cuts Kara one of those steely gray stares. "I'm warning you. Don't go feeding her with Blake's bullshit, which I assume is yours as well. You won't like the results." His fingers close on my elbow and he starts walking out. "Let's get to the room."

"That was rude," I say.

"It was honest, sweetheart," he says. "I don't give bullshit and I don't take it."

"Stop viewing me as some wimpy toddler who can't make up her own mind and needs to be protected from her own shadow."

"Wimpy toddler?"

He dares to look amused, and I'm pretty sure the sound that follows from me is a growl.

"Did you just growl at me?"

"Yes. I did."

He leans in. "Save that for when we get home."

I swallow hard on the word "home" and promise myself not to read more into our arrangement than a temporary sharing of a lot of naked moments. "Only if you save that attitude you just had for never."

"I can't promise that."

"Then I can't promise a growl later."

His eyes darken, lips quirking slightly. "I can. Count on it, Ms. Smith. But right now, my mother needs us both. She doesn't know there's something between us, though, so we need to think through how and when to tell her I'm living with you. I don't want her to think that if something goes wrong between us, she loses you. I don't want you to think you lose her, either."

"There you two are!"

Once again, Mark's father has managed to appear at a pivotal moment in a conversation between us. We turn to find him approaching with a tray of coffee.

"One of the nurses went to Starbucks. I ordered everyone's favorites." He glances at Mark. "Your mom's pretty eager to see you this morning." He enters the hospital room and Mark is unmoving, staring after him.

Reading his apprehension, I reach up and rest my hand on his arm. "She needs you. She probably regrets last night." I motion to the door with my head. "Come on. You kept me up all night—I need that coffee."

He inhales, his broad chest expanding beneath his suit jacket. "Coffee it is." His hand goes to my back and he guides me forward.

I enter the room to find Dana eagerly watching the door, her eyes touching me and then going beyond to settle on Mark.

Giving her the moment she's obviously seeking with her son, I go to where Steven has set the coffee tray on a rolling hospital table.

"White mocha for you, right?" he asks.

"Good memory," I say, smiling, always charmed by the way he treats me like family.

He lifts a cup and glances at the writing. "Plain latte with an extra shot. This one is Mark's. Dana didn't want anything."

I crinkle my nose. "Plain is just so . . . plain."

He laughs. "Yes, it is." He holds it out. "Can you hand it to him?"

"Of course." I accept the cup, but hesitate as I note the dark circles under his eyes. "How are you?"

"Tired. But I bet Dana that I'd beat you at tic-tac-toe this morning, so hand off that cup and let's get to it."

I laugh at what has become a six-month war between us. "You're on." Turning, I plan to hand Mark his coffee, and find him squatted down by Dana's chair, his head dipped low, her hand on his face as she whispers something to him. He lifts his head and looks at her, nodding and then squeezing her hand. "I love you," he says, and my heart squeezes at the rawness of the emotion in his eyes and roughing up his voice.

"I love you, too, son," Dana whispers.

Mark's gaze lifts abruptly, meeting mine, and he does nothing to mask the heartache in his eyes.

I lift the cup. "A plain latte?"

"Yes," he says, pushing to his feet and stepping toward me.

I hand him his cup, the brush of our fingers sending a shiver down my spine. And judging from the glint of arrogance in Mark's eyes, my reaction doesn't go unnoticed. Determined to put him back in his place, I say, "Plain and strong. I guess that's what a macho man like yourself needs to feel extra macho."

"Oh, how you have him figured out," Dana chimes in, her laughter filling the room.

Mark's expression flickers with a moment of pure joy at her reaction, but he doesn't miss a beat in his reply. "I prefer my coffee like I do my women—without the sugarcoating."

If I had any doubt that comment was meant with naughty intentions, the totally inappropriate way he's looking at me, like he wants to lick the proverbial sugar off me, douses it. And I have an equally inappropriate response of being warm and tingly all over.

"I'll tell you what's *not* sugarcoated," his father inserts, and aware that Dana can see my reaction to her son, I whirl around and say, "Your wife when she talks baseball with you."

He snorts. "Isn't that the truth. But not what I had in mind." He sets a pad of paper and two pencils on the table next to my coffee. "Game on."

"Tell me he's not trying to get you to play tic-tac-toe," Mark says.

"You just hate when I'm right, Steven," Dana says in reply to the previous exchange, while I nod my confirmation at Mark.

"I just let you think you're right," he counters, eyeing me and tapping the table. "Come here, Crystal Smith. Today is the day I kick your butt."

"Remember our bet," Dana says in a singsongy voice I haven't heard her taunt him with in months. "If she wins—"

"I remember," Steven says quickly.

Dana looks at Mark. "Crystal always kicks his butt."

Mark arches a brow at me and I shrug, moving closer to his father, lowering my voice. "What's on the line? Should I throw the game?"

"No," he says indignantly. "And if I think you do, I won't respect you in the morning."

"But you'd win the bet."

"Hey," Dana says, sounding remarkably energetic. "Whose side are you on?"

"I'm going to win," Steven insists. "I figured out how you beat me. My new pitcher showed me your trick."

Mark settles onto the arm of his mother's chair. "I assume you know he does this to all prospective pitchers."

"I've heard," I say.

"They need brains," his father counters, "and not the kind that recites Shakespeare. They need to be able to process and problem-solve under pressure."

"This isn't much pressure," I say, placing my X on the grid he's drawn.

"You're here by choice," Mark points out. "My father tells them if they lose, then their dreams end with the tic-tac-toe of his pencil."

"That's kind of cruel," I say, watching as Steven makes a poor choice for his move.

Mark laughs. "No wonder you like her, Mother. She's just like you. She holds nothing back."

"I find it real and honest," Dana says, and my pencil stills as Mark's words play in my head: *the only honest thing in my life.* Somehow I manage a laugh. "My brothers just call it bitchy." I glance at Steven and feel a little sorry for him as I draw a line and say, "Tic-tac-toe."

"Impossible," he grumbles, as Mark and Dana burst into laughter. Steven draws another game grid. "Again."

I sigh and we play again, with the same outcome.

He scrubs his head and then motions to Mark. "Come play, son."

Mark stands up and shakes his head. "You're just looking for an ego boost."

I claim his spot on the arm of Dana's chair and ask her, "Ego boost?"

"Mark hardly ever beats his father. It's like he has some sort of mental block. I bet they played fifty games last Christmas, and Mark only won seven or eight."

"Nine," Mark calls over his shoulder, sounding casual and accepting of his losses.

The square isn't fitting in the circle here. Something isn't right, an observation I feel tenfold when I watch Mark lose two games in a row.

"Are we ready?" Reba calls as she rolls a wheelchair into the room, and my chest tightens when I see her red scrubs.

"Ready to get it over with," Dana says. "I want to trade in my wheels for high heels."

As Mark and Steven join us, I remind her, "At least you're done for the weekend."

She nods, but her eyes are on Mark. "Remember what I said."

"I remember, Mother," he says as his father helps her into the wheelchair.

They disappear out of the room and Mark turns to look at me. When I just study him for a long moment, he arches a brow. "What do you want to know?"

What his mother said to him—but he'll tell me if he wants, when he's ready. Instead, I walk to the table and pick up a pencil, quickly drawing a game grid on the pad. I place my X. "Your move."

He narrows his eyes on me, several moments passing, and I'm sure he will refuse. Then he closes the distance between us and reaches for the other pencil. In a matter of a minute, he's beaten me.

"Why?" I ask.

"Why what?"

"Being coy doesn't suit you, Mark Compton. Why do you let him beat you?"

"Because he's my father."

"That's a nonanswer."

"You're right."

He'd vowed honesty. *I'll avoid a topic, but I won't lie.*

He changes the subject. "My mother wants us to go on to work and take care of business. She says the two of us will probably outrun her by miles."

I hesitate, not sure if I want to push, after he's just shut me down over a game of tic-tac-toe.

"She said she trusts me," he says, as if I'd asked what's on my mind. "She said she felt defeated last night and overwhelmed, and she knows it will all be okay now that I'm here." His voice softens. "And with us both by her side. You and me."

There's a stupid burning sensation in my eyes that I really don't want to become tears. Afraid to speak, for fear it might push me over the edge, I give him a jerky nod.

"So now we have to make sure it really is okay."

He's saying "we," and I don't think a man who doesn't allow people to touch him uses those words lightly. I smile. "It will be."

His eyes meet mine, and there's something so damn intense about being the focal point of his attention that always steals my breath. He takes a step toward me and I do the same. We're only inches apart, and I don't know what will come next—and his cell phone rings.

He hesitates, but reaches into his jacket pocket and glances at the caller ID. "Luke," he says. A pause. "Tell me something I want to hear, for once." He walks to the window, giving me his back, tension curling along the line of his shoulders. "No idea?" Pause. "Why?" A longer pause before he says, "Fine. Let me know the minute there's a change." He ends the call but doesn't immediately turn around.

After several seconds pass, I can almost feel my blood pressure rising. "Mark. Please. What's going on?"

He faces me, his face filled with the same tension in his shoulders. "The police won't let Luke talk to Corey. And even if they would, the kid had a seizure and is now in a coma."

"Oh God. Is he okay?"

"Stable for now, but he's had a lot of head trauma, from what I understand."

Whatever he *hasn't* said is hanging between us like a concrete block, about to slam to the ground and rattle us to the bones. "What else?" I whisper.

"I'm officially a person of interest in his attack."

# Thirteen

Crystal . . .

My heart races and my palms begin to sweat. "Why? How? Did Corey accuse you?"

"Hey there, kids," Steven says.

The greeting has me ready to scream at his knack for *really* horrible timing. Appearing by Mark's side, he slaps his son on the shoulder and gives me a wink. "Can you give us men a few minutes?"

"Of course," I say, somehow summoning a voice that sounds as casual as Mark now looks. Gone is the tension in his spine, the stress in his face. The Master has flipped a switch I used to possess, but today my legs are frozen, heavy and unmoving.

I force myself into action, but as I start to pass Mark, the magnetic pull between us nearly compels me to stop. I want to touch him, and I am certain he wants to touch me. It's a sensation I've never felt with any other human being but my mother.

The thought quickens my pace as I fight the memory of

hiding in a closet and peeking out of the door to meet her eyes. Wanting to help her, and being incapable of doing anything about the torment she was enduring except to cry. *Helpless.* And I can't bear the idea of being that way now.

Exiting into the hallway, I head for the waiting room with determined strides to find Kara, to find out just how bad this situation with the police is for Mark.

Sitting in a corner that gives her a clear view of my approach and the elevator to my left, she stands the instant she spots me and meets me in the middle of the empty room. "Is something wrong?"

"That's a loaded question," I say. "Bullets are flying at me from every direction, and I'm trying to catch them before they hurt someone. I need help."

Her expression softens. "You want to sit and talk?"

"Yes. Please."

She motions to the seats with the bird's-eye view of the elevator, but Mark will see us the instant he comes looking for me. "Can we sit in the corner over there instead?"

Understanding fills her brown eyes and she nods. "Of course."

Once seated, I get right to the point. "Mark says he's an official suspect in Corey's beating. Why?"

She flattens her hands on her knees. "Here's the thing. I'm under a confidentiality agreement, and no matter how much I want to, I can't discuss details about Mark with you without his consent." She hesitates. "And it's killing me. I want to."

"That answer *really* makes me feel like there's something I need to know."

She inhales and lets it out, shoving a long lock of brown hair behind her ear. "Okay, look. I'm walking a fine line here and talking about personal impressions, of which I have very few since I've barely met Mark. Blake, however, has met with him many times. He says Mark is like he was right after his fiancée was murdered: 'guilty, driven, and willing to go over the line.'"

"That sounds like the Mark I've come to know."

"But he's not stupid or vicious. Blake doesn't believe Mark would hurt someone innocent, or someone he sees as a victim."

"You're telling me you don't believe he is responsible for what happened to Corey."

"Do you think he is?"

"No, I don't. But I'm not so sure about Ava, and there's also a man named Ryan."

"Yes. We know him well. If he's guilty, he's covered his tracks well. If we catch Ava, she'll likely give him up. That's how it works."

"So could he have helped her escape for that reason?"

"Yes, but Corey was going to turn in evidence. It seems strange they'd let him go; something doesn't add up."

"And he accused Mark?"

"I can't—"

"If he did, he could have been threatened."

"We know. Believe me, we're trying to protect Mark, and not just because he pays us. Blake feels a special connection to Mark. I feel one to you. A person driven for vengeance walks a slippery slope. Blake left the ATF because he knew he was going to kill the man who murdered his fiancée. He would have, if I hadn't been there—and even then, it was my sister that held him back."

"Your sister?"

"Yes. She disappeared, and I knew the same man was responsible. If he was killed, I knew I'd never find her. So in the split second where Blake could have killed him, knowing he was breaking the law, he chose not to."

"Where's your sister now?"

"She's been missing for nine months."

"Oh God. I'm sorry."

"I haven't given up; we're looking for her and the man who took her. But here's why Blake gets Mark so well. Even with me trying to help Blake heal, with our love, and his fiancée being gone for years now, he still fully intends to kill that man. It's in his blood like a poison. So please believe me when I say this. You have to pull Mark back before he does something he'll regret."

"If you can't pull Blake back, how can I possibly help Mark? I can help him cope, yes, but we're not you and Blake. We—I don't know what we are."

"I see how that man looks at you. And I don't need Blake's opinion to know your influence over him. And he's protective and possessive, to the umpteenth degree."

"Protective and possessive are bone deep in that man, and he looks at me like he wants to get me naked, because that's what he does to silence the demons screaming in his head right now."

"I told myself the same thing with Blake. And I get it, Crystal. The thought of being a replacement for someone who's been lost is a strange bird to hear sing. You aren't sure if the words match the emotions they connect to. I'm sure he's fighting anything he feels for you, out of guilt, and I don't envy you this part of your relationship. It's a painful, guilt-driven path full of jagged edges that will cut you many times over—but it has to be traveled to find out what's real and what isn't. No matter what you decide in the end, *you* are the one sharing this journey with him. You are the one who can stop him from doing what he's doing."

"Which is what? What's he doing?" Mark asks.

My heart jumps to my throat as I discover Mark standing several feet away. He doesn't look happy. He motions us to the elevator, and we rise to our feet. As we walk toward him, Kara quickly murmurs, "He hired someone to track Ava. He believes she's alive, and we're fairly confident he doesn't want her to stay that way. We're desperately trying to find her before he does."

My mind instantly goes to his extra phone, and how he wanted me out of his parents' office to take a call.

Mark punches the call button for the elevator as we join him. "We're going to Riptide," he informs us, his expression as hard as his tone. He doesn't look at me, and I can almost feel the anger radiating off him.

The elevator dings and we all step into the car. Mark still won't look at me, and my urge to hug and talk to him is extreme, but it would clearly be unwelcome. When we exit the elevator we rejoin Jacob, and by the time we're seated in the Escalade, the silence is thick and uncomfortable. Mark has withdrawn physically and emotionally, and the way that it's tearing me up inside proves Kara's words. This path he and I are traveling *is* full of jagged edges, and I either have to accept that or get out. And I'm too invested in him, and his family, to choose the latter.

When we reach Riptide, the absence of the press is a relief. A member of Walker Security claims the Escalade while Jacob and Kara walk us to the entrance. Once we're all past the double doors, Mark and I continue forward. When we reach the centerpiece of the lobby, an abstract rug of grays and reds framed by four low gray chairs, I ask Mark, "Why aren't you talking to me?"

He doesn't look at me. "You did enough talking for both of us with Kara, I'm certain."

We reach the reception desk. As Beverly, a forty-something

brunette who's been here for a number of years, starts to greet us, Mark cuts through. "Do I have packages waiting for me?"

"Yes, sir," she says, sliding a large envelope toward him, and then pointing at a box on the end of the horseshoe-shaped glass counter.

"I'll be using my mother's office as my office while I'm here, and my stay will be of an indefinite length," he states. "Are there any urgent matters for myself or Ms. Smith to address?"

"Not at the moment."

"Excellent. Buzz me if that changes." He flicks me a look. "My office, Ms. Smith. We can talk there."

"Yes, Mr. Compton." The boiling tension is ready to become an explosion.

We go to the left of the desk to reach his office, instead of right to reach mine. As we enter the hallway to the east wing, Mark stops and motions for me to continue in front of him.

I shake my head, refusing to play his power game. "Together," I say softly, then add, "Mr. Compton."

"Don't push me any further than you already have, Ms. Smith."

"Ditto."

"Ditto?"

My chin lifts. "That's right."

He glances down at the packages. "If my hands were free—"

"But they aren't."

"They will be in just a few moments."

He starts walking and my breath hitches at the glint of warning I saw in his eyes. I fall into step with him, one part dread, one part erotic thrill. "Your threats don't scare me," I say softly.

He stops at his office door and gives me one of those steely gray stares. "Then you're not as smart as I thought you were."

Knowing his remark is a manipulation tool, my anger is instant. I walk inside the office, taking a battle position in the center of the rectangular room. Anticipation thrums through me in a way that I've only experienced with Mark. I'm furious, but I'm also ridiculously nervous. And aroused. How can I be this aroused when I'm this angry?

Mark shuts the door and a shiver races down my spine. The click of the lock that follows is like the erotic drag of an invisible finger along my nerve endings.

I try to focus on the room, to calm my reaction into a manageable proportion. With supreme effort I focus on something other than the man driving me insane, and force myself to picture the boldly colored red sofa and chairs behind me that I know are framed by black display shelves and past exhibit photos.

But it doesn't work. My attention is riveted by the graceful way Mark crosses the room and positions himself behind the massive L-shaped glass desk in front of me. And while I've always found this office to be pure feminine power, he's already erased that, claiming it as his. And as I meet his stare, I see all too clearly that he intends to make good on his vow to own me as well.

My spine straightens and I don't blink. My anger will not be thwarted. My need for answers is not forgotten, and my good reasons for talking to Kara are not diminished.

Mark presses his fingers to the desktop, and we just stare at each other. Neither of us speaks, and every little sound seems magnified. My breathing, in and out. The clock on the wall behind him.

His emotion twines around and around me; I'd never be able to explain to someone what I see and feel with this man. He can look at me as he is now, showing no emotion, and I still understand him. I know he's hurting. I know he's worried. I know he feels like I betrayed him with Kara, and that he doesn't see shutting me out of his hunt for Ava as the same sort of betrayal.

Part of me wants to shout at him and make him tell me everything. Another part wants to rush around the desk and kiss him, and promise him that everything will be okay.

But I do nothing. I wait.

He moves first, breaking the spell as he opens a drawer and pulls out a letter opener. Unsealing the box he'd picked up from the front desk, he pulls something out, and then rounds the desk to lean against the side near me.

He holds up a small velvet bag. "Come closer. I don't bite." Then his sensual, often brutally erotic mouth quirks. "Okay, I do bite. But since you're not afraid of me that shouldn't be a problem."

"What's in the bag?" I ask, certain that whatever he's holding is about how today's events fed his need for control. This is one of those moments where he's going to test me; one of those times I need to overcome my own past, to preserve in the present.

He sets the bag on the desk and my eyes follow, trying to conjure an idea of what might be in it. "Come here, *Ms. Smith,*" he commands.

His voice is deeper now, more forceful, and his "Ms. Smith" sends tingling sensations through my body, delivering the erotic heat that he'd promised it would last night.

I don't deny his demand, but I want answers I intend to claim. Closing the distance between us, I reach for his jacket, but don't manage to obtain my target.

Before I can blink, he's grabbed my waist, walked me backward, and set me in one of the red visitor chairs. His hands rest on the leather arms on either side of me, his big body caging mine as he leans forward. "If you have something to ask me," he says, his voice low, tight, "you ask me. Not someone else."

"I was worried sick about you, after what you told me about Corey and the police. I still am. I needed to know you were okay."

"You only had to wait ten minutes to get those answers from me. There's nothing more to tell, and she's bound by a confidentiality agreement anyway. She damn sure better not be running her mouth to anyone."

"She didn't. She told me she couldn't."

"But you tried to get her to."

"I just asked for more details on Corey, and what the police were saying about him and you."

"And since there's nothing more to tell, and she's supposedly abiding by her contract, you got fed the 'I'm like Blake' bullshit I'm sick of hearing." He doesn't give me time to deny or confirm his accusations, adding, "Don't go around me again. I told you this morning. I've trusted you in ways I trust no one, but trust goes two ways."

"You're right, it does. But if you think selective honesty is true honesty, you're mistaken. I've seen the extra phone, Mark. Are you trying to find Ava on your own?"

His eyes are hard, unreadable before he straightens. "What would you do if the person who killed someone you cared about was on the run, and was still a risk to others?"

It's not his obvious admission that he's playing vigilante that bothers me. It's his choice of wording that sends me to my feet to face off with him. "Someone you *cared* about? Don't you mean the woman you love?"

His lashes lower and he cuts his gaze away.

I make a sound of disbelief. "My God. She's dead, and you still can't say you love her."

His gaze jerks to mine. "It's not that simple."

"Yes, it is. You loved her. That's clear for anyone to see. You still do. What do you think is going to happen if you admit it? She's going to come back from the grave and demand a wedding ring? Maybe you aren't pretending to be an asshole, after all." I start to turn and he captures my arm. "Don't," I say in warning. "I'm angry for her, and sad for you."

"You didn't even know her."

"And clearly she never really knew you—yet she still dared to give you the biggest gift anyone can give. Herself."

His jaw clenches and unclenches, and I want him to admit his love for Rebecca. I want him to be the man I believe him to be. Instead, he releases my arm, leaving me frustrated, disappointed, hurt for reasons that I can't name and make no sense, and my feet can't take me fast enough to the door.

I exit to the hallway, my mind racing. Somehow, as furious as I am with Mark, I'm still thinking of the black velvet bag and wondering what was inside. This must be what happened to Rebecca. He got under her skin and seduced her just by existing. Before she knew it, she was out of her own mind and in his, just like I am, caught in the web that is Mark Compton.

Entering the lobby, I will myself to focus on the job I have to do. I stop at the receptionist's desk and wait for Beverly to end a call. "Do I have any messages?" I ask when she's free.

Her eyes go wide and she nods. "Do you ever." She sets a stack on the desk in front of me. "Thanks to all the press, there's an extra-large pile of angry customers for you today." She holds up a finger. "Oh yes, and this." She hands me a white envelope with my name typed in the center, the word "Private" on the corner.

My brow furrows. "Any idea who it's from?"

"A messenger brought it—that's all I know. Probably a reporter. They're desperate to get to you."

I sigh. "They most certainly are. Okay, thanks. Buzz me if you need me."

"Some of the staff are asking about Mr. Compton." She lowers her voice. "I think they're worried about the future of Riptide, and hopeful that his presence means it's secure."

"It's completely secure," I say. "We're thriving, despite all this mess going on. Mr. Compton's not here to save the business, but to make sure that Dana, as stubborn as she is, stays in bed and fully heals before she returns."

Remembering his softly spoken reply to his mother this morning, *I love you, too,* my anger at him goes down a few notches. I've seen him tear up over his mother, and Rebecca. He's closed off, but he's not a complete asshole. I refocus on Beverly. "I'll see if he can send out a company email."

"I feel awkward bothering him about little issues, when he has so much other stuff going on."

"If you want to buzz me first, you can."

Frowning down at the white envelope, I start walking, an odd foreboding in my belly. I suddenly want to tear it open.

Passing several employees with a quick greeting, I enter my office and shut the door. Rushing to my desk, I sit down and grab a letter opener, and my hand shakes as I pull it through the envelope's seal. Then I pull out a white sheet of paper with two typed lines on it.

You don't know the real Mark Compton.
Get out before you end up like Rebecca.

A chill races down my spine and I drop the paper, having watched enough episodes of *CSI* to know that fingerprints matter. Could it be from Ava? Or Ricco, who'd sworn to protect Rebecca from Mark, and tried to destroy the gallery as his own form of vengeance? Or a reporter who wants me to talk? Or. Or. Or. There are too many possibilities. And Mark all but admitted to me he's playing vigilante. If I go to him and he makes assumptions, where will that lead?

I pull out my cell phone and call Kara, who's still on guard here. "I just received a letter warning me about Mark." I describe it to her. "I don't want to hide it from him, but I'm terrified he could go off the deep end. Because you're right: He's looking for Ava. I'm worried about him."

"Believe me, I get it."

"I think . . . I have to tell him. He won't trust me if I don't. I'm also going to tell him that you know about it."

"Can you wait until Blake gets here? We need to get it finger-printed."

"No. He'll see it as distrust." I consider a moment. "Send Jacob in to pick it up. Mark seems to trust him the most."

"Okay."

"Thanks. For everything."

"I'm here if you need me."

"I appreciate that. I don't really have anyone else I can talk to." My best friend from college moved to Hawaii for a job. My next best friend is dating my ex's roommate.

"You have me," she says. "Hang in there." She ends the call.

I dial Mark's cell and he picks up. "Crystal," he says softly, the torment in his voice rippling through the line, and I pray I'm making the right choice.

"I have a situation."

His voice firms, turns businesslike. "What situation?"

"First, I'm okay. But I got spooked and I called security. Jacob's coming to my office, and I really . . . I need you here, too."

"I'm on my way."

I set my phone on the desk, staring down at the note again. *You don't know the real Mark Compton. Get out before you end up like Rebecca.* Whoever wrote it is at least partially right. I'm not going to end up dead, I hope, but falling in love with a man who may not be capable of loving me back.

I almost laugh at myself. Who am I fooling? I'm already in love with him.

# Fourteen

Mark . . .

I stuff the pictures of Ava and A.J. Wright inside my desk drawer and head to the door. What has shaken Crystal enough to have her request assistance from security? My mind conjures up the many possibilities Wright could create, and fear quickens my pace down the hallway.

At the receptionist's desk, an unwelcome and familiar visitor argues with Beverly. Upon my approach, Robert Murphy, a distinguished-looking fifty-five-year-old man who's both a customer and the CEO of a national television network, turns to greet me.

"Finally," he says.

"Finally?" I arch a brow.

"Are you pretending you don't know I've left three messages for you?" he asks sharply.

"Ms. Smith has taken all of his calls and messages," Beverly informs Murphy quickly.

"I have a hundred thousand dollars in auction items on the

line here next weekend. I deserve to hear from you personally, Mr. Compton."

"As a member of the media, you're doubtless aware that I've only just arrived in town. And while I'll be taking meetings, they're by appointment only, beginning next week." I pause for effect. "And for auction house business only."

"Of course it's about Riptide business." But he looks away, a sure sign he's lying.

"Then certainly, if there is something Ms. Smith has failed to address prior, I'm available to help. But right now, I have an emergency to attend to." I glance at Beverly. "Put Mr. Murphy on my schedule for any afternoon next week that he pleases."

"Mr. Compton—" he begins.

But I've already dismissed him, my long strides leading me toward Crystal's office. At her closed door, I don't bother to knock. I open it to find Crystal and Kara behind her desk, eyes locked on something in front of them. They both look up and my gaze collides with Crystal's, the impact like a hard punch in the chest.

She feels it, too. I see it in the way her eyes widen, the way her chest lifts with a breath beneath her red dress. She crosses her arms defensively in front of her, the distance between us suddenly miles, not feet, and too damn far to please me.

My gaze flicks to Kara, who holds up her hands. "I know I'm not your favorite person today, and I was going to send Jacob, but I'm ex-FBI and he's ex-military. My expertise is what's needed right now." She motions to the desk. "We have something we need you to see before I package it up."

Tension rockets through me at the certainty that whatever I'm about to discover could be related to Wright. I round the desk to stand next to Crystal and see a white piece of paper with two typed sentences in the center. My fingers curl by my sides as I read: *Get out before you end up like Rebecca.*

My reaction is instant, my emotions a tornado of dangerous debris I've long suppressed. Anger, fear, and guilt grind through me like glass.

I reach for Crystal, pulling her to face me. "I'm not going to let anyone hurt you."

Her fingers curl into the sleeves of my jacket. "I'm okay. I'm not scared. I think someone just wants to scare me into quitting."

"Which is exactly what you're going to do," I say firmly. "You've worked with Sara some. She's doing private hire work in Paris, finding art for customers and making the purchase for them. I'll send you to work with her."

"What? No. Are you crazy? I'm not going anywhere. Dana needs me, and so do you, even if you don't want to admit it."

"I happily admit it. I need you, Crystal, and I need you alive. You're going to Paris."

"No. I'm not."

"You're not working here."

"I'm not quitting, and I'm not letting you fire me. Whoever sent this threat must know I'm close to you and your family. So if they mean to hurt me, who says I'm not a target if I quit? Or even if I leave? Who's going to protect me in Paris?"

"I'll hire security."

"I'm not going. You can't make me go."

Grinding my teeth, I round the desk, trying to walk off the emotions I'm not accustomed to feeling, let alone containing.

"We'll protect her," Kara promises.

I stop walking and turn to face her. "That's what you said about finding Ava. Where *is* she?"

"I know this is frustrating."

"Spare me the automated replies. We both know that no matter how you try to protect her, you can't guarantee her safety."

"I know we'll do a better job than anyone else would. It's personal, and in the right way. For you, it's personal in the wrong way. Give us all the information you have, and let us make it count. We have to work together."

"You shouldn't need my information to do your job." And I have to decide if that means I trust them, or take matters into my own hands more than I already have. "What are you doing about this, right here and right now?"

Kara removes a pair of rubber gloves from her pocket and works one of them over her hand. "I'm overnighting the note and the envelope to the FBI lab for results."

"There won't be any prints," I say.

"You don't know that for sure," Crystal says.

"I know whoever dropped that kid off in Long Island without being seen wasn't an amateur. Professionals don't leave prints."

"We have to try," Kara interjects. "Humans make mistakes, and any chance of finding out who we're dealing with has to be explored."

"Even if you learn who did this, you have to actually find them. And considering that Ava's still on the run, my confidence that that will happen isn't high." My eyes shift to Crystal. "I *won't* let you end up like Rebecca."

"Then keep her close to you and us," Kara says. "Let us protect her."

The intercom buzzes and Crystal reaches for the button. "Leave it," I order.

"I'm not letting whoever this is stop me from doing my job," she says, glaring at me as she punches the button. "Yes, Beverly?"

"Is Mr. Compton there with you?" Beverly asks.

"I'm here," I say tightly.

"Mr. Murphy hasn't left. He says he won't until he sees you."

"I'll be right out," I say.

Crystal lets go of the button. "He's a problem looking for a headline."

"Exactly my take," I say.

"What are you going to do? He has a hundred thousand dollars on the auction table next Saturday."

"Ninety percent of our problems come from ten percent of our business. We're getting rid of the problems." I ask Kara, "Any more word from Luke?"

"Not yet, and I think it's a bluff by the police. I don't see how this kid can explain how he disappeared at the same time Ava did, if he truly intends to blame you."

"My attorney was already in the air on his way here when I heard they'd called me a 'person of interest.' I intend to have him take care of this when he lands. I'm done being the focal point for lazy law enforcement who should be looking for the real problem, not a fall guy."

"We all agree," Kara says.

"And since I understand Blake is traveling with Detective Grant, make sure he knows two things in light of these new developments. You work for the police—which means you not only won't receive any notes I have on the investigation, but you also won't work for me. And I won't be indulging Detective Grant's desire to catch up on old times. He can talk to my attorney."

"Blake stayed on with the district attorney in San Francisco because he wanted to help justice be served for Rebecca," Kara says. "He had no idea a finger would be pointed at you again."

"I wasn't asking for an explanation I've already heard. Those are simply my requirements to go forward with Walker Security."

Kara's expression tightens. "Understood on all points. We'll meet those requirements."

"I'll need confirmation when he arrives."

"You'll get it."

"I'll be waiting." I don't look at Crystal again. I can't. Not when there's something dark and turbulent brewing beneath my surface. I turn and walk toward the door.

"Mark, wait," she calls, and the instant my hand touches the knob, hers is on my arm, the impact shaking me to the core. "We need to talk," she says.

"Right now, the only thing I want to do is throw you over my shoulder, carry you to a car, and take you to the airport, where I'll put you on a private plane out of the country. So unless you want me to do what my gut is telling me to do, let me go clear my head."

"I . . . oh . . . but—"

"I'm serious, Crystal. Let me go, before I do something you won't forgive me for."

She hesitates, but her hand falls away and I exit the office. Quickly traveling the hallway, I enter the lobby to find Mr. Murphy talking to one of our salespeople, a redhead fresh out of school who looks like she wants to crawl under Beverly's desk.

I stalk forward in time to hear him say, "And what do you think about the counterfeit works? Have they all been located?"

"Mr. Murphy," I say sharply. He jerks around in surprise. "Obviously you've used your status as a customer to gain access to my staff for media purposes. I'll have Ms. Smith release you from your auction agreement; therefore you no longer have any need for concern."

His ruddy complexion turns white. "No. No, that's not what I want."

"You stated to me that you were concerned about your auction items selling poorly next weekend," I said, knowing we garner a 20 percent higher price than any other auction house. "That was your excuse for being here. I'm removing it as a reason for your return."

"It's natural to be concerned, with all of this scandal attached to Riptide. My job doesn't erase my rights as a customer."

"For the record," Crystal says, stepping to my side, "our attendance for next Saturday is up fifteen percent. The scandal seems to be good for business."

"Or the equivalent to rubbernecking." Then he seems to realize what he's said, holding up his hands. "Not that I'm unwilling to take the risk. I simply want reassurances."

"Your reassurance is Ms. Smith filling out your release paperwork, and returning your items to you in the same condition in which we received them." I glance at Crystal. "Please ensure that happens before Mr. Murphy leaves, so that a return visit won't be necessary."

"Of course."

About to head to my office, I realize he's going to create a story out of this visit, no matter what I say or do—and it won't be the one I want told. "One more thing, Mr. Murphy," I say, aware that numerous staff members are within hearing range. "You came here for a story."

"No, that wasn't—"

"You came for a story," I state firmly. "Don't make this worse by lying. I'm going to give you your story. A woman I cared very much for is dead." I draw in a breath and look at Crystal, a deep ache forming in my gut as I amend my words. "A woman I loved was murdered. Her name was Rebecca Mason, and she worked for me at my gallery Allure in San Francisco. The woman who killed Rebecca escaped and is on the run, but not before she leaked lies to the press about me to try to clear her name. On top of that, my mother is battling cancer. And during all of this we have to battle people like you, who see us as nothing but headlines and top Google positions. Still, we've managed to maintain an exceptional business at exemplary standards, thanks to an incredibly dedicated staff."

"What about the counterfeit art?" he demands. "That's not exemplary. Ricco Alvarez says you framed him."

"His lies to try to clear his own name are inconsequential and irrelevant. The facts will speak for themselves in court. Ricco Alvarez was obsessed with Rebecca to the point of being a near stalker. He tried to ruin me and my family because he wanted her and couldn't have her."

"At the expense of his career and his wealth? I find that hard to believe."

"And you find me creating that scandal, and risking my family business, more believable? You've known my family for at least five years. You can't believe that. But report what you want. Just know this: If you, or anyone else, slanders my family or Riptide in any way, I will sue for far more than the story was worth."

I turn to leave, and Mr. Murphy calls, "Wait."

I don't turn.

"You're right. I've known Dana for years. I'll let you review the segment before I run it."

I don't turn or thank him. We both know he didn't suddenly grow honor, and we both know I wasn't bluffing about a lawsuit.

I've won this round with the press. It's a small victory in a war with too many defeats—and that has to change.

Feeling that dark, dangerous edge come over me again, I swiftly return to my office and shut the door. Adrenaline rushes through me, and my head is spinning—and it's not just about having told the world what I never told Rebecca. It's about the past, the present. About everything.

I squat down, elbows on my knees, and I'm sweating, the memories pounding at my brain, loss and pain eating away at me. Who was I kidding, all those years I claimed I was in control of everything around me? I was never in control. The past was always with me. It's what has driven everything. It's why I made the decisions I did with Rebecca.

Images flash in my mind and I lower my throbbing head to my hands. The hellish past comes at me like a hard-swung baseball bat that makes me groan with the impact.

*"Stop, Tabitha," I order, as she rushes ahead of me in the deserted parking lot of the remote NYU campus property, my voice carrying a little too loudly in the silent, windless night. "It's too dark for you to run ahead of me."*

*But she doesn't listen, disappearing inside the open gates of the baseball practice field—but then, what else is new? She's like my mother, hardheaded and impossible. I trot down the pavement to catch up to her, rounding the corner of the concrete sidewalk that runs in front of the bleachers. She's walking backward, her long blond hair glistening silver in the moonlight, her soft feminine laugh a sexy tease despite my irritation.*

*"I'm right here, Marky baby," she taunts, holding out her arms, the shadows licking at the deep cleavage of her pink T-shirt that I plan to have*

*off of her in about sixty seconds. "Come get me." She darts to the left and disappears into the darkness of the bleachers, as fearless as she is frustrating.*

*I growl low in my throat and decide that sneaking out here for an adventurous fuck was a bad idea. We should have thrown her damn roommate out of her dorm room for an hour. I decide to sneak up on her, heading toward the end of the bleachers to cut around the back, when a sound stops me in my tracks. A scrape of a shoe? Then . . . a male voice? I scan the playing field, but it's too dark to see anything, and an eerie sensation crawls over my skin. Jogging forward, I disappear between the bleachers to find Tabitha—and stop dead in my tracks.*

I shake myself before the full image comes into view. *Fuck. Fuck. Fuck.* I'm not doing this. I'm *not* going there. I've only been to this place once in ten years, and I remember it well. The phone call. The club. Chris Merit walking into my office just in time to witness my pathetic meltdown, and me foolishly telling him everything about that night. When I woke up the next day, I buried the memory along with my lack of control.

But buried isn't gone, I'm realizing now. Tabitha is, though— and I swore I'd never go through that kind of pain again. But I am. And I did. And now there is Crystal.

I'm losing my mind, all over the place, bouncing here and there. I'm so far from being in control, I don't even know myself.

My phone starts ringing, and it takes several moments to realize it's the disposable one. I yank it from my pocket, and holy hell, my hand is shaking. I am so out of my own skin, I don't even know who I am. I hit the Answer button and hear, "I trust you received the file?"

"I did," I confirm, straightening to press my back against the door. "I'm taking care of payment." I will myself back to the present to focus on this critical conversation. "I have reason to believe there may be a threat to my family," I say. "I need to know if they've been spotted again."

"Not yet."

My jaw tightens. "Make sure they aren't here in New York, and make sure today."

"You think they followed you?"

"Yes. I do."

"I'll work on it and get back to you."

"No later than tonight. I need an update, even if it's to tell me you have nothing new."

"Understood. But I do have a development on Ryan Kilmer. He might have the cash to hire Wright after all."

"What does that mean?"

"I checked out those odd real estate transactions you caught when reviewing his file. You were right. Real estate fraud is the name of his game, and he's done plenty of it. And he looks to have sold a number of expensive properties to some pretty nasty people, which I'm pretty sure can be tied to money laundering."

"Pretty sure?"

"I'm gathering the data. I'll have it to you in the next few days. Do you want to reconsider the plan to destroy him, or let this information do it for us?"

"Get me the details to review and then I'll decide. Right now, go find Ava and Wright. I'll be expecting your call." I push to my feet, stashing the phone back in my pocket. By the time I'm behind the desk I've pulled out my regular cell phone, and I leave a message for my attorney to ensure he knows what's happened with Corey since he's been in the air. Next, I punch the auto-dial.

"Luke Walker," he answers on the second ring.

"Mark Compton. What do you have for me?"

"The kid's in a coma and the police have shut me out, but I'm staying here. His parents are flying in from San Francisco tonight. I want to talk to them and make sure they influence their son to be truthful."

"You heard about the threat sent to Crystal?"

"I did, and we're on it."

"I want to meet with you and your brothers."

"When?"

"Tomorrow, after those lab results are in." We work out the details and end the call.

However I look at it, I'm caught in a web of danger. And now someone has targeted Crystal as a way to get to me.

# Fifteen

### Mark . . .

I'm weeding through the financials for Riptide, impressed by how well it's performed under Crystal's care, when a knock sounds on my door. It opens and Crystal pops her head inside.

"Hey," she says.

I toss my pen on my desk and lean back. "Hey," I find myself saying. She has softened me in ways no one else could, and despite everything that happened earlier, there's no tension or awkwardness between us. No walls. No games. We really are the most honest thing I've ever had in my life.

She smiles and steps inside, lifting two bags in her hands and nudging the door shut with her hip. "It's four o'clock and Beverly tells me neither of us has eaten."

I glance at the time on my cell phone, shocked to find I've been sitting for hours. "I had no idea how late it had gotten. I was caught up in the numbers. Riptide looks good on paper. You've done well, Ms. Smith. Far better than I expected under the circumstances."

"A compliment," she says, setting the bags of food on my desk. "And here I thought you managed by intimidation."

"More like an iron fist."

"And a rulebook the size of an encyclopedia," she teases.

"I don't deny the rulebook. But I look out for my employees, and I reward them when they do well."

"So I'm learning," she replies, her eyes softening with her voice.

Our eyes meet and I can almost feel the simmering heat, which has existed since the day we met, expanding. "There's a bonus in your future," I say.

And while my mind has drifted into erotic territory, now isn't the time for that. I won't downplay what she's done professionally, and even personally, for my family. And money isn't her motivation, which makes her generous dedication to Riptide all the more compelling.

"So," she says, her softly painted red lips curving, "what does the rulebook say about sharing a meal with an employee, Mr. Compton?"

"You started tearing pages out of my rulebook the night I met you." I round the desk to stand beside her.

"Good point," she murmurs. "So let's dig in and eat before it gets cold. I hear cavemen lose their alpha if they go without food for too long."

I arch a brow, taking one of the bags from her. "Cavemen?"

"What else do you call someone who threatens to throw me over his shoulder, in front of an audience?"

"Would you prefer over my knee?" I ask.

Her eyes flicker with surprise. "Maybe I shouldn't feed you

after all," she quips, grabbing a bag and marching toward the seating area by the bookshelves.

Laughing, I watch her cute little ass wiggle for every second I can before she claims one of the two red chairs.

Already in pursuit, my cock thickens with the chase she has made more than about sex. There's something about this woman that calls to some part of me that's been long suppressed. And I can't even remember why I'd once thought that awakening was a bad thing—not with her floral scent teasing my nostrils.

"You're quite good at evasive maneuvers," I comment, claiming the seat next to hers.

She sets her bag on the small glass table, and I do the same with mine.

"I'm sure I have no idea what you're talking about," she replies, swiping a lock of long blond hair behind her ear, exposing her high cheekbones and perfect ivory skin.

She is beauty, wit, and graceful femininity. I don't know how I ever thought she wasn't my type.

"Why run, when I mentioned turning you over my knee? The shower spanking didn't seem to be a problem. Quite the opposite."

She swallows hard but doesn't back down, her eyes meeting mine as she angles toward me. "This is not a conversation people have over chicken sandwiches."

"Am I wrong about the shower?"

"No. No, you aren't wrong."

"You liked it."

"I liked that you opened up to me, no matter what you thought the consequences might be. It's the kind of honesty and vulnerability that I think is rare for you. And that's why I was able to go where we went. But this is new territory for me."

"Everything about you is new territory for me," I say. "And though there are things we should discuss, not here, not now."

She covers my hand where it rests on the arm of the chair with hers, and I understand the message. She's touching me. I'm letting her. "I know that I'm new territory for you, too."

"But?" I ask, sensing there's more she hasn't said.

"But . . ." Her hand falls away, and I feel the loss as quickly as I do the instant tension in her. She faces forward, rubbing the back of her neck.

"I pushed you too hard," I say.

"No," she counters quickly, cutting me a look. "No, you didn't."

"You just withdrew from me," I point out, prodding her to say more.

"Here's the thing," she says, turning toward me. "If anyone else had done what you did to me, I would have been freaked."

My brow furrows. "You mean the spanking."

"Yes. I mean . . . that."

"A spanking," I say. "There's nothing wrong with the word or the act. It's intimate. It's trust, and unless the person doing it hurts you, which should never be the case, it's erotic. It's supposed to turn you on. Don't let society make it taboo, so you have to feel guilty for enjoying it."

"I don't. I decide what's okay for me. And that's just it, Mark: *I* decide. The fact that I liked the spanking, or because you teasing me about another turns me on, doesn't mean I'm a submissive in training."

"The idea of me turning you over my knee aroused you?"

In true Crystal form, her chin lifts, her eyes meet mine, and she boldly, yet evasively, replies, "You arouse me." She turns away, reaching for the bag in front of her and making it clear she's done with the topic as she adds, "You have the drinks and I have the grilled chicken sandwiches." She sets one in front of her. "And since there were no healthy sides, I ordered you two sandwiches."

Trying not to smile, quite certain it might get me smacked, I start unwrapping one of the sandwiches. "That's perfect. And speaking of healthy, how's the gym at your apartment?"

"It's well equipped, but packed. I like to go late at night when it's empty, and I can have it all to myself."

I set the drinks on the table and discard the bag. "I've never been big on crowds, either." While the idea of sharing a life with Crystal is complicated in too many ways to count, it feels right to me, rather than what's safe. That's what control has been to me—safety. "And I work so much that late nights are inevitable."

"Same here." Unwrapping her sandwich, she says, "I love the convenience of my apartment's location and the shops inside the building and nearby, but I don't love that it's highly populated."

"You need a larger place, where you can have your own gym."

"One day," she says, taking a bite of her sandwich.

I'm certain she could have it now if she asked her father. "Your place is small because you pay for it yourself, correct?"

"That's right," she says. "My father insisted on helping me get into a safe, nice place to live right out of college. I insisted I foot the bill, which meant it had to be a place I could afford. We battled to come up with a place we could both live with, and our compromise was the great security and neighborhood to please him, and the small size to suit my budget to please me."

"This is where New York and San Francisco differ. That city has real neighborhoods with standalone homes."

"Which is what you have?"

"Yes. I have a home in the Nob Hill area, which I thought gave me plenty of property and privacy. But the downside of a standalone home is that it becomes a prison if the press decides to surround you." I set my sandwich down, the memories of that night and my date with the bottle of scotch cutting through my appetite. My elbows go to my knees and I don't look at her as I add, "Even if it weren't for the press, I couldn't be there now—any more than I could have taken you there."

"I know," she surprises me by saying.

I cast her a questioning glance. "You know?"

"She lived with you, so being there has to remind you of her. And I'm sure that taking me there would have come with guilt. It probably always will."

"No. Not always."

She doesn't look convinced, but doesn't push me. "What are you going to do about Allure? You can't leave it closed forever."

"I put it on the market. If I choose to go back to San Francisco, I can do shows at random venues and still make a killing."

"What you deny owns you, Mark," she says, again repeating the words I'd spoken to her, and I wonder why they connect with her as deeply as they obviously do.

I had these kinds of questions with Rebecca, but I never let myself ask them. I won't make that mistake with Crystal.

"What owns you, Crystal?" I ask, trying to understand.

Shadows flicker in her eyes as she replies, "The wrong things, but I'm trying to fix that."

"What wrong things?"

"If I could just spit them out on demand, they wouldn't own me, now, would they?"

"Truer words have never been spoken." I hesitate, fighting

the urge to push her for more. She needs to see inside my hell to allow me into hers. And I don't want her inside it. I want her far, far away.

"About Paris—" I begin.

"No," she snaps. "I'm not going to Paris or anywhere else. End of discussion."

"It would be—"

"No."

"You're ridiculously stubborn."

"You're worse."

"I'm trying to keep you safe."

"Then let me eat, before I pass out."

My jaw sets. "I'm not done talking about this."

"I'm sure you're not." She reaches for her sandwich. "But right now, I want to eat and talk business. Since you're all about ninety percent of our problems being from ten percent of our customers, I have a few to discuss with you."

"I'm all ears."

"Laura Benedict, for one."

"The name isn't familiar."

"She's a repeat customer who has tried to take advantage of us in your mother's absence."

"What are the dollars and cents?"

"In five years, she's never amounted to more than thirty thousand in profit for us."

"And she's a bitch?"

"A bitch with PMS year-round."

"What do you want to do about her?"

"Put her in her place, with the understanding that I can drop her if I have to."

"I saw the financials. Do what you have to do, but don't let me get blindsided. Let me know in advance, in case she comes to me."

"My one hesitation is her big mouth. She'll tell the world we parted ways and come up with some dramatization worthy of Netflix."

"If we let everyone with a big mouth intimidate us, we'll both be walking around with no balls."

She starts laughing and our moods lighten. "I swear, sometimes I think your mother has a removable set she installs at work."

"My father's," I joke.

"Mark," she chides. "I can't believe you said that!"

"If I'm alpha, then he's beta. You must see that."

"He's the head coach of a baseball team. That's pretty alpha."

"And he coaches like a beta—which is why my mother is always trying to be his alpha."

"Right." She sighs. "That brings me to an important topic."

"My father's balls or my mother's?"

She laughs. "Stop. No. Well, maybe your mother's. She's decided to go on a little outing tonight, and your father needs us to tag along."

"What happened to her barely being able to get out of bed?"

"You," she says. "Having you here means everything to her."

"Oh hell," I say, my hands settling on my thighs. "I know a suck-up, prep-me-for-what's-coming-speech when I hear one. What is she up to?"

"Your father is having pitching practice tonight, and she wants to go watch."

I shake my head firmly. "No. We are not going to the practice field. She's exhausted, and it's freezing outside."

"It's indoors. They've installed some sort of net inside the gym."

"She still doesn't need to be there."

"She doesn't have treatment on Saturday or Sunday. She can rest."

"No." I reach for my phone. "I'm telling her no."

Crystal grabs my wrist. "Mark, you can't do that."

I cut her a look before I can stop myself. "Why the fuck not?" I demand.

"I know you're worried. But she said she's learned that life is short, and she's been by your father's side far too little. She doesn't want to have regrets. You have to let her go."

The words send a shock wave through me, and my hands are suddenly on Crystal's shoulders. "Has she decided she's dying?" I ask hoarsely. "Does she know something I don't know? Do you?"

"No! It's not that—I promise. This is good. She says she's decided to live, and I admire that. It's something I haven't always done."

I push to my feet and cross the room, knowing what my mother's doing. This is about me shutting out baseball and a past that was once my future. This is about her trying to bring me back home in every sense of the word.

But Crystal is right. I can't deny her, no matter how painful this is for me. My mother just guaranteed that denial is no longer in the cards.

"What time do we need to be there?"

"Pitching practice starts at six thirty. I talked to Kara and she arranged to have someone she trusts here for closing. She's going to escort your parents to the campus. Jacob said he'd drive us and stay with us the rest of the evening."

"Isn't my father worried about the press at the campus?"

"He's had that handled for weeks now. It's not a problem."

I study her a long moment. "You decided we were going before you told me about this."

She rises and walks toward me, sliding her arms under my jacket and around my waist. I pull her closer. "You told me once your mother was the only person you couldn't say no to," she reminds me.

I cup her head and lower my mouth near hers. "Apparently now there are two of you."

"Should I say I'm sorry?" she whispers.

"I'm not sure why you would be." I kiss her, losing myself in the sweetness that promises something more than the bitterness of the past when this night ends. "Just know this." The look that I give her leaves no doubt that I have plans for her. Dark, hot, intense plans. "I'm going to need more than a simple fuck when I finally get you alone."

She smiles. "One thing I never expect from you, Mark Compton, is simple."

"Good," I say. "Because it's about to get damn complicated."

# Sixteen

Crystal . . .

A half hour after I leave Mark's office I'm sitting at my desk, trying to finish up some important paperwork before we leave for the practice. Not an easy task, when I'm still a mix of nerves and arousal over Mark's promise of more than a "simple fuck" when we get home. Even more, though, I'm worried about the past he's facing tonight—which clearly provoked that promise. I know that his mother knows what she's doing, so all I can think is that she wants to force him to heal.

My cell rings, with Kara's number on the screen. "This is Crystal."

"It's Kara. I'm at the Comptons' place now. I wanted to arrive early and scope out the building. Unfortunately, since I'm here, she wants to leave early. Something about keeping her husband from missing some sort of drills."

"Is her nurse going with you?"

"Not that I know of."

"Put her on."

Dana begins by saying, "I'm not letting Steven leave his practice to come here. And if I don't surprise him and go early, he will."

"But Mark and I would both feel better if you had us there to take care of you."

"I'm fine. Kara is with me, and I'm just going to be sitting. Not climbing the Empire State Building."

"You weren't fine yesterday."

"But today I am."

"What about your nurse?"

"I don't need her, and she's off anyway."

The rest of the conversation pretty much goes her way. When we hang up, I make a beeline to Mark's office. I knock, go right in, and motion for him to stand with my hands. "Up. Up. Hurry. We need to leave early. Your mother insisted Kara take her to the practice now, so your father won't feel he has to leave to get her. She's not taking her nurse."

Looking puzzled, he doesn't move. "Are you sure we're talking about my mother? The one who could barely move yesterday?"

"I know. I thought the same thing. She says she's fine today—and I can vouch for her being as feisty as ever."

"Well, that's good news, at least."

"You still aren't getting up! What if she gets weak and needs help?"

His intercom buzzes. "It's your father, Mr. Compton."

"Put him through."

I perch impatiently on the edge of a chair, trying to follow the conversation.

"Crystal just told me," Mark confirms to his father. "She's worried Mom's too weak to be there without us." He listens a moment. "You're sure? And you have security in place to handle reporters?" A few seconds pass before he nods. "Okay. Yes. If you're sure." His eyes meet mine. "I'm really coming, Dad." Another pause, and this time Mark's lashes lower, sheltering him from my probing stare as he replies, "I know. It has. I will." He hangs up the phone, and I don't miss the way he drags out the process, studying the desk a few seconds too long before he focuses an unreadable look on me. "My father says he's not even involved in the earlier practice she's trying to make sure he can attend. His base coach is running it. He'll be free to take care of her."

Sighing, I relax. "Thank goodness."

"All is well," Mark assures me. "And since we have a little time . . ." He opens his desk drawer and reaches inside, shocking me when he sets a black pouch the size of his palm on the desk. "Come here, Ms. Smith."

My fingers dig into the arms of the chair. "No."

"*Come here*, Ms. Smith."

"What are you going to do?"

His stare is a pure, white-hot challenge. "What do you want me to do?"

"That's not the same bag as before."

"This is one of the items from the bag. I'm going to show you the rest later."

"Why?"

"Because I said."

"That's not a good reason."

"It's the only reason you're getting. Come here."

"Shouldn't we be leaving? Just to be safe."

"*After* you come here."

There is something about dominant Mark that does funny things to my body. Heat rushes through me, and my skin warms all over. It's arousing. And confusing. Why do I want to do what he demands? Can I take orders and still be my own form of alpha?

I study him, this man who affects me like no other, this man who is not my type at all.

I find myself standing without consciously deciding to do so, but I manage to delay my advancement. Pressing my fingers to the edge of the desk, I make darn sure we're clear that *I'm* making this decision, not him. "I'm going to come over there—but only because you're really sexy right now."

He laughs, low and deep, and the sound is sin and sex. "Is that right?"

"Yes. It's because I want you—and only because I want you." With those final words of bravado and my pulse jumping like I'm skydiving without a proper parachute, I walk around the desk.

Mark rolls his chair back just enough to allow me to stand in front of him without touching him, then rolls forward, trapping my knees with his, his hands settling possessively on my hips. "No one talks to me the way you do."

"No one tells you you're sexy?"

"I don't invite conversation with women. Or anyone, for that matter."

"Like the way you don't like to be touched?"

"That's right. But every time I'm with you, Ms. Smith, you yank out another page of that rulebook." He wraps his arm around my waist and pulls me sideways onto one leg. There's something immensely erotic about sitting on his lap, how the delicious male scent of him surrounds me, and the thick ridge of his erection presses against my hip. He reaches up, his fingers caressing my cheek, then finding my hair, and a light tug leads my mouth to his. We breathe together and I don't know what is happening to me with this man. He's both night and day, good and bad, in all the ways every girl wants a man to be bad.

His lips brush mine, a soft caress. I feel him like hot sun blistering my skin in one moment, and a cool breeze soothing the burn the next. I feel him in every part of me. I want him next to me, inside me, everywhere. I *need* him everywhere.

"You," he whispers, "are like a drug."

"Is that good or bad?"

"Both, in all the right ways." It's as if he's heard my thoughts about him.

I've never been so connected to a man, so in the same place, at the same time.

He strokes hair behind my ear, then drags the velvet bag to the edge of the desk. "Open it. There's something for now, and something for later."

My throat goes dry at the "later," due to his warning that he wants more than a simple fuck. "This part of you makes me very nervous," I tell him.

He frames my face with his hands and stares at me. "I'll push you, but I will never, ever hurt you." He scoops up the bag and hands it to me. "Open it."

Nervous, but ridiculously aroused by this little game we're playing, I open the bag and reach inside, my hand trembling a bit. I dump the contents onto my palm. Two small balls, about twice the size of a pencil eraser.

"What are they?"

He turns one over, showing me the opening on the back. "To cover your nipples."

"Clamps?"

"No." He rolls them in my palm. "These are soft plastic with no clamping. Just some suction." He takes them from me and positions my backside against the desk, his hands returning in that possessive way to my hips. "All they're going to do is remind you that I'm thinking about licking them, every second we're not alone."

My lashes lower with the rush of sensations his words create. "You probably shouldn't talk to me like that."

"Why is that?"

I look him in the eyes. "Because we have to leave."

His sexy, sensual, so-damn-scrumptious mouth curves. "That's the idea in doing this now." He tugs down the zipper at the front of my dress to expose my lacy red bra, which he shoves down in a swift, easy move. His thumbs stroke my nipples and I have to press my hands to the desk to keep from touching him.

One of his hands cups my breast and he leans in and laps at the already stiff peak, making my sex spasm. I bite my lip and moan, already wet and aching, wishing he were inside me right now. He licks the little plastic ball and then places it on my nipple. I suck in a breath and there is pressure, but as he promised, no pain. His tongue flicks the plastic, sending darts of sizzling pleasure to all parts of my body.

His eyes meet mine with heat and possessiveness that match his touch, and I'm all for being possessed right now. He was right. He will own me, and I might just like it. He leans down, his blond hair tickling my skin, his tongue lapping at the other nipple before he draws it deeply into his mouth. I grab his head and hold him to me. When he lifts his head, his mouth finds mine, kissing me deeply, passionately before he licks the other ball and places it on my swollen nipple.

The intercom buzzes, and he surprises me by hitting the button. "Jacob from Walker Security would like to see you," Beverly announces.

"Send him back," Mark replies.

"What?" I say. "No!" I try to move away but he holds me. "I didn't lock the door, Mark!"

"We're done." He pulls my bra up and zips my dress. "And now, Ms. Smith, every time your nipples chafe, think about all the ways I might fuck you when we get home."

A knock sounds on the door.

"Come in," Mark calls, and I glower at him as I stand up.

"I was *not* ready."

"You will be, though, I promise." He smiles.

"You really are an asshole, Mark Compton."

He laughs as Jacob enters.

"I hear you might want to leave early. What time were you thinking?"

"I believe we're ready now," Mark replies.


We exit Riptide to a fresh crush of reporters that slams us with reality, leaving fantasy back in Mark's office. By the time Jacob has us en route to the NYU athletic facility off Fourteenth Street, Mark's mood is notably darker. Whatever he's facing tonight from his past has clearly hit him. He's reserved, barely speaking to Jacob, but I'm encouraged by the way he keeps me close, molding our legs and hips together, his fingers resting on the inside of my knee.

Jacob parks by a side door near a gymnasium and exits the vehicle, but Mark remains where he is, all hard lines and tension. I silently settle my hand on his leg. Baseball is clearly a part of the past he doesn't want to revisit, but can't escape. I wonder if that's the reason he moved to San Francisco, and not his need for individual success outside the umbrella of Riptide and his mother.

He finally seems to shake himself into action. "Leave your coat here," he says, shrugging out of his own. "You won't want to deal with it inside." After helping me with mine, he opens the door. Stepping outside, he guides me out of the backseat and into the cold, dry night. My hand settles on his chest, his erratic heartbeat thrumming beneath my palm.

"When was the last time you were here?" I ask.

"Ten years ago."

It's a number I've heard him mention on numerous occasions, and it stirs many questions that I don't ask. He's fighting some internal battle, and he's trusted me enough to allow me here with him. He'll talk when he's ready to.

"Have you gone to your father's games?"

"Yes. But I stay away from here." His hands come down on my shoulders. "I'm going to want to touch you in there."

It's an admission that this trip is stirring his inner demons, and I want to help him. "Then touch me."

"I'm certain my mother doesn't know about us. She'd have already said something to me, and probably you as well. Let's hold off until tomorrow."

"We should go inside," Jacob says, glancing around us, reminding me of the danger Mark is certain exists.

Mark scoops my hand from his chest and surprises me by bringing it to his lips and kissing it. The tiny act of tenderness reveals so much about what's beneath his steely shell.

Jacob joins us and we walk to the door. Inside the small hallway, a guard assigns us badges. I hear Mark inhale a moment before we round the corner, and in unison we stop and take in the view before us. In the center of a yellowish orange floor is a catcher in full gear, kneeling in front of a huge net while a pitcher throws him a fastball. A half dozen players in uniforms are lined up to the left and watch the action. Mark's father, dressed in jeans and a team shirt, is standing a few feet from the players with two other men in similar attire, apparently other coaches. On the opposite side of the room, Dana and Kara are seated in cushy folding chairs rather than on the hard bleachers, with a few extra chairs waiting for us.

Dana spots us and waves, her expression lightening and her energy level remarkably high. I lean in closer to Mark. "Her nurse thinks that her sleeping all the time has been more about depression than physical exhaustion. I'm beginning to think she was right, and you were the cure."

"Whatever the case, it's good to see her looking better." He steps backward to where Jacob is talking to the guard, and I watch them huddle together before Jacob disappears out the door. Mark turns and his father spots us, waving his greeting as well. We both wave back and Mark rejoins me.

"Everything okay?" I ask.

"It'd be better if I was licking you all over right now."

His hand comes down on my lower back, scorching me with erotic promise as he urges me forward, my nipples swelling beneath the soft plastic enclosing them. I want him suddenly, intensely, and I'm sure it shows on my face.

I step away and he laughs, low and deep. "Problem?"

"I thought we weren't touching?"

"I cheated."

Pleased that he's being playful, I egg him on. "I'm going to make you pay for teasing me."

"You can try."

I purse my lips. "Game on, Mark Compton. Game on."

We're both laughing as we reach Dana and Kara. Kara stands up, offering me her chair as she moves to the bleachers.

"What's so funny?" Dana asks, smiling as she glances at us, and I'm happy to see pink color in her cheeks.

"Your son's bad jokes," I say, casting him a taunting look.

He laughs again and Dana lights up. "Oh, do tell," she says. "I love a good naughty joke."

Mark claims the other seat next to his mother and covers her hand. "I'm your son. I don't want to hear that from you."

"I guess we both have to accept that we're adults, now, don't we?" she asks. It's clear that she's referencing his club activities, but it's framed as acceptance, not disdain. "And," she adds, "if you won't tell me the joke, Crystal will." She looks at me. "Right?"

"Right," I say, moving my chair so that it's angled toward them both. "Here it goes."

"Crystal," Mark says, his eyes steely.

I grin, loving how I have him in suspense. "It is a *very* bad joke, Dana."

She waves it off. "Please. Tell me already."

"If you're sure, then," I say, "here goes. So . . . there's a mama tomato, a papa tomato, and all their baby tomatoes. They all go out for a walk, and when the youngest tomato falls behind, the mother yells 'catch up!'"

Mark shakes his head. "I did *not* tell that joke."

Dana laughs and kisses his cheek, whispering something in his ear. His lashes lower and a smile lingers on his lips. "Yes," he says, and he leans in and whispers something to her.

As I watch them nestled together, their closeness, their love, really get to me. Any question of why I've fallen for this man has faded. He's sexier than ever, and I'm more emotionally invested than I thought possible. And I want to know what happened ten years ago that made him incapable of showing his love to Rebecca, while he gives and receives it freely from his family.

"That's Joey Macom," Dana says, settling back in her seat and pointing toward a player who's about to pitch. "He's your dad's new recruit. He says he's wild but powerful. I say anyone who's wild should have worked that out before reaching this level."

I turn my attention to Joey and watch him throw a few crazy pitches. "He slouches," I say. "I've never seen a pitcher do that, and I've been to my share of Yankees games, thanks to my family's baseball obsession."

"One of his legs is stiff," Mark says without looking at me. "It's affecting his posture and his results, and I can't believe my father can't see that. He would have been all over me for that."

"He's distracted because of me," Dana says. "I want him to go out on top. You have to shake him back into focus, son."

Mark squeezes his mother's hand, but he's watching the pitcher. He shakes his head as Joey throws another crazy pitch. His leg starts bouncing, a sign of nervous energy and a fight for willpower. Mark's dying to get up and tell his father what's wrong, already completely absorbed in this world though he hasn't been here in ten years. Now that he is, he can't suppress what's in his blood.

"Mark!" his father calls out, motioning him over.

I hold my breath, waiting for his reaction.

One second.

Two.

Three.

Mark stands up, but I don't let out my breath until I see him walk toward his father.

Dana relaxes, too, apparently on eggshells like me. "Thank goodness. I was afraid he'd refuse."

That's a strong word. What the heck happened ten years ago?

Mark is halfway to his father when he stops, then he starts walking toward the door. "Oh no," Dana murmurs. "I was afraid of this."

I stand, intending to go after him, but he's headed toward Jacob. They meet midway across the gym and exchange a few words before Mark heads back in our direction, a fast-food drink in his hand. "What is he up to?" Dana murmurs.

I have a feeling I know, but I wait, watching his long, graceful stride, the way he owns the space around him. The way I bet he owned the mound when he pitched.

He stops in front of us, his eyes meeting mine in a warm flicker of a moment before he crouches in front of his mother. "A milk shake," he announces, handing her the drink. "I'm here, and we both know that's what tonight was about. Now you drink the milk shake." He pushes to his feet and shrugs out of his jacket, which he hands to me.

I accept it, our fingers brushing beneath it, his eyes telling me the touch is intentional. And at the moment, I don't care that he's winning our little game. I *want* him to win.

He turns away and jogs toward his father. Dana and I watch as he talks with the coaches, and I can't help checking out his nice, tight backside, imagining him in baseball pants.

"Drink," I order without looking at Dana.

"Yes, Ms. Smith," she says, laughing.

I cut her a look. "Was that a Mark joke?"

"Of course not," she replies glibly. Then smiles, elbowing me. "Of course it was."

We laugh and I'm reminded of how much I love this woman. "It's good to see you energetic again."

"I'm tired, but I'm faking it."

"You couldn't have faked it a few days ago."

"I guess a mother's soul is always lighter when she has her child home." She motions with her chin toward the practice area.

I return my attention to the center of the gym to see Mr. Compton's sleeves rolled up, his tie loose, as he demonstrates a pitching stance to Joey, his knee high to his chest, posture perfect.

"I didn't think I'd ever see that again, after his injury," Dana murmurs.

"I didn't know he was injured." Somehow that doesn't feel big enough for Mark's reaction to coming here tonight.

"Well, it wasn't really an injury. More . . . an event."

"I kind of thought so."

"He hasn't told you?"

"No."

"You aren't going to ask me?"

"It's his story to tell when he's ready. If he ever is."

Her eyes soften and she takes my hand. "That's a perfect answer, and he's getting there. Tonight shows that."

"I hope so," I say, my attention returning to Mark as he demonstrates the way Joey should set his leg.

"You love him," Dana says softly, and my gaze jerks back to her.

"What?" I ask, trying to figure out what I'd done to bring on such an observation.

"You love him."

"I . . . Dana, I—"

"It's okay. I love him, too, and I haven't seen him this relaxed in a long, long time. I wasn't sure I ever would again. I believe you're the reason."

"No. No, it's not me."

"You're just a coincidence?"

"It's Rebecca. He loved her. He lost her. I'm here, and he needs me to get to the other side."

"The other side is you, Crystal. You can't see it, but I do."

"I don't know what I am, or what we are. But I don't want to lose you if I lose him."

"Well, my vote is for you keeping us both, but I won't let you lose me if you don't. Not because of Mark, and not because of damn cancer."

I drape my arm over her narrow shoulders, her thin body downright frightening, and I nudge the shake to her mouth. "I'm going to hold you to that."

"I'll drink. I'll drink." She draws on the straw. "I expect you and Mark to stop pretending you aren't seeing each other now."

"Happily. And I guess this is a good time to tell you he's staying at my apartment."

"Even better. Now I know where he is at night." She takes my hand. "Oh, honey, please hold on to him."

I'm not sure I could let go if I wanted to.

# Seventeen

Mark . . .

I'm surprisingly removed from the past as I stand next to my father and watch Joey throw a few improved pitches. There seems to be a freedom in facing this that I didn't expect, and I'm embracing it to the fullest.

I'm about to walk over to Joey and give him a pointer when Crystal stands and begins to sashay toward me across the gymnasium, looking like a blond bombshell in her red dress, with curves from here to Texas. I don't miss how every male head in the room turns to watch her the way I am, the same way everyone had turned to look at Tabitha. The truth is that Crystal's fiery, sexy, and defiant nature is very much like Tabitha's had been, only ten years more mature.

My father nudges my arm. "She's a looker, that one. Like your mother."

"Yes, she is," I say. "And so is Mom."

"Have you told Crystal?"

I don't have to ask to know he means the events of ten years before. "No."

"Are you going to tell her?"

My answer comes with remarkable ease. "Yes."

He claps a hand on my shoulder. "That's a good choice. *She's* a good choice."

"Yes," I say in agreement again. "She is."

Crystal stops in front of me and hands me my main cell phone. "Your phone was ringing."

"Who was it?" I ask, thankful I'd stuffed the disposable in my pants pocket.

"I respected your privacy and I didn't look."

"Your mother would have looked," my father says, "even way back in our dating days."

Crystal grins. "I find that so easy to believe."

My father turns somber. "How is she?"

"Good," Crystal says. "Tired, but the best I've seen her in weeks."

"Did she drink the milk shake?" I ask, tabbing through my missed calls.

"With a little needling I was happy to provide," Crystal responds.

"I'm sure that was difficult for you," I reply dryly. "Because you're so soft-spoken and hesitant about pushing people."

Crystal's blue eyes twinkle with good humor. "And here I thought you didn't know me."

My father yells something at the catcher and I take the opportunity to softly say, "I do know you—but not as well as I plan to."

"That boy needs to pay attention," my father mutters, settling back into our conversation.

"I need to step away and take a few phone calls," I announce.

Crystal's brow furrows. "Problems? Who called?" The urgent lift to her voice tells me it killed her not to look at my phone, but she'd still resisted.

"Blake, and my attorney, Tiger."

"Crystal can stay here with me while you talk to them," my father offers.

One of the players gives her a once-over that makes me want to go shake him, and I say to hell with discretion. I grab Crystal, pull her to me, and kiss her, making damn sure everyone knows whom she belongs to.

Afterward, she grins. "Good thing your mother already knew about us."

"And now everyone else does, too." I set her right next to my father. "Watch out for her," I instruct him.

My father chuckles. "Gladly."

Not giving Crystal a chance to tell me she doesn't need watching, I waste no time striding away to the opposite side of the gymnasium. Punching my voice mail button, I listen to Blake's message as I lean against a wall of folded bleachers.

"I'm here, and so is Detective Grant. I told him to contact Tiger, and I'm warning you that he wasn't pleased. I'm headed to the hospital and I thought he'd join me, but he didn't. I'll call you if I find anything out. Otherwise I'll see you in the morning. And don't fucking keep my wife out too late. You have Jacob. I haven't slept with her in two weeks."

My phone beeps with a call from my attorney, and I answer to hear, "Fucking Detective Grant won't take my calls."

"I take it you got my message?"

"I got it and I'm headed to Long Island. I talked to Luke Walker

203

and he's still being shut out, but I set up a meeting with the Long Island PD for tomorrow morning. And I told them this is a bunch of bullshit. I'm as sick as you are, of you becoming everyone's fall guy."

"That's the least of my worries with Ava on the loose."

"Let me do my job. I'm here for a reason."

Crystal starts walking toward me and I say, "Call me if anything changes." I slide my phone into my pocket.

"Is everything okay?" Crystal asks as she steps to my side.

"Blake wants his wife home early since he hasn't slept with her in two weeks, my attorney is meeting with the Long Island PD tomorrow, and the asshole detective who made my life hell over Rebecca is in town. But nothing significant has changed."

She leans a shoulder on the wall, facing me, and I do the same. "Your mother's doing better. That's pretty significant."

"Yes," I say, reaching up to catch the long blond hair that's managed to attach itself to her lips, lips that I want to kiss and feel on several places on my body. "And now we're out of the closet with her, and pretty much everyone."

"Yes, we are. What was that kiss all about?"

"The caveman in me felt the urge to stake my claim among the other wannabe cavemen."

"Is that right?"

"I did it. I'll own it." We're silent for a moment and there's this level of understanding between us, a sense of knowing each other in ways beyond words, that I'd never thought I wanted in my life. But I want it now, with Crystal. "I'm sure you got an earful about me and baseball from my mother tonight."

"No. She was excited to see you here, but I didn't want her to tell me the details of why you've stayed away. I told her that was your place, if and when you wanted to tell me."

Her respect for my personal demons reminds me again of her own. She'd once claimed we were too alike to be compatible, two bulls after the same red flag. I'd agreed then, but I'm beginning to think that what makes us alike, the scars beneath our need for control, are what pull us together.

She runs her fingers down my cheek and traces my lips, as if she's absorbing who I am, what I am—when I'm still struggling with that myself.

I capture her hand in mine, feeling as if showing her my past is a window into the future. "Come with me. I want to show you something."

Leading her toward a door, we exit into a corridor that leads to a large reception area with offices with half-glass walls lining the hallway behind it. I lead Crystal to the office farthest in the back, flipping on the light and illuminating a basic desk, a small, round table that could be in a cafeteria as easily as here, and an array of pictures on the walls of sports heroes my father has met.

Crystal scans the room while I claim one of a cluster of weathered, hard chairs sitting around the desk. "Your father's office," she guesses.

"Yes." I wave at the wall to my right, where my father still proudly displays several pictures of me pitching on the mound.

Crystal immediately moves in to get a closer look, studying them intently for some time before facing me. "You played for your father."

"Another yes." I lift my hand to her. "Come here." As soon as she's within reach, my hands settle on her hips and I maneuver her between my legs, her hands on my shoulders. "You're not going to ask even one of the many questions I know you have?"

"No. You don't need questions. I think . . . I think you need answers that only you can give. We find those answers in our own way that we can live with, or we don't find them at all."

There's a flicker of something dark in my mind, a brief flashback that I shove aside before it takes hold of me. Yet another confirmation that the past absolutely owns me, and has for too long.

"Ten years ago I was pitching for NYU, under my father as a coach, and I had the attention of the right people. There were scouts circling as intently as the press is now. I was going pro. The only question was with whom. I was that good. And that's not ego; it's a fact. I was, and then I wasn't, and then everything changed. And . . ." I hesitate, that dark spot in my mind again stirring memories that I'm not prepared to sort through in a public place, especially with my mother and father nearby. I stand up and say, "And that's where the past ended and the present began."

She reaches up, cupping my cheek, silently telling me that she gets it, and knows I'm already at my limit. I lean into her touch, cupping her hand with mine, my eyes seeking hers, the connection triggering an unfamiliar warmth in my chest that has nothing to do with desire. "God, woman, what are you doing to me?"

"Nothing you aren't doing to me."

I stare into her blue eyes and see the trust there, the understanding I'm not sure I deserve or ever will in this lifetime, but I want to. God, how I want to—and there are suddenly things I want to say to her, about us, about Rebecca, and about my past. But there isn't time—or maybe this is simply the wrong time.

My forehead settles against hers; my hands go to her waist and caress upward, fingers curving the swell of her breasts, working their way to the hard covers over her nipples. Her breath hitches, the sound driving what I already feel. "I really need to be inside you right now."

She jerks back and says, "Not in your father's office," as if she believes I might intend just that.

It's tempting. So damn tempting. I lean in, brushing my lips over hers, still teasing the hard tips covering her nipples, intentionally creating a sweet friction in her body that I want to lick away.

She moans and the sound thickens my cock. I dip my tongue into her mouth again for one last sweet taste of her to hold me over until we're finally alone. "Let's go tell my parents good-bye and go home."

"Yes," she agrees. "Please."

My lips curve. "Please. I like how that sounds. And 'Please, Mr. Compton, lick my nipples' would be even better."

"Not going to happen."

I press my cheek to hers and nip her ear, whispering, "Challenge accepted."

We walk back to the gymnasium to find it all but deserted, and hurry toward my parents.

My father hands me my jacket, which I slip on. He's quick to discover that we've been in his office, and he draws Crystal into conversation about the photos. I'm equally as quick to hug my mother. Holding my arms, she tilts her face up to study me. "How are you?"

"Far better than expected."

"I know there's a part of the past you don't ever want to think about," she says. "But I want you to have that special baseball bond with your father again while he's still here. You both need that." She softens her voice. "And you know the counselor said there are stages of healing, and you never let yourself go through them all."

"I am now."

"Because of Crystal," she states.

"Because you and Rebecca made me realize life is short."

She looks at me closely. "Don't forget that with Crystal."

"I don't intend to."

"That's the most positive answer I've heard from you in ten years. Are you two coming by the house tomorrow?"

"Probably late. We have prep work for next week's auctions, which reminds me: Crystal's done very well. Today I reviewed the financials that you haven't been able to look over. Riptide is kicking ass and the scandal has created buzz, not a mass exodus. Next week's RSVPs for the auctions are up fifteen percent."

Crystal comes to our side, and I wrap my arm around her shoulder. "I was telling my mother how well you've taken care of Riptide."

"I knew you were a superstar, my dear," my mother proclaims proudly. "And you've done this all on your own. Sounds like you need to do a little nose-rubbing to your father and brothers."

"Oh, I intend to," Crystal assures her. "I'll be doing just that on Sunday night."

"What's Sunday night?" I ask.

"My birthday is next Saturday, during the auction, and Thursday and Friday will be crazy busy, so my family's having a little birthday dinner for me at my father's place Sunday night. Want to come along?"

Pleased at the invitation to meet her family and discover the foundation that made her the woman who has turned my world upside down, I am quick to accept. "Looking forward to it already."

"Sounds like enough testosterone in one room to damage a woman's ovaries," my mother quips, sounding very much like her pre-cancer self. "And remember, my dear son," she adds, "you're not the pack leader there. Her father is. No matter how much you want to show your dominant tendencies, you respect his first."

"Such love, Mother. I can barely stand it."

My mother smirks. "I still love you, you arrogant ass."

Crystal chokes on laughter and my father drapes an arm over my mother's shoulder. "Handing out compliments again, I see." He lifts his chin at Crystal. "Welcome to the love factory."

Crystal takes the intended bait. "Love factory?"

I explain: "That's what he called our house when I was growing up. Usually after my dear mother told me I needed to 'suck it up and move on' after a bad game."

"Wallowing in negativity never works," Dana says, "so yes. I told you to suck it up." She leans into my father. "And I really need sleep."

My father kisses her head. "The car is ready to go." The two of them head to the door, toward Kara. Jacob holds up a hand, signaling for us to wait until my parents have departed for our turn.

My hands settle on Crystal's waist. "While we wait," I say, "what do you want for your birthday?"

Her hands settle on my arms, and I don't get the playful reply I expect. "The same things you want, I suspect. Your mother to be well and Ava to be captured."

"We'll blow out some candles and make those wishes together."

"I'd like that," she says. "And how old will you be on your next birthday, Mr. Compton?"

"Thirty-five, Ms. Smith, and you'll be twenty-nine."

"You looked at my file."

"Of course I looked at your file. You're running Riptide."

"*We're* running Riptide."

"I'm not responsible for the balance sheet I looked at today. That's all you."

She tilts her head and gives me a curious look. "For a man as arrogant as you, Mark Compton, you aren't quick to steal someone else's thunder."

"Contrary to my mother's belief, I'm not arrogant, I'm confident. True confidence means you're prepared to work hard enough and smart enough to make your own thunder. You don't need someone else's." Jacob motions us forward, and I wrap my arm around her. "Let's get out of here."

After we return our badges at the guard post, Jacob leads us down the hallway beyond. Opening the door to the parking lot, he stops us with a hand as he scans for trouble. After he waves us forward, he opens the back door of the Escalade for us. I help Crystal into the vehicle, and as I prepare to join her I hear, "Mr. Compton."

The familiar voice to my right grinds my nerve endings, and Jacob and I both jerk in its direction. Detective Grant steps out of the shadows. "Detective," I say to him shortly, giving his tan trench coat a once-over. "You're looking very Inspector Gadget."

"Compliments will get you nowhere, Mr. Compton," he chides.

"Nevertheless, I find it hard to resist a well-deserved one when it's due," I reply dryly. "How exactly did you find me here?"

"Process of elimination. It's how I operate, picking away at people, things, and problems, bit by bit."

"Which would be effective, if you chose your targets effectively."

"I was right about Ava killing Rebecca, and right about her using her young employee to finish her dirty work."

"But she got away. Didn't she?"

"Yes. She got away, and there lies the problem. It's a huge one, to you especially, I'm sure. One that could, say, make you want to take matters in your own hands."

"What I want is justice, and the security of knowing my family is safe."

"I hear you might hunger for a side of vengeance with your justice."

I manage not to stiffen. Did Blake tell him that? "I'm not sure anyone who's lost someone they loved doesn't have that emotion."

"Now you loved Rebecca? I thought she was just your sex slave."

The insult is a jab in my heart, but I manage not to react. "What is it you want?"

"I thought I'd give you a heads-up about tomorrow's meeting with the Long Island PD for your attorney. Per Corey, he and Ava were blindfolded and beaten. She escaped and rescued him, dropping him off at the hospital. But before she left him, he says she bid him a tearful good-bye and apologized for underestimating the violence you were capable of, implying that you were their captor."

Another setup by Ava? "If you study people as you say, then you must be smart enough to know I wouldn't bring trouble home with my mother fighting for her life."

"Ah, but you'd have to bring it here, *because* you have a mother fighting for her life."

The nerve he hits is deep and angry, and I actually find myself swaying toward him, even taking a step.

Crystal is suddenly by my side, her hand gripping my arm. "Let your attorney handle this, Mark."

"Or you could just go all vigilante on me," the detective taunts.

Every part of me wants to throttle him, but I clamp down on the emotion. "Let's go," I tell Crystal, giving him my back as I help her into the Escalade. I join her without another look at the detective.

As Jacob joins us I already have my cell phone out, dialing Tiger. The instant he answers, I say, "Detective Grant paid me a visit."

"When? Where?"

"Just now, at my father's sports facility." I relay the conversation.

"But he didn't say Corey saw you, correct?" Tiger asks.

"Correct."

"Then it's hearsay and they can't do shit to you. And he knows it. That's why he showed up. He knows this all has to be wearing on you, and he was trying to set you off and get you to do something erratic. I'll handle it. You stay away from it. This is my show."

"Right." I end the call and I hear Jacob on his phone, relaying the details of the incident to someone. Ava and Wright may be trying to destroy me, but they aren't the masterminds. It has to be either Ricco or Ryan.

I look down to find Crystal's hand on my leg and I can feel her willing me to look at her, but I don't. I'm thinking about the letter she received, and how easily she could be in the line of fire, if she isn't already. And my parents, as well.

Removing the disposable phone from my pocket, uncaring if Crystal or Jacob hears what I have to say, I punch the auto-dial. At three rings, I hear, "I got nothing, man. Ava and Wright are ghosts."

"Don't tell me you 'got nothing.' She's here in New York. Find her. And there's a hundred thousand dollars in it for you if you get me conclusive evidence of who's behind Wright's involvement." I punch the End button.

"Care to tell me who that was, and who Wright is?" Jacob asks, eyeing me from the rearview mirror.

"Not yet." My hand covers Crystal's, and I'm not letting go.

# Eighteen

Mark . . .

The ride to Crystal's is dark and tremulous. I am not where I need
to be mentally; I'm inside my own head, guilt driving me nearly
insane. The emotions I've spent ten years denying are shredding
me into pieces I can't hold together. I'm on the edge of the present
and the past, weaving between control and no control at all.

When Jacob stops at the front door we exit into the bitter
cold, me still holding on to Crystal's hand. After he makes sure we
enter safely, we continue across the lobby to the elevators. Crystal
doesn't push me to speak and I don't look at her, willing myself to
get right in my head before we're alone.

Inside the elevator I lean on the wall and enclose Crystal in
my arms, feeling one dominant need: to control everything around
her, including her, to ensure that nothing hurts her. Though this is
the same flawed thinking I've used for ten years, it's what I know,
and who I am.

"Mark," Crystal whispers softly, and I meet her gaze, mine

unguarded. I let her see the dark need in me, the possessiveness. I want her to know what's coming. I want her to see this is a part of me that won't go away. It's how I steady myself when my world is spinning.

Our floor number dings and I cup her head, kissing her fast and hard, then release her to close my hand around hers and lead her out of the car, down the hall, and to her apartment. *Our* apartment right now, and it's remarkably easy for me to think about spending every day with this woman. I won't lose her. I won't.

She digs her keys from her coat pocket and her hand shakes. I grab the keys. "I'm making you nervous." Her lashes lower and I curse. "Of course I am. I'm making *me* nervous."

Her gaze lifts. "You aren't making me nervous. It's the unknown. You're on edge, and you need things I don't know how to give you. Simple fucking is all I know."

"Do you want to know more?"

Her hand goes to my arm. "I want to know you."

It's everything I wouldn't have wanted in the past. Now, the part of me that wants to chain her to a bed, spank her, and make her submit shrinks into the shadows—but it's not gone. I slip my hand to her hip and pull her close. "Then the answer is yes."

"Yes," she repeats.

"Then I'll take care of the rest." I unlock the door and push it open.

She inhales, a sign I'm coming to know as her means of calming herself and gaining control. She holds the air in for a moment, and on the exhaled breath she walks inside.

I pursue her, reaching for that comfortable part of me that's more primal beast than man; a place where I can reclaim control by showing Crystal the pleasure of letting it go. Safety is letting me have control. Tabitha ran off. Rebecca left. I didn't have control then, and I don't now. I didn't intentionally bring Crystal into this. She was already inside my family and my work, and I can't simply send her away to keep her safe. So I need control. I have to have it.

Crystal hesitates in the hallway, and there's a spike of unease around her that with anyone else, I wouldn't pause for. I'd order them forward, intentionally making them walk in front of me. But this is Crystal. The nervousness radiating off her rushes into me, and I'm instantly snapped back to man, not beast. That easily, I'm reminded that she is like no other woman I've ever known. And apparently, no matter how on edge, I am no version of myself that I was before her.

My hand settles on her back, gently urging her forward, and I'm a tightly paced step behind her. The curtains are open, the moon and stars illuminating the room and making artificial light unnecessary. We stop in the bedroom beside the bed. She faces me and I her, her back to the mattress. Again I find myself acting outside my Master instincts. Instead of ordering her to do something intensely erotic, I cave to the urge to caress the shadows sculpting her high cheeks, her luminous skin, and I hope the touch offers her a sense of security as I take her into a new world. My world, where I'm done denying that I want her.

I cup her face and rest my forehead on hers. Damn it to hell. Control is the answer. *It's the answer. Focus. One. Two. Three. Four. Five and fucking six.* "Reach into my right coat pocket," I tell her, my voice remarkably calm considering the chaos in my head.

She does. "The bag," she whispers, holding it between us.

I laugh at the way she says it. Though it's tight and unfamiliar, it's still a laugh, something I've never done during any Master/submissive game.

She glances up at me and I say, "It's not a bomb, sweetheart."

"That's up for debate after I see what's inside."

I cover the bag and her hand with mine. "You can always say no to this, now or later."

She studies me closely. "Who's more on edge? You or me?"

"Me." I shrug out of my coat and then my jacket, tossing them on the bed.

"I know you didn't have Corey beaten."

"If I thought you believed I did, I wouldn't be here." I take the bag from her and set it on the bed, returning to caress her coat over her shoulders. She slips it down her arms, and I catch it before it falls, tossing it on top of mine.

We stand face-to-face, staring at each other. Her trying to read me, me trying to stop thinking about her trying to read me, and just get to the craft of fucking. "I've been thinking about getting you naked all day long." I tug her front zipper down to her waist, granting me a delicious slice of skin.

"I generally think you have on too many clothes," she replies, her voice a soft rasp of desire.

My gaze lifts to hers at the uncensored comment. *Always honest.* She is who she is. And that, to me, is even sexier than the sexy-as-hell red lace bra now exposed, the material barely covering her nipples.

"You're going to get plenty of me naked tonight, I promise you." My gaze lowers to the swell of her breasts and I trace the line of lace, letting the material and my fingers tease her nipple covers.

Her breathing deepens in response, a subtle sign of hyper-arousal that tells me I affect her as deeply and intensely as she does me. *Honest.* The word rolls through my mind again, followed by another. *Trust.* Suddenly, I know *that's* what I need tonight. That is what is driving me. I need to know that, after everything I've told her about how I behaved with Rebecca, she knows I won't hurt her, and I won't let anyone else hurt her. And I need to know she can still see the man I want to be, not just the one I let myself become.

Gently, I settle my hand on the side of her neck. "Trust me," I murmur softly. "Give yourself to me, Crystal, and I won't make you regret it."

She tilts her head and studies me a long moment, and I find myself holding my breath, waiting for her decision. I've used seduction to gain control many times, and played erotic games that ensured it. And though the chemistry between us is strong enough for me to do that now, it isn't what I want. Her freely offering it is the only option for either of us.

Understanding and acceptance fill her face. "I trust you, Mark Compton. And I want *you* to trust you again."

I inhale sharply at the depth of her ability to see inside my battle, which has become our battle, as well. "When I tell you to do something, you do it. There's a price for hesitation."

"What kind of price?"

"Nothing I won't announce in advance, and even that, you can decline. It's always your choice. But don't take the power of saying 'no' or 'stop' lightly. I don't. If you speak those words, I *will* stop. So make sure that's what you really want. Understand?"

"Yes," she says firmly. "I understand."

Desire rips through me and I move backward, leaning on the wall to the bathroom.

"Undress," I say softly.

Her hands slip beneath the shoulders of her dress and she pulls the sleeves down her arms. She shimmies the dress down her hips, leaving herself in tights and her bra. Without hesitation, she reaches for her bra.

"The tights first," I tell her, saving the bra, and the nipple suction cups beneath it, for the moment when I have total control.

She does as I command, sitting on the edge of the bed to roll them away, taking her panties with them. I watch the silky expanse of pale skin appear, the triangle of blond hair in the V of her body, heat stirring in my own, cock thickening, but I don't move. I wait. Watch. Anticipate the way she'll taste, smell, and feel.

Task complete, she starts to stand, but I stop her. "Stay right there." She sits back on the bed, unhooking her bra. Arching her shoulders, she drags the lacy material forward, freeing her breasts, and gasping as the nipple covers tug with the release of the pressure the bra created.

I push off the wall and walk to her, going down on one knee in front of her. I reach for the bag and set it on her knees. "Open it."

She inhales, and on her exhale she reaches for the string tying the velvet closed. She tugs and the bag opens, revealing a pair of three-inch-wide red leather cuffs with silver clips. She stares down at them, unmoving, unspeaking. Several moments pass and she doesn't look up.

"Crystal," I say, but she doesn't respond. I'm not sure she's even breathing.

## Crystal . . .

The room closes in on me, the past a wicked gloved hand wrapped around my throat, making breathing and thinking nearly impossible.

"Crystal," Mark says again and I tell myself to look at him, telling myself I'm strong enough not to show my panic.

"Ms. Smith."

My gaze snaps up at the sharp command in his voice. "Crystal," I correct.

"Who owns you, Crystal?" he surprises me by asking.

I blink. "What?"

"Who owns you?"

"I do."

"Not tonight. Tonight, I own you."

Unbelievably, with the outrageous declaration that should have me fighting mad, that gloved hand slides away from my throat. I trust Mark, even if he doesn't. And if he owns me, the past doesn't. I almost sag with relief. "For the night," I concede. "You own me for only this night."

He agrees, tossing aside the velvet bag and picking up the cuffs. "Set your hands on your knees."

I glance at them and back at him. "I think I'm more of a silk tie kind of girl."

"Silk ties require knots, and if you want to get free I can't do it quickly." He shows me the silver clips on the side of the cuff, using his finger to flip one back and forth like a light switch. "You say you want to be free, and you're free."

"You promise?"

"You have my word."

"What are you going to do to me?"

"If I were to tell you, it would destroy both the anticipation and the freedom that full trust gives you, and us. Rest your hands on your knees."

He wants trust. He needs trust to heal. I need to get over my fear of being trapped, to heal. I flatten my palms on my knees.

"Turn them over, wrists up."

I do as he says and I expect him to attach the cuffs, but instead he leans down and kisses one of my wrists. His tongue flicks the sensitive skin, sending shivers up my arm and tightening the suctions on my nipples. Lingering there, he drives me wild with erotic sensations as he drags his lips up and down my arm, inhaling deeply as he returns to my wrist, his brow furrowing as he glances at me. "Why do you smell like jasmine and rum?"

"Jasmine and rum?" I laugh, a ball of tension in my belly dissolving at the unexpected comment. "I have no idea about the rum. My shampoo and bubble bath are jasmine scented. The perfume roller I keep in my purse is vanilla."

He brings my wrist to his nose again. "Rum."

"Vanilla," I say.

He flattens my hands back on my knees. "Whatever it is, you smell good enough to eat." I squeeze my thighs together a little tighter at the erotic words that have me thinking about all the places his tongue could soon be; I'm distracted enough that I'm shocked when the first cuff closes around my wrist. The second cuff follows, and my laughter fades while my heart does this crazy fluttering thing that can't be good for me. I inhale to calm myself, a technique a therapist I saw in my teens taught me.

Mark snaps the clasps into place on the cuffs, his gaze lifting sharply to mine. "Why is your leg trembling?"

"Adrenaline," I say, pretty certain that's what has my heart jumping around as well.

He laces the fingers of one hand into my hair. "Are you scared?"

"No. Yes. No. Damn it—I keep sounding indecisive with you, and I'm never indecisive." I try to be clear. "I'm not scared of you. The lack of control thing is an issue for me."

His expression tightens. "We don't have to do this."

"I want to," I say quickly, aware that he's reading my reaction as a lack of trust. I laugh nervously. "Unless you'd rather skip the cuffs and look for the rum? Preferably with your tongue?"

He releases my hair and reaches for the clasp of one cuff to free me. I grab his hand. "No, I was joking. I'm okay."

"You don't seem okay."

"We both have some things to work through." Seconds tick by, and I am certain he's waiting for more—but like him, I'm not ready.

"I've said this before, but I want to be *very* clear. You are freedom to me, Crystal. A place I can be the man beneath the Master. Where my pain isn't my weakness. I want to be that with you, but to do that, you have to be willing to be vulnerable."

"I really do that for you?"

"Yes. That's why I say this is honest. We're honest and real, and those are things I've missed in my life. Let me show you how experiencing an intense, erotic scene ensures there's no room for anything else."

"You never leave room for anything else. But does 'intense' mean pain?"

"It doesn't have to, but it can."

"Pain to you is what?" I ask, the cotton in my throat making my voice gravelly.

"It depends on the person and the scene. A spanking can come in many erotic forms. You can add flogging or clamping or both. Caning is the most intense, reserved for people who are on the more extreme end."

"I don't even want to know what that is."

"You don't have to know. I wouldn't do anything I didn't

give you a chance to decline. And once our mutual perimeters are set, a Master is supposed to know when, and what, is too much. That doesn't come without nurturing the bond and taking things slowly."

"Between Master and *submissive*," I say, concerned that that's where he's taking this.

"Between two people, Crystal. Even without the BDSM elements, good sex is about caring enough to learn about the other person. And letting go of control isn't a chore for a natural submissive. You aren't that. But letting go for a few hours doesn't make you a submissive. It gives you relief from the pressure of always trying to maintain control."

"When do *you* get that relief?"

He cups my face. "When we make love. I only make love with you. That's the trust I give you."

My doubts fade. He's intense. We're intense together. There is no room for the past. "I'm giving you trust. I wouldn't let anyone else cuff me. No one."

He brushes his lips over mine. "And I won't betray that trust."

# Nineteen

Crystal . . .

Mark's kiss lingers on my lips, his hands on my face, but it's his words that really get to me. *We make love.* I know this doesn't mean we have a future together, but it tells me that we're more than these leather cuffs—and that dissolves the prickling sensations and warms me inside.

I know he wants to protect me. I know he doesn't want to hurt me. *I'm okay. I can do this.* I can overcome my past and finally leave it behind me.

My bravado fades the instant Mark's hands slide away from my face, his body no longer touching mine. My gaze drops to the cuffs around my wrists and the prickling begins again, the urge to jerk against them almost too much to resist. I'm cold and on edge; dark shadows cloud my mind and transform into flickering images. I inhale, fighting this damnable weakness. I just want it to go away.

Mark's hands cover the leather, enclosing my hands. "Look at me, Crystal," he says softly.

His tone pulls my gaze upward, and I'm instantly trapped in his spellbinding steel-gray eyes. "Stop thinking about the cuffs. Start thinking about me owning you. Me fucking you. Me licking you until you're whimpering with pleasure. That's what this is about."

I shake my head. "No. It's not. It's about control that you have, and I don't."

"You're right. *I'm* in control. The monster I know you're fighting is not. And don't tell me there isn't a monster. I've seen it in your eyes."

I try to remember what I've told him in the past, but I can't think. Not naked and bound and staring into his eyes. "We all have monsters."

"But not everyone has the kind of monsters that I do. And you do. *I know,* Crystal. It's how we connected in the beginning. It's what gave me the freedom to be man, and not Master, with you. So whatever your monster is, I'm not letting it have you. You need to own it—and tonight, I own you. But until I know your monster, I'm only going to push you so far."

"No," I say quickly. "No, I don't want that. I want you to just make me stop thinking. Don't coddle me. Don't act like I can't handle this. You don't know my history. I do."

"Exactly. I don't know. And I'm not pushing you to tell me, any more than I'm pushing you somewhere you might not be ready to go."

This is why I don't do men like Mark. They want to decide for me. They want to control what I think I can handle. I cut my gaze, wishing I'd never gone down this path.

His fingers slide under my chin. "Whatever you're thinking about, stop."

"I'm thinking you're like every controlling man I've ever known. You think you know better."

"You aren't going to goad me with that remark, little one. Not even close. One minute you're afraid—"

"I'm not afraid."

"—and one minute you're not. We can always go deeper later. But we can't come back from me taking you too far too fast, and you shutting me out."

"I won't."

"All right. Then right now, you think only about what I give you permission to think about." He lifts my arms and presses my hands and my bound wrists behind my head. With my breasts thrust high in the air, I am instantly in the moment, aware of the vulnerability I've allowed myself with him. He holds on to the cuffs, his eyes meeting mine. "Don't move them unless I tell you to move them. Understand?"

There's a strong tug on my sex, and it becomes clear that while being trapped is hell for me, being this man's captive is more than a little sexy. "Yes," I whisper. "I understand."

"Good," he says. "Now. Back to what you have permission to think about." His gaze lowers, caressing my breasts, then lifts. "My tongue on your nipples. My tongue licking your clit. My fingers inside you. The many places my mouth can, and will, explore every part of you." He leans in and nips my bottom lip, the bite making me yelp. "And," he continues, his voice lowering to a velvety smooth seduction, "the many ways I can make your need for pleasure hurt so good. And I can, Crystal. I promise you, I can."

I moan at that naughty little promise of what is to come, and then gasp as he plucks off the shells on my nipples. The throb is instant, and I reflexively begin to lower my hands.

"Don't," Mark warns, his hand catching my elbow. "I said not to move them."

Inhaling, I force myself to fully reset my hands behind my head, and "Good girl" slides from those dangerous, provocative lips. My response isn't the indignation I expect, but something unfamiliar and erotic. I am hot all over, so very, very hot, that I want to rub myself against him and force him to take me now.

"There's a price for disobeying," he reminds me, his tone low and absolute.

"What kind of price?" I ask, remembering the threat of him turning me over his knee.

His lips, oh those seductive lips, curl. "My creativity is endless." He's quick to shut me down, telling me, "Open your legs."

I hesitate, swallowing hard at the command that will leave me fully exposed, then shocked when he suddenly twines a rough hand in my hair above the cuffs.

"Don't hesitate. I say. You do. I reward you with pleasure. Understand?"

"Yes," I whisper, aroused by the erotic tug of my hair in a way that the me I know would never feel.

"Yes, *Master*," he corrects.

My reply is instant. "No. I'm not—"

"Ms. Smith—"

"No," I repeat, my tone sharper this time. "I am not calling you Master. And don't you *dare* force me to say it in some moment of near orgasm, or I swear I will punish *you*."

He stares down at me, his face hard, unreadable, and my heart is beating so fast it might explode from my chest. Suddenly, he smiles and shocks me by kissing me, deeply, passionately, *intensely*. "Did you know," he says when he lifts his mouth, leaving me gasping for more, "that when I'm playing dominant, I never kiss in a scene?"

Surprised at this admission, I want to ask why he kissed me, but he's already moving on. "And 'no' is no. I told you that. You don't have to call me Master." His lips curve. "Just as long as you know I am Master."

My brow furrows. "That's—"

He kisses me again. "Nonnegotiable. You belong to me tonight. Remember?"

The words do funny things to my belly, and though I'm still confused by the kiss and his confession, my reply is immediate. "Yes. I remember."

"Say it."

"I belong to you," I willingly say, leaving off the "tonight" without intentional thought.

His mouth lingers near mine, his breath a warm, sweet promise I can almost taste, and I know he's noticed my admission.

I know he's waiting for me to correct it, and so am I. But I don't. I can't. He is more to me than just tonight.

Slowly, his hand slides from my face, his palms settling on my knees, his eyes meeting mine. "Open your legs, Crystal. I want to see and taste you."

"Yes," I say softly, and then, remembering that he never kisses in a scene, I surprise us both by adding, "Master," and opening my legs.

His eyes darken, his expression pure possessive heat that sends a shiver down my spine. His hands begin a slow path from my knees upward, his thumbs caressing my inner thighs. Goose bumps lift on my skin and my nipples are still so oversensitized from all the hours wearing the tips over them that they burn from the distant touch. His path feels eternal, as if he'll never reach the place I need him to be—but finally his thumbs stroke over my clit, then caress the slick, wet heat beyond. I bite my lip at the long strokes of his finger, back and forth, until he's pressing inside me, and it kills me that I can't arch into his touch without falling.

His tongue teases me with a quick flick of my nub and I whimper shamelessly. He looks at me with primal, white-hot desire. "I want to taste you, Crystal. And I want it badly enough that I'm not even going to make you ask for more. This is for me."

If the eroticism of his words isn't enough to undo me, his mouth is. He closes it over my sex and sucks deeply. My head falls backward, resting on the heavy leather of the cuffs, as I feel the wicked play of his tongue in intimate, perfect places.

And even as it tortures me, his fingers are still inside me, pumping, stroking. His tongue begins this swirling motion, around and around and then up and down, and . . . Oh God. He's right there where I need him—and then he moves. Then he's back. The cuffs are a heavy weight on my arms, reminding me not to move, but then *he* moves, and I'm going insane. This time when he's back where I need him, my hands come down on his head.

His mouth is gone instantly and he's on his feet, pulling me with him. Shocked, I lift my eyes to meet his, and in that instant, I know he's teased me on purpose. This was a battle of his will over my control, and his will has won.

"You disobeyed," he states. "You'll now wait to come." He loosens his tie and pulls it free of his collar. "It's my turn now." He wraps the red silk around my neck. "You keep it. We might need it."

A shadowy place in the back of my mind stirs but I reject it, focusing on him unbuttoning his shirt and shrugging out of it, his broad chest expanding with the movement, the light blond hair dusting his muscular torso. My mouth is dry, and I'm all about fully appreciating his body—but he doesn't remove his pants. He walks behind me, and as I turn, he sits down on the bed.

He grabs my wrists and pulls me close, my knees against his right thigh. "I'm going to spank you. Then I'm going to fuck you until you come. Understand?"

Adrenaline surges through me, and in shock I automatically answer, "Yes," forgetting the "Master." I think I've forgotten my own name.

I have a second of realizing the impact of my "yes" before he pulls me across his lap, my cuffed wrists dangling toward the floor. His hand comes down on my backside and he starts to rub and rub. I squeeze my eyes shut and I grab the silk tie, holding on for dear life. He keeps rubbing and in my mind I start saying, *His hand, his hand, his hand.* I don't know why I'm repeating it. And then there's the first smack—the sting, the arousing, painful bite of his palm. Then another. And another.

I can't breathe. I can't think. My heart is doing that wild fluttering thing again. Everything spins and burns, and I don't exist outside the here and now and him.

Abruptly, it's over and I don't know if I want to laugh, cry, or orgasm. He lifts me, and as quickly as he'd put me over his lap, my cuffed hands are pressed between his chest and mine, and his fingers are in my hair and he's kissing me. Hot, wild, crazy kissing me. I whimper, actually whimper with the taste of him that is dominant, hot, and impossibly right and wrong at once.

Then I'm flat on my back on the bed, and he's licking my clit and I'm coming unglued with the sensations ricocheting around my body. I need more and more, but I'm not sure my heart can take one more second. Still I arch my hips, reaching for it, and him, and yes, more, and he's sliding his hands beneath my sore backside, lifting me, licking me.

My orgasm comes over me like a rainbow of sensations, the build to bliss and the shattering ride over the other side overwhelming my body. I reach for his head but my fingers only find his hair. I jerk with the impact of my release, shaking before it finally begins to ease.

I hear him unzip his pants and feel him push them away. I'll finally have what I need most. He drives into me, hard and deep, and I spasm again around him. He begins to pump into me, our harsh breathing filling the room, and it's as wild as the kiss after the spanking, as intense as he promised. I meet his thrusts with my own, feeling the edge of that rainbow again.

I spasm, oh how I spasm, deeply, almost painfully, and he lets out a guttural groan that's so fierce and hot, it makes me moan. He drives into me one last time and I feel his release as I shatter into my own.

As I slowly come back to reality, Mark rolls to his side, pulling my back to his front. His powerful leg twines between mine, and my cuffed arms come to my chest. He strokes my hair. "Are you okay?"

"Yes," I say, my lashes fluttering, limbs heavy. "Just so very tired."

"An adrenaline spike will do that."

"Yes," I whisper, unable to open my eyes. I think the bed shifts, but I'm too relaxed to check. So . . . relaxed. I feel Mark pull out of me, then open my eyes to watch him stride into the bathroom in all his naked, masculine perfection. I bet he really looked good in baseball pants.

He returns, his eyes meeting mine, and I suddenly realize that

I'm cuffed, and he spanked me. I also told him that I belong to him. That's the part that really gets me, and makes me look away. The mattress sinks in with his weight and he presses the towel between my legs and embarrassingly, but sort of sweetly, cleans me up.

He stares down at me. "How are you?"

"You already asked me that."

"Actually, I asked if you were okay. How are you?"

*In love,* I think, but instead I say, "Good."

"Just . . . good?"

"Yes." I lift my arms and show him the cuffs.

He reaches down and frees one of my arms, his eyes darkening. "Leave the other on, in case we get the urge to play again."

"Again?"

He grabs a pillow and spoons me again, wrapping his arm around me and twining my legs with one of his once more. "That's right," he says near my ear. "I can't seem to get enough of you."

I smile, pleased with this answer. "I guess it's mutual."

"It had better be. And just for the record, you taste like honey, but you smell like jasmine and rum."

"Vanilla," I whisper.

"Sweetheart," he says. "There is *nothing* vanilla about you, or us."

I'm smiling all over again, letting my lashes lower, and feeling the weight of the cuff on my wrist. He's right. We are not vanilla. And I do believe I like it.

### Mark . . .

I absently caress Crystal's naked hip, inhaling her sweet scent and listening to her steady breathing. She's exhausted, and while adrenaline has something to do with it, I also suspect the insane hours she's been working to run Riptide and support my mother are the real culprit. And me. This woman is a part of our lives in every possible way, and I don't deserve her. I want to, though. God, how I want to.

"I belong to you." She said it like she meant it. And I'm going to make sure she does.

She twitches sharply, murmuring something in her sleep I can't make out. Another twitch, and her voice lifts. "No. No. Stop! Let her go. Let her go! No!" She jerks to a sitting position, her breathing coming in heavy gasps.

My hand goes to her arm. "Easy, sweetheart," I say, in eerie remembrance of doing the same with Rebecca after her many nightmares. "You had a bad dream."

She looks at me uncomprehendingly, her mind still in the nightmare. "Dream?" she repeats, lifting her hand to her face, the cuff dangling off her wrist. She jerks it in front of her and stares.

"Crystal—"

"Get it off! Get it off!" She turns to me, grabbing my arm, not even realizing she can just pull it off herself. "Get it off *now*!"

"Easy, sweetheart." I grab her arm.

"Hurry! *Now!* I'm going to . . . I need— *Hurry!*"

I unlatch the cuff and she scrambles off the bed and runs into the bathroom, trying to slam the door behind her. I follow her and find her trembling on the floor by the toilet, her knees to her chest, her head on her knees. This strong woman who's gotten me through so much is trembling.

Snagging her pink silk robe from a hook, I kneel in front of her and wrap it around her shoulders.

"Hey," I say, using her greeting.

She doesn't move. "I can't talk right now."

"Then we'll just sit." I join her on the floor, leaning against the wall beside her, my hip and leg pressed to hers.

She lifts her head, angling her body next to mine. "Why are you on the floor?" she demands, looking appalled despite the tears streaking her cheeks.

I caress them off her face, wondering what kind of monster torments her this badly. "Because you're on the floor."

She swipes at her cheeks. "I so hate you saw me like this. And stop being crazy, Mark. Get up."

"The only thing crazy would be getting up without you." I soften my voice. "Do you want to talk about it?"

She presses her hand to her face, then curls it at her mouth. "No. Not now. Not yet."

The inference that someday she will is enough. "I just need to know one thing."

Her gaze meets mine, the torment still there. "What?"

"Did I set this off? Did the bondage?"

"I have these nightmares." Her robe starts to fall and I reach for it, catching it for her.

"Put your arms in, sweetheart."

She stares at me, and I can see her trying to read me—which is ironic, because for once, I'm an open book. After a moment she shoves her arms inside the robe and I tie it at her waist.

And I don't question why, deep down, I'd already known. I love her.

"How long have you had the nightmares?" I ask.

"Since foster care."

It's easy to figure out that something of profound impact happened to her then. "You freaked out over the cuff even though your hands were free. I need to know, Crystal. Did the bondage trigger the nightmare?"

She hugs herself tightly. "Neither. The nightmare triggered my claustrophobia."

"What? Fuck, woman. I just cuffed you and spanked you."

"And I liked it. You are not my monster, and you never will be. You're why I was smiling when I fell asleep."

She's deflecting, and I can't let her. "How long have you had the claustrophobia, and how bad is it?"

"Since I was a teen. I was in a haunted house with my brothers, and the small space made me hyperventilate so badly, they thought I was having a heart attack."

"Why didn't you tell me?"

"Because I want to get over it, and these nightmares," she blurts out. "I want it all gone."

I drag her to me. "Then let me help you. Whatever's haunting you, we'll fight it together. But I have to know what it is to help."

"Like I know your secrets?"

"We need to sit down over a bottle of scotch, if that's what it takes, and get both of our pasts on the table. We're going to fight together."

"Until *you're gone*. And you will be, and I can't manage like that. Like you said, I own my monsters. I have to deal with them."

"I'm not going anywhere."

"Until you're gone," she repeats, as if I haven't spoken.

Something in her eyes, in her tone, slams me with the realization of just how alone she was in her youth—and how easily she must believe I really will leave.

"I'm falling in love with you, Crystal. I'm *not* going to hurt you."

A stunned look slides over her delicate features. "What? No. No. You just said that you don't know how you feel."

I silently curse those words, lacing my fingers in her hair. "When I said I didn't know what I was feeling, or if it was about you or her, that was about denial, fear, and guilt. And in case you didn't know, I master denial far better than I do you.

"I'm not falling in love. I *am* in love. I love you, Crystal Smith." My gut clenches with the fear I've spent a decade hiding from. "I *love* you, and it scares the hell out of me that I might lose you."

She covers my hands with hers. "You won't. And I don't want to lose you, either. I couldn't have done those cuffs with someone else, but everything is different with you. I trust you. And I love you, Mark Compton."

My mouth comes down on hers, a hot claiming of my woman. *My woman.* Not my submissive. She moans, wrapping her arms around my neck, and I cup her backside, lifting her, urging her legs around my waist.

I carry her to the bedroom and lay her down on the mattress, me on top of her. "Whatever hurt you, we'll deal with it. And nothing, *nothing,* is ever going to hurt you again. You have my word."

# Twenty

⁓

Mark . . .

I wake Saturday morning to Crystal curled against my side, and the feeling is surreal. For a half hour I don't move, just holding her and replaying the night before. We'd ordered takeout from her favorite Italian place and watched reruns of *Seinfeld,* and her amusement and her pleasure from my liking it led to a lot of laughing, fucking, and talking about nothing serious.

My plan to wake Crystal at nine, to be at work by ten, is destroyed by a series of 8:30 a.m. calls from Blake and Jacob that entail coordinating an eleven o'clock meeting at Riptide. I'm finally free of the conversations and about to join Crystal in the shower when my cell buzzes again. This time it's Tiger ranting about being squeezed out at the Long Island PD thanks to Detective Grant, whom he proceeds to call every four-letter word in existence.

"I might have some proof for you today that I couldn't have been involved," I say cautiously, not wanting Crystal to find out about Ava and Wright by overhearing me tell someone else.

"What proof?"

"I'll let you know."

"Then I'm not counting on it." He adds, "But I'll get my meeting today—and by the time Detective Grant gets back to San Francisco, he'll be lucky if he has a job."

I set my phone down, thinking I can catch the last of Crystal's shower, just as she exits the bathroom wearing a black fitted dress, tights, and her hair already sleekly styled. Glancing at the clock, I see that it's nine fifteen. "This morning didn't go as planned."

Crystal's gaze slides up and down my naked body and she lets out a regretful sigh. "No. It did not." She bites her lip and inspects my thickening cock, which gets even thicker while she watches.

"Go make coffee, woman," I growl. "I have a meeting you're about to make me miss."

She laughs and leaves, pausing at the closet for her shoes, giving me a moment to appreciate the way the dress hugs her heart-shaped backside. A cold shower it is, I decide, and enter the bathroom.

As I grab a towel off the rack afterward, my gaze lands on her pink robe, jolting me with the memory of Crystal sitting on the floor trembling. Cursing, I step to the bathroom sink, my mind replaying our conversation last night. *I don't want to lose you, either,* she'd said. *I wasn't afraid of the cuffs because I trust you.* I don't deserve her trust. I should have seen her hesitation over the cuffs as a problem, and I don't believe for an instant that they didn't contribute to her nightmare.

I walk to the suitcase I'd stashed in the closet the night before and bend down, unzipping it and digging into a pocket. My hand closes around Rebecca's journal and I pull it out, staring down at the red leather cover. "I need to do this," I whisper, squeezing my eyes shut against the ache in my heart. "So I can't hurt her like I did you."

Standing, I seek out Crystal and find her with her back to me as she fills a cup with coffee. A knock sounds on the door and I grimace, certain it's Jacob with really bad timing. Crystal turns and smiles when she sees me, but it fades as she notes my solemn expression. Her gaze drops to the journal she'd once opened and begun reading, mistaking it for something I'd left for her. She swallows hard and sets her cup down. "What are you doing?"

Another knock sounds and I ignore it, walking to the island separating us and setting the journal down. "I need you to read this."

Shock rolls over her face. "Why? Those are her private thoughts."

"I was a bastard to her, Crystal. You need to know who I am capable of being. But I have to warn you, she details the sex. And it was all about sex and dominance. It's not an easy read, even for me—and I lived it."

She inhales, straightening her spine. "When I was fifteen, I rebelled against all the protectiveness of my father and brothers. I think I also secretly wanted them to prove that they loved me unconditionally. I skipped school, got horrible grades, and shoplifted even though I had all the money a girl could want. My father put me in counseling and private school, and the counselor and I connected, which was good. But even more, I knew my home wasn't temporary.

"My point is that I am not that girl now, so I don't need to read the journal." She rounds the island and wraps her arms around me, tilting her chin up to look at me. "I know who you are with me, and who you are with your family. And I like that man. I love that man."

"Crystal—"

My cell phone starts ringing, and now there's pounding on the door. A second later, Crystal's cell phone starts buzzing on the counter.

"We're scaring Jacob," she murmurs, "but you don't scare me."

As I bring her mouth to mine, the distant sound of the front door opening is followed by Jacob shouting, "Crystal!"

"Security must have let him in," she says, and calls out, "In here!"

Footsteps pound, and Crystal and I face the doorway as Jacob bursts through with his gun drawn.

Blake Walker, whose long, dark hair spills out of the tie at his nape, follows, using his gun to scan the room. "What the fuck is going on?"

"Coffee for the road, anyone?" Crystal asks, walking around the island to pick up the pot.

Blake Walker throws so many F-bombs you'd think he was going for the New York record, which has steep competition. Crystal laughs every time I grimace, and I'm damn glad when we arrive at Riptide.

Crystal exits and I follow, my hand going to her back to urge her toward the roped-off security area.

Jacob and another security guard frame us, protecting us from a few piranha reporters. We've just entered the security area when I hear "Mr. Compton."

I glance in the direction of the guard who called my name, going downright icy when I see the familiar man next to him.

"Any idea why Ryan's here?" Jacob asks suspiciously.

"I don't care why he's here," I reply. "He's leaving." I walk toward Ryan, Jacob keeping pace with me, and I'm aware of Blake hurrying in our direction. Apparently they aren't sure I won't kill the man. I'm not, either.

I step close to him, my voice low, tight. "What are you doing here?"

"We need to talk."

"No. We don't."

"Is everything okay?" Crystal asks, coming to my side.

Ryan's eyes light on her, his lips twisting evilly. "Crystal Smith."

It's a seductive threat I don't miss. "Escort Ms. Smith inside, Jacob."

There's amusement in Ryan's blue stare. Jacob steps between him and Crystal, obviously understanding why the hell I want her out of here. Blake steps to my side. "Shall I drag him out of here by his attitude or his ass, Mr. Compton?" he asks, leaving no doubt he witnessed Ryan's short address to Crystal.

"We have business," Ryan snaps. "Are we doing this out here, or inside?"

"We aren't doing anything at all." I lift a hand toward Blake. "Escort him by whatever you wish." I head for the door.

"Someone dirtied up my financials," Ryan calls out loudly. "Do you want me to tell the press who I think did it?"

I pause but don't turn, my lips curving into a brutal twist. "If you want to announce the mismanagement of your business in the financial capital of the world, enjoy yourself." I enter the building, where Crystal is waiting for me.

She looks at my face and shakes her head. "Oh, no. What did you do, Mark?"

"Not enough. But I'm about to." Knowing Crystal's determination for answers, I grab her arms and carefully set her aside, and I head toward the conference room.

All three of the Walker brothers are tall, dark, and in my face from the moment they enter the Riptide conference room. I swiftly dismiss their questions about Ryan and everything else until we are all seated, and I'm in full command of the room. I claim the head of the rectangular table, and Royce and Blake are quick to claim the seats to either side of me. Luke sits next to Blake and Jacob next to Royce.

"Do you have the lab results?" I ask, getting right to the point.

"They're clean," Royce replies curtly. Everything about the man is gruff. "But you won't be, if you pursue the poison-pill vengeance that my brother did. It's our job to save your ass, Mr. Compton."

Luke leans forward. "What we are trying to get across is that Ryan showing up and throwing around accusations that you're after vengeance—when Corey's already saying you beat the shit out of him—isn't in your favor."

My lips thin and I fix Royce, the brother in charge of Walker Security, in a hard stare. "You want to save my ass? Find Ava. And don't give me 'we've been trying.' Try *harder*. And while you're at it, link Ricco or Ryan to Ava." I glance around the room. "Can any of you tell me you've done any of these things?"

"No," Blake answers for them all. "And we're pissed off as a motherfucker, too. If they can be found, we will find them."

"That's what I used to think. Then I hired someone else who got the job done."

"Who?" Royce snapped. "And define 'got the job done.'"

"There's a group of 'treasure hunters' I've hired in the past to locate high-profile art pieces. Pieces that collections keep underground, so to speak, to prevent theft. Their success rate has been exceptional, so I was more than willing to see what they could do outside the art community."

"That's who you were talking to on the phone last night, after your father's practice," Jacob says.

"Yes," I say. "My objective for the hunter I'm working with was to find Ava, and to prove Ryan was involved in Rebecca's murder. He failed to connect the dots with Ryan."

"So you decided to financially ruin him," Blake concludes. "Which is why he was here today." He runs a hand through his hair now neatly tied at his nape. "I can't fight a small amount of admiration. And it's better than killing him."

Royce growled, "It's still illegal."

But it feels good, I think, still fighting with myself over what I'm about to do. I flip open the folder in front of me and remove a stack of documents. I hesitate, then remind myself that this is the fastest way to protect Crystal, my parents, and my employees.

I set the documents in front of Royce, effectively giving up my role as vigilante. "There should be enough there to arrest Ryan for money laundering. It also proves he had cash no one thought he had. In a couple of days I'll have a deeper file, but I want him off the streets now—not later."

Royce grabs the paperwork and thumbs through it. He glances up at me. "It's enough. I can get this to the right people and make it happen."

"Today," I say.

"It's likely to be Monday."

"Not good enough."

"Today," Blake agrees. "I saw his interaction with Crystal this morning. I don't trust the bastard."

"Let me make this perfectly clear," I say, my irritation grinding through my tone. "I want to kill him. You say you want to protect me from myself. So get him off the streets."

Royce clenches his jaw. "I'll make it happen today."

I reach into my folder again. "Next topic. Ava." I toss the picture of her and Wright on the table, and Royce picks it up as I continue. "I scanned this and sent it to my attorney a few minutes ago. She's alive and on the run with a deadly mercenary named Wright. From what I understand, he comes with a price tag few can afford."

Royce passes the photo to Luke, who looks at it and sets it down. "When was this taken?"

"A few days ago, in Texas. And now that Corey claims Ava is here, we have to assume the man in the photo is here as well. And Wright is not a man to be taken lightly." I hand a file to Royce. "His detailed history is inside, but I'll summarize. Killed his own mercenary team. Hired assassin. Coldblooded killer. Like I said: He costs money."

"Ricco—and now Ryan, it seems—fit that profile," Royce says.

"Once Ricco found out Ava killed Rebecca, he would have had Ava killed. I can't believe he's behind this while she's still alive."

"Or," Blake says, "Ava seduced Wright and she's pulling his strings."

"I considered that," I reply, "but my hunter says Wright is

missing an emotional chip. He'd fuck her and slice her throat in the same ten minutes."

"Then we get Ryan off the streets," Luke says, "and we get him to call off Wright."

"Houston, we have a serious problem," Jacob says, holding up the photo. "Remember I told you that Crystal had an incident with a man on the street?" He holds up the picture. "She said he had a big scar on his cheek—like Wright."

My blood runs cold and I dial Crystal. "I need you in the conference room immediately." I end the call and glance around the room. "She *will* be protected. You know Ava and Wright are in town. We can't be sure Ryan will confess or call Wright off, especially if he was prepaid to do something. *Find them.*"

Luke shifts in his chair. "If there's anything the Walker men understand, it's protecting our women. We'll protect her."

"Yes," Royce agrees. "We'll do whatever it takes to keep her safe."

"Can we talk to this 'hunter' ourselves to speed this process up?" Blake asks. "If he's got connections we don't, we need to be working with him."

"Right now," I reply, "I find dividing my resources creates peace of mind. I need you to do what you do, and he'll keep doing what he does. If he gets a lead, I'll pass it on."

A knock sounds on the door and Crystal enters, pausing as everyone turns their eyes on her. "Why do I know this is bad news?" she asks, shutting the door behind her.

I stand up and motion for her to join me. The mask of indifference I wear like a second skin doesn't fool her; the instant my eyes meet hers, she pales and closes the distance between us. "What's happened?"

"We need you to look at a photo and see if it's familiar." I indicate my chair.

Her brow furrows but she sits, and I kneel beside her and open the folder to a large picture of Wright.

She stares down at it for a moment. "Who is this?" she asks me.

"Do you know him?"

"Yes." She glances at Jacob and back at me. "He's the man I saw outside Riptide when I was with Jacob."

# Twenty-one

Crystal . . .

I turn over the photo of the man with the scar, and shiver. There's something about him that spooks me, and I don't get spooked. "Who is he?" I repeat.

"Everyone out," Mark orders, pushing to his feet.

The entire room is standing in a blink, making tracks for the door, but Royce lingers. "I'll call you after that situation is handled."

Mark gives him a nod. "The sooner, the better."

"Agreed."

By the time he's followed the rest of the men into the hallway and shut the door, I'm on my feet, too.

"Tell me what's going on."

"The man in the photo is a high-dollar mercenary who's traveling with Ava. We don't think he's working for her. We think he was hired by someone with deep pockets."

"What exactly does a mercenary do? Did he help her escape?"

"This one is a high-paid assassin. Killing people is what he excels at, and someone with a lot of money obviously contracted him."

I lean against the conference table. "Oh God. He was in my face, standing right here." I hold my hand an inch from my face. "Right here, Mark."

I welcome the way his big body frames mine, his hands on my shoulders, steadying me. "Ryan is being arrested on money laundering charges, and we think he's behind this. That gets him off the street."

"It doesn't get that monster off the street, or Ava."

Mark cups my cheeks. "I need you to go to Paris until we catch this guy."

"I'm not going to Paris." I pull his hands from my face and try to push away from him, but he doesn't budge. "Don't do this now, Mark. This is one of those rare times I can feel trapped very easily."

He instantly steps back and I dart away.

"I've been fine through all of this. Completely fine, but what if that man comes after my family? I have to warn them. I have to go see my father today."

"We'll go see him together."

"No, we won't. He'll hate you before you ever have the chance to defend yourself. I need to see him myself. I need to call him and figure out when we can meet." I press my hand to my forehead. "I don't even want to go to his house tomorrow night. That's going to bring attention to my family, but he's going to insist." I shake my head. "I can't go see him. That's not safe. I have to call him."

"If I could turn back time and make this go differently, I would."

The rough quality of his voice stills me, and I meet his eyes. "I know. This isn't your fault." I wrap my arms around him, inhaling that wonderful, masculine scent of him that somehow soothes my frazzled nerves. "I just can't lose my family." I step back and draw in a calming breath. "I need to make the call here. I have two employees in my office going over paperwork."

He kisses my forehead. "I'll shut the door on my way out."

I walk to the opposite end of the long table, where a phone sits, and dial my father's cell number.

He answers in two rings. "Well, hello, honey. Since my caller ID says you're calling me from work, I assume you haven't decided to slow down."

"I'll take time off when you take time off."

"That's not the answer I wanted to hear."

"I have a huge auction next weekend."

"What's wrong?"

I frown at the phone. "What makes you say something is wrong?"

"I know you. It's in your voice."

I dive right in. "You know that the woman who killed Rebecca is on the run, but now it seems she's teamed up with some sort of mercenary. He . . . I had a brush with him a few days ago. Outside the gallery. He came right up to me and smiled, and then just walked away. I didn't know who he was then, but—"

"You're quitting. Right now. We'll get you out of the country."

"You'd clearly get along well with Mark. He wants to send me to Paris."

"That SOB is why you're in trouble. He's not sending you anywhere."

"This isn't his fault, Dad. You know that. You're being protective and I appreciate that, but—"

"You're quitting, Crystal."

"No, I'm not. It solves nothing. Dad, I'm in love with Mark, and if the plan is to hurt him, I'll still be a target anywhere I go."

He's silent for several heavy beats. "You love him."

I think of the way he sat down on the floor with me, the way he tried to get me to read Rebecca's journals to bare all to me, and my answer is easy. "Yes. I love him."

"You've never said that about a man before."

"I've never felt it before." Then I laugh. "And he can pay his own bills."

He doesn't laugh. "I want to meet him. Bring him tomorrow night."

"Maybe I shouldn't come. I don't want to bring attention to you."

"You're coming, and you're bringing Mark Compton. I have plenty of security. I'm going to send someone over to you."

"I have security people all around me, Dad. Mark won't let me breathe without someone supervising."

"Who's handling the security procedures?"

"Walker Security."

"I've heard of Walker. I'll be checking them out quite thoroughly."

We chat for a few more minutes and end the call. I was wrong when I said Mark and I were two bulls after the same red flag. He and my father have become the two bulls, and I'm the red flag.

I exit the conference room to find Mark leaning against the wall, and I walk over to him. "He wants us to come tomorrow night. It's not going to be an easy meeting."

He wraps his arm around me and holds me close. "I can handle it. Royce called. They used Ryan's credit card to track him to his hotel."

"Can they legally do that?"

"I really don't care. He was at the Omni hotel, a few blocks from here."

"Where you were staying before you moved in with me?"

"He knew it was my place of choice. Royce pulled strings to pick him up for questioning about Corey. They'll build the case for the money laundering while he's there."

"Good. No word on Ava or the mercenary?"

"Wright is his name, and no. No word on either of them, but we have a lot of people working on this. Now that Ryan is being arrested, we suspect the police will be brought in on the entire plot."

"Which is what?"

"Hurting me. And I can only assume that's because I applied pressure to expose Ryan as being involved in Rebecca's death. I think we should go home and stay in tonight. I'm telling my father I need to stay away from NYU until this is over." He strokes my hair. "Ryan's in custody. They're going to make him talk."

His voice is strong and confident, but I sense his unease. I know he's worried there's a whole lot more trouble headed our way.


Much later in the evening, Mark and I have eaten the sandwiches we picked up on the way to the apartment and managed to end up naked in the bedroom, where he is tender and loving and . . . vanilla.

By the time we're headed to vanilla event number three, my fear is confirmed. Because of who he decided I was last night, he can't be himself, and we can't be the us that we were becoming. Frustrated, even hurt by the way the past is invading my future, I shove him to his back and straddle him. "I wish I'd never told you about my claustrophobia. Stop treating me like I'm breakable."

"I have no idea what you're talking about."

I let out a growl. "You don't wear naïveté any better than you do vanilla. Either fuck me like *Mr. Compton*, or don't fuck me at all." I climb off him and scramble across the bed, barely managing to escape his reach.

"Where do you think you're going?" he calls out as I dart away.

"To take a bubble bath. It's what we delicate girls do." I try to slam the bathroom door but he's there in a blink, catching it before it shuts. "This is why I don't tell people I'm claustrophobic, or that I was a foster kid, Mark. They feel sorry for me, or like you, they think I'm fragile."

"You think that I think you're fragile?" He sets me on the bathroom counter. "You want to be pushed, I'll happily push you, sweetheart. I was just letting your pretty pink backside recover." He steps back and leans on the wall, his shaft thick, his eyes hot with challenge. "Touch yourself. I want to see you make yourself come."

My bravado fades instantly and I feel the blood leave my face. Mark closes the gap between us, grasping the counter on either side of my hips. "Remember what I said, Ms. Smith. I say. You do."

"Yes, but I've never . . . Not for someone else."

"Because delicate girls never do."

Before I can make a smart remark, he takes my hand and presses it between my thighs, using my fingers to explore the swollen, slick seam of my body. The effect is pure erotic thrill, proof that his skills at seduction and control are revved to full throttle. And he's not done.

Claiming my free hand, he molds it to my breast, kneading and stroking my nipple. The double assault of pleasure has me on sensory overload, and my lashes lower with the impact. "No," he orders roughly. "Eyes open. I want to see you, and you to see me."

My eyes snap open, and he wastes no time pushing for another reaction. He, *we,* stroke deeper into the slick heat of my sex, pressing two of my fingers inside my body. I gasp, and not just from the nerve endings we awaken. From the *intensely* intimate experience of touching myself with him. But even more so, it's the possessive demand in his eyes that says if he wants to own me, he can and will. Pleasure blossoms, thick and sweet, a burn in my belly, a tingling sensation in my nipples. Inhibitions fade, and when his hands leave my hands, settling on my knees, I continue to touch myself, letting him watch. Letting myself go where I would go if I were alone. And I like the tension in his body, the hunger in his expression, that says maybe, just maybe, I own him, too. He leans in and kisses my neck, trailing his lips downward, until he's licking my fingers where they cover my breast, his teeth scraping the nipple. It pushes me over the edge and into orgasm with barely a warning; I stiffen as my body clenches and spills over into spasms.

Mark doesn't give me time to revel in the sensations, lifting me and setting me on the floor, then turning me to face the mirror. A few strokes of his fingers between my thighs follow, quickly replaced by the hard drive of his cock stretching me, pleasing me. The thick pulse of his shaft presses to the deepest parts of my sex, creating a fierce physical need. *Everything* about him makes me need. And need more.

My head drops forward and his fingers instantly twine into my hair, pulling my head up. "Look at me," he tells me, thrusting harder, deeper, as if punishing me, the movement an erotic tug on my scalp. I can hear my own panting, the raspy, urgent whimpers I make. And that mirror is a window to *his* need, his passion and demand. Seeing this, knowing I've created it, sends me over the edge. Without warning, no chance to delay and savor our shared pleasure, my sex spasms and my eyes close. But this time, Mark doesn't seem to notice. As I am lost in my release his hands leave my hair, bracing against my hips for a fierce, final thrust.

I'm in the aftermath of the desire-filled escape that he so easily creates, my knees weak. I'm about to collapse when Mark catches me, steadying me. Once I'm steady he pulls out of me, leaving me gasping with the suddenness of the action. The sticky, wet proof of our intimacy is instant, and I grab the towel on the sink.

Mark's eyes meet mine in the mirror. "Still feel delicate?"

"Not at all."

"Are you sure? Because—"

"I'm sure." I turn in his arms and wrap mine around his neck. "I need to know you can handle my past, and not do what you did tonight."

"I can handle anything you need me to handle."

My past simmers on my tongue, but I contain it, still uncertain of its release after the reserve he showed tonight.

He *is* a Master. It's still a part of him, no matter how he's softened.

# Twenty-two

Crystal . . .

Sunday morning begins with Mark receiving a million phone calls. I hop into the shower to get ready for my spa day with Dana. By the time he heads to the bathroom, I've showered and dressed in dark navy jeans, a "Pink" brand T-shirt, and pink Keds.

I'm in the kitchen, coffee cup in hand and wondering about Wright, when Mark walks in and proves he does faded jeans and a navy blue Ralph Lauren shirt as sexily as he does suits. "I'm coming with you to my parents' house," he announces.

I crinkle my nose. "You want to be at our spa day? You realize it's hair color and nails and other girly stuff, right?"

"Wouldn't miss it," he confirms, walking to the cabinet for a cup. I watch as he fills it. "You were on the phone a long time."

"I wanted to get everything out of the way before we're with my mother. To summarize: Wright is already on the FBI's wanted list, but they've now issued a bulletin that he's potentially been spotted with Ava, who is also on the list."

I inhale and let it out. "But no news on where they're at."

He gives a grim shake of his head. "No news."

I nod, and hyperfocus on refilling my cup to keep my mind from going crazy, thinking about how Wright scares me. "What about that detective who tried to ambush you at NYU? Has he backed off, now that Wright is in the picture?"

"My attorney is in Long Island dealing with him, but no. He thinks I created the story to get attention off me."

I set my cup down, indignant for him. "He can't be serious."

"I wish he wasn't."

"So now what?"

"Royce wants to talk to your father's security people."

I feel the blood drain from my face. "Why?"

"He's just trying to make sure everyone is on the same page and safe. Can you call your father and arrange it?"

I grab my phone from the counter. "Yes." The knot in my stomach seems to be growing by the second. This hired professional killer, who has me, and the people I love, on his radar, terrifies me.

Hours after arriving at his parents' place, I've managed to set everything aside and laugh with Dana and Mark. Dana's hair is colored, mine is cut, and both of us have manicures. By the time the stylist has left, Dana is smiling but worn-out. With plenty of time left before our evening dinner with my family, Mark and I settle on either side of Dana on the bed to watch television. When she flips the channel to the movie *Message in a Bottle,* Mark grumbles, but he endures. It's charming, sweet, and sexy, and I wonder how he managed to keep this part of him alive, when he'd wrapped himself in hard control for so many years.

It's a good day that's made even better when Asher, the tat-tooed employee of Walker Security I'd met a couple of days before, drops by to let us know he's located the press leak in the building. Turns out it's the mailman, who has been "dealt with." We cling to the small piece of good news as if it's a big breakthrough.

Later in the afternoon, Mark and I stop by a specialty retail shop he favors, and he purchases a large selection of clothes, having brought a limited quantity in his suitcases. Aside from how inti-mate the shopping experience feels, it delivers a sense of security I don't realize I need until I experience it. He's filling the closet here with me, intending to stay in New York.

Too soon, it's time to head to my apartment—*our* apartment—and change out of our jeans to something nicer for the family dinner. Mark dresses in black slacks and tailored white dress shirt, going sans jacket, while I choose a casual red dress to match his tie. The red had been Dana's suggestion to bring us luck, which I fear we're going to need tonight.

We arrive at my father's penthouse suite overlooking Central Park at seven o'clock on the dot. "Should I ring the bell?" Mark asks, after I stare at it for a full sixty seconds.

I turn to him. "He's going to be protective."

He caresses my cheek. "A good father should be."

The door opens and I jerk around guiltily, as if Mark and I are teenagers who just got caught kissing. My father and stepmother stand in the entryway, him looking his normal tall, elegant self in gray dress slacks and a white button-down, his salt-and-pepper hair slicked back. My stepmother, Anna, looks pretty and conservative in a long blue floral skirt with a light blue silk blouse, her raven hair tied at the nape.

"Mom and Dad," I begin, "this is—"

"Mark Compton," my father supplies, offering his hand. "I've heard a lot about you."

Mark shakes his hand. "Not all good, I'm sure."

My father tightens his grip and holds on, pinning Mark in a direct stare. "She's in danger, and I don't like it."

Mark doesn't miss a beat. "Neither do I, Mr. Smith, and I'd send her out of the country if she'd go."

I groan and move forward to hug Anna, whispering, "Help! I've fallen and I can't get up."

She laughs and I follow her down the short hallway, which is floored with the same gorgeous black African wood that runs through the house. Pausing as we reach the contemporary living room furnished in soft blues, I glance behind me. Mark and my father are huddled together, speaking softly.

Sighing, I turn back to Anna. "They're either going to throttle each other, or plot my deportation."

Evidently not worried about either possibility, she motions me forward. "Leave them to work it out. The boys are hanging out in the kitchen, ready to pounce on the lasagna when I take it out of the oven. It should be ready in about thirty minutes. Just enough time for everyone to chat and have a drink before we start."

"The boys?" I tease at the reference to my two older brothers. "Daniel and Scottie are both in their thirties."

"Scottie is barely thirty and Daniel is only thirty-two. That's young."

"Then I'm a baby."

She wraps her arm around me. "Exactly," she says, proving how much she feeds the overbearing macho male attitudes in this house. "That's why they all want to take care of you."

In the kitchen I find Daniel and Scottie leaning on the island that's the centerpiece of the gray and white tiled room. They'd done exactly the same thing when I'd cooked for them years before.

"My two Twinkies," I tease, noting they're both wearing navy blue, Daniel in a sweater and Scottie in a button-down.

They straighten to their freakishly tall heights to greet me, both with wavy brown hair and green eyes. "We might look alike," Daniel comments, "but I got all the brains."

Scottie grimaces. "People who have to claim their own brilliance rarely possess it, and after what you put on her cake, I'd say 'stupid' fits. She's going to make you pay." He points to the giant chocolate cake sitting in the center of the island.

Anna holds her hand up and shakes her head. "I've already yelled." She heads toward the oven. "Loudly," she calls over her shoulder.

"Now I'm afraid to look." I move to the island and grimace as I read, "Soon to be an Old Maid."

I give my brothers a scathing look. "And you both wonder why I won't work for you? I'd be taunted half the time, and bossed around the rest."

"Hey now," Scottie objects, holding up his hands. "I had nothing to do with this."

"Oh, please. Daniel just thought of it first. And for both of your information, not every woman needs a man to take care of her. I hope you both end up with a strong woman who teaches you a lesson or ten."

"I think I'm at about ten."

The sound of Mark's voice makes me turn. While his comment is a compliment, there's an edge of possessiveness to his tone and the way his hand settles on my lower back. Like he doesn't like something in the exchange. And of course he doesn't. He's as protective as they are.

"And apparently," my father adds, "we won't be convincing Crystal to come to work for us anytime soon. I've just been told that Riptide profits are up substantially under her management."

"Little sis is kicking some ass," Scottie says, always the positive one of the group, though still dominant. He just comes at people with a coaxing hand, while Daniel and my father give them a shove.

Daniel focuses a hard stare on Mark. "You must be the notorious media magnet."

Mark takes the punch on the chin. "Not by choice. I prefer privacy for me and those around me, but it's not been easy to manage these past few weeks."

"Sex scandals tend to create problems, I imagine," Daniel replies dryly, and it's all I can do not to shake him.

If the flex of Mark's fingers on my back is any indication, he feels the same. "Under the circumstances," he says, his tone low and tight, "I really don't give a damn about sex scandals. I care about the murdering bitch who created them and is now on the loose."

The room is stunned into silence by the bold rebuttal, but bold and honest is everything my father has always preached. Scottie grins. "Mark Compton, I'm Scottie Smith. The younger, more forward-thinking brother. I hope that they catch the bitch in question—and as for the press, I hear ya, man. They're like a one-night stand that just won't go away."

"Scottie!" Anna exclaims from behind him. "That's inappropriate."

Scottie grins and my father chuckles. "Well, he *is* right, Anna." My father lifts his chin at Mark. "I'm sure Mark here agrees."

"I plead the Fifth." He glances at my father. "You're going to get me in trouble, Hank."

"Smart man you've got there, Crystal," Anna says, glaring at my father before she turns to open the refrigerator.

I'm having a happy few moments, absorbing Mark being on a first-name basis with my father in record-breaking time, when Daniel pushes off the island and grumpily announces, "I think I'll go have a drink." He cuts behind us and disappears.

Scottie sighs. "He had a bad day in the stock market. I'll go toss that drink down his throat." He takes off after Daniel, and my father glances at Mark. "Welcome to my home, in all its colorful glory."

Mark gives him an understanding look. "You don't know colorful until you spend a few hours with my mother."

Anna joins us. "Crystal has told us so much about Dana. How are her cancer treatments going?"

"Better, now that Mark is here." I wrap my arm around him. "He's totally turned her spirits around."

Mark drapes an arm around my shoulder. "I want you both to know that Crystal has quite possibly kept my mother alive. Your daughter is special, and so is what she's done for my family."

My father's eyes meet mine. "I know it is—and I know *she* is. Many years ago, she kept me alive."

My heart squeezes and I go around the counter to hug my father. He buries his face in my hair and whispers, "I'm so damn proud of you."

"Thank you, Daddy."

He leans back, his expression going from soft to hard as he releases me and focuses on Mark. "Hurt her, Compton, and I'll hurt you."

Approval fills Mark's eyes, and it pleases me, as I know it will my father. "I'd expect nothing less."

It's a perfect answer, but my father quickly makes it known that he is *not* going to let Mark off that easily. "I still have questions."

I pat my father's chest. "Of course you do. You always have questions." I flick a look between the two men. "I'll let you two work it out."

I move to the counter and face Anna. "What can I do?"

"I just need to make a salad. Can you slice the tomatoes?"

"Of course," I say, moving to the fridge.

"You invest all that money you make?" my father asks Mark, as I set several vegetables on the counter and find a knife.

"How do you know I have money?" Mark counters, not missing a beat.

"I had you investigated a couple of weeks ago."

I whirl around, the blade in my hand. "You did what?"

My father glances at the knife. "Easy there, baby."

"I'm serious, Dad. You had him investigated?"

"Hell, yes. You work for him under unusual circumstances."

"I'd do the same," Mark comments.

I turn my full attention to Mark, the Master himself, and grimace. "Yes, you would. Yet I'm in love with you. Someone help me; I need a sanity pill." I go back to my tomatoes.

Anna snickers, and Mark dives back into the verbal wrestling match with my father. "In answer to your question, yes, I invest."

"Any tech stocks in your portfolio?" my father asks.

Anna and I exchange an eye roll at my father's obvious baiting.

Mark throws the bait back in my dad's bucket. "Are you asking if I invest in your company?"

"Exactly."

"I did, but I sold it last year."

"Why?"

"Better numbers elsewhere. I'm holding out for your next financial report to opt in again."

Ouch! I glance over my shoulder at the same time my father looks in my direction. "He's honest. You know I like honest."

I let out a relieved breath. "Yes, I do."

"And now I know why she has no filter," Mark comments.

"I have a filter," I argue. "And a brain to know when to use it. I just choose not to with you."

"Don't I know it," he comments dryly.

"She had to learn to speak her mind to survive around here," my father says. "And for the record, I'd really like to comment on the stock situation but I can't. We can talk after the report." Then he says, "Now, on to the most important topic of all."

I hold my breath, waiting for what's coming.

"Is your father going to go all the way to the championship this season?"

I smile and return to my chopping.

"If he doesn't," Mark replies, "my mother will get well just to kick his ass."

"That's the truth," I mumble.

My father chuckles, something he rarely did before Anna came into his life. "You know," he says, seeming to think out loud, "if anyone can convince Crystal to go to Paris, it's her."

"That's it," I say, abandoning my slicing duties to face both men, hands on my hips. "You two plotting against me is not the kind of bonding I was hoping for. It's my pre-birthday celebration."

Anna joins me, proving that her pride in being the keeper of family traditions will not be tested, even by a Smith and a

Compton. "It's her birthday party," she states. "I've worked hard to make tonight special."

My father, the man who taught Daniel how to be a hard-ass, softens instantly. He winks at Anna. "And you did a wonderful job. We'll go join Daniel and Scottie for a drink so you can't hear us talking."

Mark gives me a wink of his own and follows my father.

Great. Now they've moved to another room, where I have zero control over where they go with this Paris conversation.

Anna steps to my side. "Mark sure won your father over quickly."

I cast a suspicious glance at the doorway. "Yes, he did."

Fifteen minutes later, the table is set and Anna sends me to round up the men for dinner. I walk out toward a double stairwell and head down to the level where the den—and the bar—is located. I'm on the final step, still hidden by the wall, when Daniel's voice lifts.

"I'm protective and I won't apologize for it," he says. "She watched her damn father beat her mother to death. So I'm telling you, man: You hurt her, you'll live to regret it."

I suck in air and grab the railing, feeling like I've been kicked and betrayed. *Damn you, Daniel!* This isn't how Mark was supposed to find out about my past!

I turn and run back up the stairs, desperate to get away before someone sees me. I reach the main level of the house and Anna is in my line of sight, headed my way. Needing a few minutes alone, I round the railing and begin climbing the stairs to the next level.

"Crystal!" Anna calls from behind me, but I keep climbing the stairs, fighting the same windstorm of emotions I felt often those few years when Daniel had lived with me. He'd shoved family down my throat, when I'd had one foster family after another take me in and throw me out. Even Angela, Hank's first wife, had died before the adoption. I'd liked her, and wanted her to love me.

Back then, it seemed like everyone eventually left me. I wasn't ready to open my heart to have it ripped to pieces all over again, certainly not because Daniel ordered it to happen.

I clear the final step, entering what my father calls the Observatory, where a glass wall and various telescopes offer a view to be envied. Walking to the glass, I press my hands to the surface, knowing that it's hurricane-proof and I won't fall. But as a teen I hadn't known, and there were many times I leaned on it and hoped I'd fall.

Behind me there's a soft sound and awareness rushes over me, telling me Mark is here. I feel this man in ways I've never felt another human being—and never wanted to. I didn't want to need anyone and end up ripped to pieces again.

He steps behind me, but I can't look at him yet. I think he knows and understands. He knows what hell feels like.

His hands come down on the glass beside mine, that spicy, masculine scent of him a soothing balm. "You okay?"

"I'm angry that Daniel told you."

"He spat it out before I could stop him. I didn't ask, Crystal. I wouldn't do that to you."

I turn and flatten my hands on the solid wall of his chest, his warmth radiating into my palms. "I know. Daniel gets in his fierce mode and tries to rule the world, and it's always his way or no way."

"Come sit," he urges, drawing me by the hand.

I nod and he leads me to one of the four oversized chairs in the room, where we squeeze in, facing each other. Mark trails a finger down my cheek. "You didn't answer my question. Are you okay?"

"I wasn't ready for this. I'm still not ready."

His hand rests on my hip. "This doesn't mean I don't touch you. We aren't shut down by this."

I want to believe him. More than he can possibly know. Cotton forms in my throat and I face forward, staring at the twinkling city lights in the ink-black night. "My father beat my mother often," I force out, saying what I've never said out loud to anyone. "I'd hide in the closet. So . . ." I inhale and let it out, my eyes burning from just thinking about what I'm about to say. "My mother always acted like it didn't happen the next day—until she couldn't pretend anymore." I look at him. "The night she died, he started beating her with a belt, and her screams were bloodcurdling. I was crying, and shouting her name. I think I knew on some level that he was different that night, angrier in some way."

I face forward again. "My shouting got his attention and he came after me with the belt. He'd never touched me before, but he intended to now. I saw it in his eyes. My mother must have, too, because when I ran and hid in the closet, she attacked him. He turned on her and"—my voice hitches—"he beat her until . . . she died." Tears flow and I swipe at them. "Sorry. I haven't let myself think about this in years. And I've never told the story to anyone."

He takes my hand. "Don't be sorry. Don't ever be sorry."

An old ache rips through me and my tears flow more freely. "She lay there limp and pale. And he turned to me and told me it was because of me. Then he left. Walked out of the door and never came back. I mean, they arrested him and he's in jail, but he just . . . left her like that."

Mark tilts my chin in his direction, wiping away my tears. "It wasn't because of you. You know this, right?"

"Yes. But I didn't know that as a child, or even a young teen. My first couple of foster homes were disasters. The first one, the husband and wife had a fight and I jumped on the husband. The second, pretty much the same story. After that, they wouldn't let a couple have me. I ended up with an elderly woman for years. She was a sweetheart, but then she had health issues and I was back without a home."

"Ah, sweetheart. I knew it was bad, but I had no idea how bad."

I'm suddenly angry at the tears that are making him feel sorry for me. I straighten. "It was bad, but I'm blessed, Mark. I ended up with a wonderful family that many don't have, and that includes Daniel. He's a bulldozer but he means well. Even when I'm pissed as hell at him, I love him."

"And they all love you—especially your father."

"He likes you, too. How'd you manage that?"

"I'm fairly certain it was when I told him I love you enough to take a bullet for you."

My eyes burn again. "You said that to my father?"

"Yes. And I meant it." He brushes hair behind my ear, his look tender—and worried.

I grab his hand, worried about where his mind is going. "He never hit me. My counselor thinks it was the closet that causes my claustrophobia. You're not going to be afraid to touch me, are you? I *liked* it when you spanked me."

He wraps his arm around me and pulls me close. "You're mine, Crystal. I'm going to touch you."

"You know what I mean."

"There are all kinds of ways we can get around actual bondage. I'm creative." He nuzzles my neck, goose bumps lifting as he adds, "If you aren't convinced, I'll convince you."

My lips curve. "I'd like to be convinced." And I'm only half joking. I do want to be convinced. "I want to defeat the claustrophobia. I don't want that man to still have that control over me. I want to control me. I want the cuffs. I want you."

He frames my face. "I don't need the cuffs. I just need you."

## Mark . . .

When Crystal and I finally return downstairs, Daniel pulls her aside to talk to her, and I walk to the giant stone fireplace in the downstairs den and stare at the flames. I've never felt as protective of anyone as I do now of Crystal, and my mind races with ways to make this nightmare end. Ways to lure Ava out of hiding.

"Would you like a drink, son?" Hank asks, coming to my side.

"I'd prefer to stay clearheaded."

"She told you everything," he says flatly.

"Yes."

"And you're ready to bolt."

I cut him an irritated look. "Not even close."

"Then what's the problem?"

*Me. I'm the problem.* I face him, ignoring the question, and I change the subject. "We can't bully her into going to Paris."

"Why the hell not?"

"She's a control freak. She needs to know everyone around her is safe. The mercenary or Ava could hurt her, yes—but if they hurt anyone she cares about, it will destroy her. And being in another country, not knowing what is happening—or worse, finding out something has gone wrong—would tear her to pieces. She'd blame me and us."

"She'd be alive."

"But would she be living? There's only one good answer here. Ava and this mercenary have to be captured before they hurt someone else."

"Yet they are on the loose, and my daughter is evidently on their radar."

"You think I'm not living that hell right now?" I scrub my jaw. "I need to go make a phone call."

He studies me a moment. "My office is the first door to the right outside the kitchen."

I nod, but exit the penthouse for the hallway, dialing my "hunter," and I repeat the offer of a small fortune to find Wright and Ava.

"I'll happily take your money, man, but Wright is a master at staying off the radar. I do have one interesting piece of information, though. I linked Ricco to Wright. It took some digging and there were aliases used, but Ricco hired him several years back for a job. I have proof of the transactions. So it's not Ryan you're dealing with here. It's Ricco."

Alarm bells go off. Ricco has deep, deep pockets, and he controls his funds—not some gangster types we now think Ryan might be associated with. "Are you sure?"

"Positive."

"Then why is Ava still alive? Ricco was obsessed with Rebecca. He wouldn't help her killer."

"Your guess is as good as mine. Maybe Wright is amusing himself with her, in which case she'll end up dead."

Or Ava did what many think is impossible, and successfully seduced Wright. "What job did Ricco hire him for before?"

"No details on the job itself."

My lips thin. "Get me proof on Ricco, and find Ava and Wright. Update me tomorrow." I end the call and lean against the wall.

If Wright is the master of staying off the radar, right now I'm the master of nothing. I've only felt this helpless one time before, and it didn't end well. I can't sit here like a duck on a pond.

I dial my ex-customer, the head of the television network, and offer him an interview. If I can't find Ava, I'll bring her to me.

Next, I dial my attorney. I'm going to need him.

# Twenty-three

Crystal . . .

When we arrive home from my birthday celebration, Mark takes me to bed, insisting he's going to make love to me, not fuck me. Turns out vanilla with Mark is never vanilla, and those hours in bed are some of the most intimate we've ever shared.

But in the morning light his mood has changed, leaving him distant and on edge. He's silent on the ride to work, but his hand is on my leg. Mixed messages—the man is forever confusing. Once we walk inside Riptide he quickly disappears into his office, and I can't help but worry there's something going on with the Ava situation that he doesn't want to tell me.

At nearly lunchtime, I'm in the lobby to greet a customer when I hear Beverly announce my father's call to Mark. A moment later, Royce Walker walks into the lobby for a scheduled meeting with Mark. Thirty minutes later, I've finished with my customer when Beverly calls me to the reception desk, lowering her voice to a hushed whisper. "That TV network executive you had a run-in with is here again. He's in with Mark, and so is Royce Walker, as well as some FBI agent."

I pray this means there's good news, but the odd way Mark was acting this morning still worries me. "Thanks, Beverly. There's a Cecelia Mercury coming in. She's worth millions to Riptide. Buzz me in Mark's office when she arrives."

I head toward the hallway, trying to seem calm and cool when there is so much adrenaline pumping through me, I think my heart might explode. I stop at Mark's door and knock. He doesn't answer. I knock again, and when there's still nothing, I peek inside— and find it empty.

The conference room is the only other place he could be, and sure enough, the door is shut. I knock, and almost instantly, Jacob opens the door. A moment later Mark appears, stepping into the hallway and shutting the door rather than inviting me inside.

I hug myself, crossing my arms over my pale pink dress. "What's going on?" I ask, my stomach in knots.

"I'll come find you when I'm done."

"No. You'll tell me now."

"Crystal—"

"Don't shut me out. Don't do that to me. Has something happened? Is someone hurt?"

His hands come down on my shoulders. "No one is hurt, or in any more danger than they were yesterday or the day before. I'm simply taking steps to end this nightmare once and for all."

"What steps?"

"I need you to trust me."

"You say that too often, Mark. If you won't tell me, I'll talk to my father. I heard him call you."

"Damn it, Crystal." He scrubs a hand over his face and pulls me to the end of the hall, lowering his voice. "Ava's erratic; she snaps easily. So we're trying to come up with a way to use the press to bait her."

"Bait her?"

"Yes. But we can't figure out how to be sure it's me she comes after."

"That's insanity. You could end up dead. Wright is with her."

"We have to take control, Crystal. Doing nothing isn't working, and no decisions have been made."

"And you decided I shouldn't be a part of those decisions, obviously."

"I was going to bring you in after I had a solid plan, which isn't yet."

"After—right. Because I can't possibly be your partner. I'm your possession. You'll tell the woman how things will be after you've decided." I try to step around him.

He catches my arm. "That's not how this is. The idea of losing you destroys me." His voice is low, gruff. "I knew it was going to scare you, so I wanted to have a workable plan before I came to you. Right now, I don't."

"Crystal."

Mark steps aside at Beverly's urgent tone and I bring her into focus. "Ms. Mercury is here, and she's not in a very pleasant mood."

"I'm on my way." I whirl on Mark. "Ms. Mercury is worth millions to Riptide. You go plot our certain destruction. I'll go try and fund it."

I leave, knots in my stomach, fear in my heart. He's going to get hurt—and as furious as I am with that man, I can't bear the idea of him getting hurt. I turn around, returning to the conference room door and opening it.

I glare at the room that includes Kara, Jacob, Blake, Royce, and a few other men. "I'm the logical target. Ava killed Rebecca. We do an interview and make me the bait. It's the best way to end this."

Mark stands up from the conference table. "Actually, that's an option we've talked about," he shocks me by saying. "But there's a condition that I told everyone you wouldn't consider."

"What's the condition?"

"You agree to go to Paris, while an FBI agent pretends to be you."

My heart sinks. How am I supposed to walk away and hope everyone I love is safe? But how do I ignore a chance to end this, when even I've said it's the most logical choice?

"Fine. I'll do it."

My meeting is tough but it ends well, and I walk my client to the lobby. As soon as she departs, Beverly flags me down. "Mr. Compton needs you in his office."

"Thank you, Beverly," I say, walking toward my office, not Mark's. I need a minute to process Paris, and his planning all of this behind my back. The instant I walk into my office, my cell phone rings and I don't even look at the caller ID. Of course it's Mark. I answer with exaggerated formality, "This is Ms. Smith."

"Ms. Smith," says an unfamiliar male voice that sends a chill down my spine. "There is a bomb in your building. Walker Security isn't as good as they think they are."

I am instantly reeling, the world spinning under my feet. "Who is this?"

"You have exactly two minutes after we hang up. Exit the building and turn right, then turn into the sandwich shop next door—or the building will be detonated. Do not put on your coat before you leave. Do not carry anything out with you. If you allow

anyone to stop you, everyone is dead. If anyone steps into the sandwich shop that we think is following you, everyone is dead. Make
sure they don't. Ready, set—"

"Wait," I say. "Security will follow me."

"That's why you have two minutes, not one. Create a disruption. Use your brain. Go." The line goes dead.

I stand there in shock. I'm not sure. *Think. Think. Think.* How
would a bomb get inside the building? It could be the mail. Or
in someone's purse. Or what if he hired one of our employees?
Or it's on top of or beside the building? Oh, God. The options
are too many. I can't risk thousands of lives for mine. My mind
races for a way to warn everyone.

Paper. Pen. I write a note.

*Bomb in building. Evacuate now. They made me leave and said if
I'm followed everyone will be killed.* My mind races.
*I'm hiding my phone on me so I can be traced. I love you, Mark.
Please tell my family how much I love them. And this is NOT your
fault. It's NOT.*

I throw down the pencil and look for a place to hide the
phone, and decide on my bra. Turning off the volume, I stuff it
awkwardly inside.

I dart for the door and try to be calm as I enter the hallway,
walking swiftly when I want to run. In the lobby, I make a mad
dash for the reception desk. "Is everyone still with Mark?"

"Yes. They're still in there."

"Good. Tell Mark I'm headed to my meeting but I left an urgent message on my desk."

Her brow furrows. "On your desk?"

"Do it *now*, Beverly," I order harshly, and since I'm never snippy, she jerks into action and punches a button.

I draw a breath and do the only thing I can. I walk toward the exit and act like it's perfectly reasonable for me to leave without a coat, giving a friendly nod to the two guards inside the doorway. Outside I don't stop to greet the two guards to my right and left, and they don't stop me. *Thank you, thank you, thank you.* I make it to the end of the roped-off walkway, and my luck runs out. One of the two guards steps in front of me.

"Where's Jacob?" I demand, aware my two minutes must be up. "I have a meeting and I'm freezing." I hug myself. "My coat is inside the Escalade."

"I haven't heard anything about this, ma'am."

I glance at my watch, acting irritated. Riptide pays these guards. They consider me a client, and they're not ex-FBI or ex-ATF. They are foot soldiers, so to speak. "I have a meeting with a big client in fifteen minutes and I'm late. Please find out where the heck Jacob is, or get someone else to escort me. You know I can't leave on my own." I move outside the ropes and give the street my back, facing both guards, looking at them both expectantly, when I'm really preparing to dart away.

The second guard gives me a puzzled look. "Jacob is inside, in a meeting."

He's more informed than I thought, but I recover quickly. "He was supposed to leave the meeting to escort me. *Please* tell me he didn't forget. This meeting is worth millions to Riptide. Mr. Compton will be furious with him, and me."

"I'll call Jacob," the second guard says.

"I'll get one of the other men to pull up the Escalade," the first guard offers.

"Thank you," I reply to both. "Hurry. It's freezing."

They both reach for their phones, and the instant I spot a good cluster of people, I dart into the midst of it, hearing their shouts. "Ms. Smith!"

My heart is racing and I can barely catch my breath, but I keep moving, never looking behind me as I enter the restaurant.

The instant I step into the doorway, a jacket is draped over my shoulders from behind, a hood pulled over my head.

A strong male hand closes on my arm, his face covered by the same kind of hoodie as the man on the street had worn. *Wright.* I know in my gut this is him, and I'm terrified, certain I'm not making it out of this alive.

"Walk forward," he commands, and I do as ordered. I remind myself I still have my phone and I left a note. But suddenly I'm trembling, and I can't stop. I want Wright to think it's because I'm cold, but it's fear, which I can't afford. I have to get free. I want to scream for help—but the bomb is still a threat.

We pass the register and go to the back exit onto another street. The instant we're on the sidewalk, he drags me into the crowd. "Why are you doing this?" I ask.

"I kill people who talk too much," he murmurs. "And so you know, I've never set off a bomb. I want an excuse to do it." He stares forward, his face still hidden. "Give me one."

I shut my mouth, but I panic when we head toward the subway. My cell phone can't be tracked there, and any hope that anyone will find me is about to be lost. We head down the stairs. I consider fighting and yelling for help, but I don't do it. I'll wait until we're out of the subway. I'll give Riptide time to evacuate and then I'll scream for help. I'm going to make this work. I'm going to get out of this.

The next few minutes are a blur as we pass through the turnstiles to the trains and I'm pulled onto a car. Still my captor doesn't look at me. He stares forward, holding on to me with one hand and a pole with the other. Three trains later, nothing has changed. He still holds me and the pole, and we've done a circle, looping back to a train station that puts us only a few blocks from Riptide.

It gives me hope. I'm close to help. I just need to get away. And it's time now.

We clear the platform from the train and he seems to sense my shift in mood, yanking me around to face him, looking at me for the first time, his eyes black, cold, and brutal. The jagged scar down his face is somehow a promise of pain. "You scream," he murmurs in a soft, lethal hiss, "you do anything I am not happy about, and I will slice Mark Compton's throat if it's the last thing I do in this world. Understand?"

I go cold as ice. "Yes. I understand."

He doesn't move, staring me down, the crowd bustling round us, and I think he'll never stop looking at me with those cold, black eyes. Abruptly his hands go to my waist, his lips twisting as he starts caressing my body. While he makes it sexual, his intention is clear. He's looking for something, and he finds it. He caresses my breast, sickening me with the touch, demolishing me with defeat. He grabs my phone and drops it to the ground.

He leans in close, his hot breath on my cheek. "I'm smarter than that, bitch." And then he's dragging me along again. The next few minutes become a blur, my mind going wild. He's going to rape and kill me. I saw it in his eyes. I have only one way to survive and keep Mark safe. I have to kill him first. It's a crazy thought that almost has me spurting laughter, like a crazy person. I think I might be crazy right now.

We exit to the street again and walk several blocks, and I try to think of ways to kill him. I took self-defense classes, but I don't know how to kill. Survival is all I can think. *Put him down, and then figure out the rest. Survive. Don't give him a chance to tie you up or you'll die.*

We're nearing Rockefeller Center, directly across from Riptide, and I start to fear that he wants to be around to enjoy the explosion. But he turns into a pizza joint connected to the subway, and immediately goes to the stairs leading down to the seating area and train tunnel. My heart stops when he heads to a bathroom instead of the exit.

This is it. This is where he's going to do it. I fight the urge to scream for help, reminding myself about Mark. I have to take this bastard down. I have to be stronger than my fear.

He shoves me inside the small bathroom and leans on the door, holding it shut, holding my arms behind me, taking away my foolish idea that I could defeat him. Panic over the trapped sensation radiating through me is nothing compared to what I feel when a gorgeous brunette steps in front of me. "Ava," I whisper, though I've never seen a picture of her.

"Yes, my sweet. I am Ava." She cups my cheek, caressing it, sending a shiver through me. "So you're Mark Compton's flavor of the month."

"What do you want?" I ask, trying to buy time, though I don't know what for. I can't get out of this. I can't get away. But still, I try. "Why are you doing this?"

"Because it amuses me to hurt him. And what amuses me, amuses the man holding your arms. That's real love, darlin'."

She punches me, sending pain splintering through my head. I gasp and another blow comes. Then everything goes black.

# Twenty-four

∽

Mark . . .

I'm climbing the walls, losing my mind with worry over Crystal. I pace the small office a mile from Riptide that's being used for emergency personnel and authorities. My staff has thankfully been evacuated, as are all nearby businesses, while the bomb squad does their job. But I'm going insane, and the fact that we were fighting shreds me all the more.

Royce is on the phone with the feds, trying to get an update on the ping for Crystal's phone, and I listen, hoping for good news. He ends the call and shakes his head. I turn away, my hand in my hair, my eyes burning. An hour and a half has passed, and not one ping. Damn it, I had a plan. I was going to end this.

"Crystal's father and brothers are trying to get past the blockades," Blake says, from a cluster of people in one corner.

I'd talked to Hank an hour ago. He'd barely spoken, but I'd felt his anguish, his absolute torment. He'd trusted me to protect his daughter. I'd failed her and him.

Kara bursts through the front door of the office. "They found her," she says, sounding winded. "She was in a bathroom a few blocks away. She's on her way to the hospital."

Relief and terror grip me. "What does that mean? What's happened to her?"

"Beaten badly," she says tightly, "and I don't know the extent of her injuries. They couldn't tell me. Jacob's pulling up to the door to take you to her."

Terror defeats relief as I head for the door, Blake on my heels. I can't breathe with the thought of losing Crystal. I *can't* lose her.

"I'll get her family to her when they arrive," Royce calls behind me.

I nod but don't look back. I just need to get to Crystal. Outside, sirens are flashing everywhere, and Jacob pops the front passenger door for me. I climb inside.

"You okay?" he asks.

"I am as far from okay as I could possibly be."

He pulls onto the street, navigating through the blockades. "I have your back, man, and I'll rip out Wright's throat if I get the chance. I'll even hold him and let you do it, and tell everyone with a problem to fuck off."

I nod but say nothing else for the eternal fifteen-minute ride. We pull up to the emergency room door and park, both of us exiting in a rush. Another vehicle pulls in behind us and Blake appears.

With Jacob and Blake by my side, I tell the receptionist, "My wife was brought in. Crystal Smith."

The woman looks at the computer screen. "I'll have someone come out and talk to you."

I step to the side of the desk where she motions for me to stand.

Blake and Jacob follow me and Blake says, "We're using satellite and camera footage to try to track Wright and Ava. We also have men questioning Ricco back in California about the tip you got about him and Wright working together in the past, but we could use any proof you have to pressure him."

I reach into my pocket and hand him my disposable phone, no longer worried about anything but making this end. "That's my hunter. He was supposed to have the proof delivered to me today. If he gives you any trouble, find me."

Blake gives me a nod. "I'm going to talk to security, and get Crystal set up in a protected area with Jacob by her door."

"Mr. Smith."

Forgetting Blake and Jacob, I turn to find a man in scrubs and rush over to him, my chest unbearably tight. "How is she, Doctor?"

"Are you the husband?"

"Yes, but it's Compton. Mark Compton. She kept her maiden name."

"Well, Mr. Compton, your wife was badly beaten. We're doing a CT scan and diagnostics, but I already know she has a serious concussion. She's unconscious but her vitals are stabilized for now."

"But she's going to be okay?" I ask.

"She's in critical condition, but we're going to take good care of her."

It's not the definitive answer I want, but it's the only one he offers before he leaves. Turning, I find that Hank, Anna, Scottie, and Daniel have arrived. I inhale and walk forward, giving them the news I've just heard.

"I knew we shouldn't have let her take this job," Daniel growls.

"Shut the fuck up, Daniel," Scottie snaps while Hank cuts

Daniel a hard look. "He loves her. He's blaming himself plenty without you doing it for him. Believe me, I know."

Hank places his hand on my shoulder and gives his sons our backs. "You didn't do this, son. Don't do that to yourself. I've been there."

My eyes burn, and I don't give a shit who knows. Hank might have lost a wife, and he knows the natural guilt most people feel, but not nearly as well as I do. "I should have sent her to Paris."

"I would have convinced you and her that she needed to leave. Neither of us got the damn chance."

"Where is he?" my mother demands.

I twirl around to find her and my father entering the ER. "My family," I tell Hank. Grabbing Crystal's note from my jacket pocket, I hand it to Hank and leave to greet my parents.

My mother throws her tiny body against mine, hugging me, and her frailness reminds me how close I am to losing not one, but two women I love. She leans back to study me. "Tell me she's okay."

"They're not saying anything certain yet."

Her eyes widen in fear, but then she grabs my arms. "This is *not* a repeat of history. You are *not* going to lose her."

My eyes burn again. "I've never needed you to be right as much as I do now."

"I'm always right," she assures me. "You know I am."

My father gives me a hard hug and I catch a glimpse of Hank over his shoulder, staring down at the note Crystal had left. I know what's he's doing—the same thing I did for the past two hours. He's reading it over and over, clinging to anything that is a piece of Crystal.

I break away from my father as Blake and Jacob join us. "They're going to move her to a secure wing of the ICU as soon as she's able," Jacob says. "The doctor will update you there."

Then my family and Crystal's pile into a waiting room, hoping for good news.

It's ten years ago, all over again. The only difference is that my parents and Crystal's get along well, while Tabitha's family had always hated me. I never knew why they didn't want Tabitha with me, when she was the one always diving into trouble, but in the end, I proved them right. I was trouble.

I start to pace, the time feeling like hours, though only minutes have passed. At some point Blake shows up and pulls me to the corner of the waiting room. "No bomb."

I inhale this bitterly hard-to-swallow news. Crystal had self-lessly left the building to save everyone inside, for nothing. "Tell me you have something on Ava and Wright."

"We've got some tips we're working on. I'll let you know soon."

"I don't know how I can let the staff go back to work. Hell, some of them may quit—and who would blame them?"

Blake sets his hands on his hips. "Bomb threats happen."

"They're smart enough to know this is related to everything else I've had going on."

"I agree. Today was an obvious, direct attack on you personally. They didn't just go after your woman, but also created a disruption to your business, which hurts your family. *But* there was *no bomb.*"

"There could have been."

"No. We have the place too well locked down. But if it'll make you feel better, we can add dogs. I suggest that you close tomorrow, and when you reopen, we have the dogs in place, and we don't allow outside visitors until we've assessed this situation more. We can even take care of notifying employees for you."

"Do it. And I'm going to cancel Saturday's auction if you don't have good news about Ava and Wright by Thursday. It's too high profile, and too many people could be hurt."

"Isn't that a huge income day for Riptide?"

"I don't give a damn about the income."

"Maybe that's exactly what this is about: cutting you financially. Canceling this auction Saturday will do that. And Ricco already tried to bring down Riptide with the counterfeit artwork. More and more, this lead you have on him makes sense."

"Except I can't dot the *i*'s on him working with Ava. The entire reason he hates me is his belief that I hurt Rebecca. Yet he knows that Ava killed her. It makes more sense for Ava and Wright to be working alone—even if they started out under Ricco's control."

"What if Ricco is keeping Ava around just long enough to keep attention off himself?"

I inhale and let it out. "Maybe."

"Mr. Compton?"

At the sound of my name, I turn and rush to greet another man in scrubs. I assume he's Crystal's new doctor. Both families crowd in behind me.

"Your wife has a concussion, but it's not as severe as we first thought. She remains unconscious but we've medicated her heavily for pain. We're going to keep her in the ICU for now."

"So she's going to be okay?" I ask, trying to get the answer I didn't get from the previous doctor.

"I'd be surprised if we don't move her to a regular room in the morning."

I let out a breath. The room erupts in sighs. "Can I see her?"

"I'll have the nurse take you back in just a couple of minutes." He disappears back down the hallway, and I turn to face the crowd of family.

Hank steps close to me. "Husband?" he asks softly.

"Yes," I say without hesitation. "I plan to be, if she'll have me."

My mother hugs me. "I told you. Everything is going to be okay."

"Mr. Compton?"

I turn at the sound of my name again to find that the nurse has already arrived. "You can come back now," she says as I identify myself.

Hank steps forward. "I'm her father. Can I come, too?"

"Yes, but only two at a time. Everyone else needs to wait."

Hank and I fall into step, not speaking as we walk the long corridor. When we turn left I spot Jacob hovering outside a door that has to be Crystal's, and I am reminded that Wright is alive and well while Crystal is in a hospital and suffering.

It's not over. Not until he and Ava are captured.

At the doorway, the nurse motions us forward. Jacob gives me a look that says I'm not going to like what I see. Dreading what is to come, but anxious to see Crystal, I step forward—and stop at the sight of her swollen, black-and-blue face. Hank sucks in air beside me, as shocked as I am.

I don't think I breathe for a full minute, and I barely remember moving, but suddenly I'm sitting on the side of her bed, touching her, kissing her cold hand, trying to warm it. Across from me Hank is doing the same, and the sight only serves to choke me up more.

Hank starts talking to her, telling her how brave she is, how amazingly strong she is. I force myself to stand up and give him space, when all I want to do is hold her. One by one, her family and mine come into the room, until they all seem to understand I need some time with her alone. My father brings me food, but I can't eat. I sit in a chair beside Crystal, holding her hand, not planning to let go. Not now or ever.

I whisper, "You're going to Paris when you wake up if I have to kidnap you to make it happen." I say this at least ten times. I think it a thousand. Every second of the many hours that pass, I pray for her to wake up, drilling the nurses frequently about why she remains unresponsive. They assure me that she's fine, but I'm not convinced. She doesn't move at all. She's like stone.

Long before evening comes and visiting hours end, my mother's forced to go home to rest, my father with her. Crystal's father and brothers remain until I convince them I'm not going anywhere. I remain in that chair by her bed, where I will stay as long as she's here.

"Mark."

I glance at the door, surprised to see Hank. I thought he'd left ten minutes ago. He walks around the bed and gives me back the note, pressing it into my palm and holding my hand a moment. "It's clear that you love her, and that she loves you." Then he turns and leaves. I close my hand around the note and hold on to it, and Crystal.

It's the middle of the night when something tickles my head, and my eyes jerk open with the sensation of fingers on my hair.

"Crystal!" I sit up with a jolt to find her eyes open.

"Bomb," she whispers. "Is . . . everyone . . . okay?"

I hit the intercom buzzer for the nurse. "She's awake," I announce, then answer Crystal's question. "Everyone is safe. You're safe. You're beat up, but you're going to be okay."

She swallows hard and nods, and I'm hit hard again by her selflessness. Beaten up, in ICU, she's worried about everyone else.

She tries to lift her hand. "My throat. Need . . . water."

"We'll ask the nurse if you can have some. You scared me. I thought I was going to lose you."

The night nurse, Bella, a grandmotherly type, rushes into the room and scoots me out of the way. She talks to Crystal and checks her vitals, asking where she hurts.

"My head."

"That's normal. You have a concussion and lots of bruising, but nothing that won't heal."

"Water," Crystal says again. "I'm . . . so thirsty."

"Let's do ice chips for now; we need to make sure you tolerate it. Throwing up would not be fun now." She pats Crystal's leg. "I'll be right back."

I go to the side of the bed again. "It's good to see you awake. It's the middle of the night, but your family and mine were here for hours and hours."

"Dana . . . was here?"

"Of course she was here. You're the daughter she never had."

She tries to smile and grimaces. "Ouch. I feel swollen."

"Ice chips have arrived," Bella announces, returning. "You are swollen, honey, but like I said, it's nothing that won't heal." She sits on the bed and helps Crystal suck on a couple of broken-up ice cubes. When those are gone she says, "Okay, I'll leave you to your doting husband now. We'll try some water in an hour or so if you want it."

The nurse leaves and Crystal's lashes flutter. "Husband?" she whispers.

I settle back into the chair and take her hand. "Yes. Husband."

Her lips curve a tiny bit and her eyes shut as she slips into deep breathing.

I sit down and hold her hand. "Rest," I say, unsure if she can hear me. "I'll be here if you need me."

I watch her sleep for several minutes and eventually lower my head again, exhaustion taking hold with the first bit of peace I've had since her attack. Listening to her breathe, I'm so thankful she's alive.

"Not . . . your fault," she whispers, and I lift my head to find her eyes shut, not sure if she really said it or not.

Crystal wakes at three in the morning with a nightmare, screaming and bringing hospital staff running. They sedate her and she rests, but I'm certain she is haunted not just by Wright and Ava, but the past they had to have stirred. That *I let* them stir. By six o'clock her blood pressure is high, so she's kept in ICU, and I worry that she's still having nightmares, her reactions suppressed by the drugs.

By midmorning Wednesday we've moved to a regular room, but she's still struggling to eat and sit up due to the throbbing in her head. Our families come for frequent visits, but she wants sleep more than she does talk. Still, by midafternoon she agrees to meet with Royce and the FBI agent working the case.

Listening to her recount the details of her attack guts me.

When we're done, I step into the hallway with Royce and the fed, Joe, who leaves Royce and me to talk. Royce updates me. "Ricco isn't talking, but we don't need him. A lead turned up Wright in a Queens hotel, but Ava isn't present. We're watching him, hoping she shows up before we arrest him. We don't want to spook her into running."

My relief is a complete physical rush like nothing I've ever experienced.

"It's not over yet," he cautions. "Ava's still a problem, and still a psycho bitch from what Crystal just said."

"Could Wright have killed her?"

"If Blake's theory is correct, that she was being used to divert attention from Ricco, it's possible Wright was done with her. But if that's the case, why is he still here? He's smart. He doesn't get caught, because he doesn't overstay his welcome—and he has this time."

This is a cold slap of reality I don't need right now. "Make sure you're watching my family and Crystal's."

"We're all over them, and Wright. And we're only giving Ava twenty-four hours to show up or we're arresting Wright. I'll keep you posted as things change."

He departs and I enter Crystal's room, finding her missing. I walk to the open bathroom door to find her staring at herself in the mirror.

"I look like a monster," she whispers.

More of the past comes back to me, pounding at my temples, bleeding into my sanity. I step behind her, my eyes meeting hers in the mirror. "You look like the woman I love."

She turns and faces me, her hands coming down on my arms, and I feel her touch like a punch in my chest. Too easily, she could have been gone—and I'd have never had this moment with her. "You do love me, don't you?" she asks.

I draw her hand in mine and kiss it. "With all that I am. I should have forced you to go to Paris."

Her fingers trail through the stubble on my jaw. "I would have been furious."

"But safe."

"And maybe it would have been your parents, then. I can't

293

regret it being me. And I'm ready to put it behind me. It's over and I'm fine, and one of us has to get back to work. And while I'd be the bigger attention grabber for the auction Saturday, I think it might have to be you."

"I'm canceling the auction."

"What? No! I've worked on that for months!"

"Wright and Ava are still on the loose. They found Wright, and they're watching him. But Ava is missing. I'm not making the same mistake I made with Paris. No auction. No exposure. No one else gets hurt. The end."

She tries to argue. She doesn't win.

# Twenty-five

Mark . . .

Early Wednesday evening, we're told Crystal will stay one more day at the hospital, and I have no option but to go to Riptide to take care of business. Kara joins Crystal to keep her company, and as extra security. As they chat about makeup options to cover Crystal's bruises, I reluctantly stand to leave. "I have to go, but I won't be long. I'll bring my work here."

"You'll bring me my files for the auction?" Crystal asks anxiously.

"Yes. And I'll call and personally apologize to everyone, and reschedule it."

"I can help. I *want* to help."

I lean down and kiss her. "You can *rest*. How about I bring us some dinner from the Italian place you love?"

"Yes, please." Her hand covers mine. "I'd like that."

"Good," I say. "I can't believe I almost lost you." I brush my lips over hers and reluctantly release her, then lift my black quilted

Ralph Lauren coat from the back of my chair. Shoving my arms inside it, I add, "I shouldn't be more than an hour or so."

"Be careful," she calls as I exit into the hall and pull the door shut.

Jacob stands and faces me. "Ready to go?"

"I am, but you aren't. You're staying here to protect her."

"Kara's here."

"And she's covering my spot inside the room. You keep your spot outside the room. Ava and Wright are targeting her. I want her safe."

"Then let me call another driver."

"No. I don't want anyone protected less for me. I'm getting in the truck and getting out at Riptide. It's safe. And frankly, if Wright or Ava wants to come at me, bring it on." I hold out my hand. "I need the keys to the Escalade."

He doesn't look pleased. "Have one of the guards downstairs walk you to the vehicle, and call me when you arrive at Riptide. I'll have someone meet you to walk you in."

"Fair enough."

Still, he doesn't hand me the keys. "Do you know how to shoot a gun?"

"Yes. I know how." The reason I learned is ten years old.

"Then take the Ford Focus I just bought, not the Escalade. There's a Glock in the glove box registered in my name." He hands me the keys. "I'll have the guard downstairs take you there."

My lips twist. "I can only hope that I need it."

I arrive at Riptide without incident, dodging the press at the door. Once I'm at my desk, I coordinate rescheduling the auction for a month away with critical staff, deciding to offer our clients a higher percentage of the sales for leaving their items with us. And while several employees have issues to deal with, everything is remarkably fine.

Fifteen minutes before I'm ready to leave, I order dinner for Crystal and me, having it delivered to security at Riptide. Part of me wants to tempt fate, though, and invite trouble by going to the restaurant myself. I want to be the bait that draws out Wright and Ava. No one else.

But I reel myself back in, aware that anything happening to me would hurt Crystal.

I'm pulling into the hospital parking lot when my phone rings with an unknown number. I'd normally let it go to voice mail, but it might be about Crystal, so I hit the Answer button.

"Mark." Ava's voice crackles through the line, and I stiffen. "I didn't kill Rebecca. It's all a setup. They're trying to kill me. I need help. I can prove everything."

"Where are you?"

"I'll meet you. But—"

"Where the fuck *are* you, Ava?"

"I need assurance that you'll protect me. He's trying to kill me. I'll get you proof."

"Get me proof and I'll protect you," I say, knowing there is no proof, wanting to strangle the bitch.

"Promise me you'll give me a chance to show you the proof before you turn me in."

*Or kill you,* I add silently. "I promise." She's silent. "Ava—"

"I'll call back." She hangs up.

"Fuck." I hit the steering wheel. "Fuck. Fuck. Fuck."

I begin to dial Jacob, but hesitate, my chance at vengeance burning in my heart like a new love I can't resist. She killed

Rebecca. She almost killed Crystal. I pull into the parking garage, sitting there and contemplating my next move.

Suddenly something bangs against a window and I jump, finding Ava pounding on the passenger door. It's all I can do not to open that glove box, and I force myself to get out of the car so I won't, slamming my door and rounding the trunk to confront her.

She whirls on me, a disheveled mess in jeans and a T-shirt, her hair wild, face filled with bruises that are at least two days old. "They're going to kill me!" she says.

"Who?"

"Ricco. Wright. You have to get me out of here."

The sight of her, the sound of her voice, is acid in my soul, and I've never hated the way I hate her in that moment. I walk up to her and grab her hair, shoving her against the window. "I'll kill you."

"You said you'd help."

"You killed Rebecca. You almost killed Crystal."

"No, it was Wright. He did it all."

"No. *You* did this." I'm shaking, and my hand is on her throat, and I'm not sure how it got there. In a moment of sanity, maybe the last one I have, I click open the trunk and drag her over by the neck. I shove her inside and shut the door.

For several seconds, I lean on the top and try to calm my breathing. A small slice of reality hits me, and I realize I have no idea if anyone has just seen what I've done. I have no idea why I've even done it.

I turn, scan, and, finding no prying eyes, I start walking.

## Crystal . . .

I'm sitting in a giant hospital lounge chair, starting to worry about Mark, when he walks into the room. "Leave, Kara," he orders gruffly. "Shut the door behind you."

I'm not sure who is more stunned, me or Kara, but she stands. "Is everything—"

"Go," he growls.

Kara leaves and the door shuts behind her.

I straighten in the seat, my head throbbing with the movement. "What's happening? Is someone hurt?"

"Not yet," he says, walking to the window and leaning on the ledge, darkness beginning to fall just beyond the glass.

"Ten years ago," he says. "I need to tell you about ten years ago."

"Okay," I whisper, not knowing what's triggered this, and holding my breath for more.

He turns toward me, his hand covering his face for a few moments before he drops it. "I was in love with my college sweetheart. Her name was Tabitha. She was like you. Blond, gorgeous, and full of life." He laughs without humor. "Rebellious. Always rebellious. I couldn't control her, and I didn't want to. I liked her wild spirit. We were going to have it all, we thought. I was going pro. She was going to be a cheerleader."

He looks at the ceiling, the seconds ticking by. "One night before graduation, both of our dorm rooms were occupied by our roommates." His eyes level on mine. "We decided to go to the baseball field to be alone. It was dark—too dark. We shouldn't have been there. She took off into the darkness, and I ran after her."

He looks away. "I went under the bleachers to find her. A group of men had a hold of her."

I gasp. "Oh God. No."

"I launched myself at them, and the next thing I knew I was being crushed by baseball bats. They beat me badly, and then they tied me up and made me watch when they raped her—and then beat her, too."

My heart breaking for him, I start to get up. But he holds up a hand. "Wait. There's more—and I've never made it through this story." I nod and sink back onto the chair.

He continues: "I woke up to find that she was in a coma, and my arm would never be the same. I didn't care about my arm. Tabitha was alive, but her face needed reconstructive surgery. She needed me. I didn't need baseball.

"When it was over, I still thought she was beautiful, but she didn't. She hated me, and she blamed me. She said it was all about my baseball. I tried to work through it with her. I went to work at Riptide to be close to her, but she didn't care. She hated me, and I was such an ass that everyone at Riptide hated me as well."

It all finally comes together. That's why he'd left New York. "Did they catch the people who did it?"

"Years later—and it turned out Tabitha was right. The attack was masterminded by a competing pitcher who hated me." His jaw clenches. "It was all about jealousy."

"Where is she now?"

"She became an alcoholic, and several years ago she drove her car into a telephone pole in New Jersey and died. That was three months before I met Rebecca. At that point, I couldn't fall in love with her. I never told her why. I'm not sure I even admitted it to myself."

I wipe away tears as he continues.

"And then Rebecca died, and it was once again rooted in jealousy. And then you almost died, due to Ava's jealousy all over again. I can't let you die, too. So I have to do everything I can to stop it from happening."

He wants me to go to Paris. That has to be what this is. "None of this is your fault, Mark. And I'll go to Paris if you really need me to."

"That's not what this is about. Ava," he says tightly, "I saw her tonight."

"Where? When? What happened?"

"She's in the trunk of the car."

My hand goes to my mouth. What has he done? I stand up. "Is she dead?"

"No—but I want her to be. I want her to be dead so badly, I can taste it."

Tears pour down my cheeks. "I know. I know, Mark—but you *can't* kill her."

I close the space between us and he drags me to him, burying his face in my hair. "I can't lose you, too."

"Then don't go to jail. She wins that way. She separates us." I pull back, needing to see his eyes. "Let's tell Jacob. Let's put her behind bars, and let them arrest Wright. Please."

He hands me the keys. "Tell them to go get her, before I do."

I rush out the door to find Kara and Jacob standing there, looking shocked at my arrival. I hold out the keys, my hand trembling. Jacob reaches for them and I grab his hand, stepping closer to him and lowering my voice. "The trunk," I whisper. "Ava is alive and in the trunk."

"Oh my God," Kara gasps, grabbing her phone and dialing.

Jacob takes the key from me and starts running down the hall.

I walk back into the room. "It's done," I say, and we fold each other into our arms. And I pray that his healing begins now—as it did for me the day I met him.

# Epilogue

*Christmas Eve . . .*

### Mark . . .

Crystal and I have an hour before we're due to meet my family at her parents' house for a Christmas Eve dinner, and a celebration of many things. Dana has completed her radiation treatments. Wright and Ava copped plea deals and gave up Ricco, who'd admitted he'd been using Ava to steer attention away from himself. Our rescheduled auction was a massive success. Even Daniel is coming around, and has started to speak to me in full sentences that don't sound like attacks. But before we attend the party to celebrate all these successes, I've teased Crystal with a surprise.

The driver I've hired for the night pulls up to a high-rise building Crystal has admired on several occasions. As we exit into the chilly night Crystal pulls her coat snugly around her slim-fitted emerald-green dress, while I opt for just my suit jacket.

After clearing my ID with security at the door, we go inside, bringing the giant Christmas tree decorated in all red into view, the top climbing into the ceiling between two wood-railed stair-wells.

"It's beautiful," Crystal says, lacing her arm with mine. "My mother would love to see this."

"We can bring her tomorrow." I lead her to the elevator and we step inside, where I punch in a code to allow us to travel to the sixty-eighth floor.

"How do you know the code?"

"I made special arrangements."

Her brow furrows. "Now I'm really curious."

"You're supposed to be."

She leans in to me and smiles. "Does it involve floggers?" she asks, having gained a liking for that form of pleasure quite recently.

I stroke her cheek, where the last remnant of a deep bruise remains, my gut still wrenching at the hell she'd endured. "You'll have to wait and see."

The doors open and we exit into a massive living room with four huge white pillars, a white-faced fireplace, and huge windows overlooking the city.

She glances at me, obviously curious about the lack of furni-ture. I motion her forward. "Go inside."

Biting her lip, she enters the room and stops, and I know that she's seen the small box in the center of the room. "That doesn't look like a flogger."

I move ahead and pick up the velvet box, waiting for her to join me. She takes tentative steps forward and I can almost feel her nervous energy mirroring mine. She stops in front of me and I see tears pooling in her eyes. But she has a right to cry. We've been through hell and back together, and we're stronger for it, seeing a counselor, working through the hell of our pasts.

"I put my house in San Francisco on the market, and this apartment can be ours if you like it, but it doesn't have to be. We can shop and find whatever you want. What's important to me is we find the perfect place for us."

I open the box, revealing the Tiffany diamond inside. "I never thought I was the marrying kind of man, but you've changed me. You have made life so much better." I go down on my knee and take her hand. "Please spend the rest of your life with me. Will you marry me, Crystal?"

Tears stream down her cheeks. "Yes. Yes, I'll marry you."

A deep warmth spreads through me. Setting the box down, I slip the ring on her finger.

She stares down at it. "It's gorgeous. So very gorgeous."

I push to my feet and enclose her in my arms. "Like you."

"Like *you*. I'm a lucky girl." Then mischief fills hers eyes. "Can you imagine everyone's face if we end the ceremony with 'You may now spank the bride'?"

I laugh, something I do a lot since meeting Crystal.

Life is so much better—and so are the spankings.